# Delicious Romance

*"They say a way to a man's heart is through his stomach, what they failed to mention is that there was another way, a way I never knew existed and that was the smile of a beautiful woman and the gleam in her eyes. I knew three women in my life and one of them always did things to me when she looked at me that I could not explain. My name is Tony Cross, that one woman in my life is Annie Roberson and when we were together, boy could we cook."*

# Delicious Romance

Stephen Vasilas

Rev. date: 03/14/2014

**To order additional copies of this book, contact:**
Xlibris LLC
1-888-795-4274
www.Xlibris.com
Orders@Xlibris.com
540401

# DEDICATION / ACKNOWLEDGEMENTS

I want to dedicate this book to my mother, Lillian Vasilas,
for all of her help and support over the years.

I also want to say, thank you, to my wife, Darla, who edited this work and
translated it from gibberish to English. My thanks also go out to
Sue Wachter, who gave me her support and occasional story ideas.

# PROLOG

*"LOOK! A ZOMBIE!"*

AS THE TORNADO ripped through the town of Pine Lake, it destroyed everything in its path. A young couple was running, trying to stay ahead of it. The boy had a grip on the girl's hand . . . knowing that if he lost her, he would not be able to handle it. The couple was Tony Cross and Annie Roberson. Annie was having trouble keeping up with Tony. Debris was flying all around them and the sound of the wind was deafening. Suddenly Tony realized that he was no longer holding Annie's hand and turned just in time to see her being sucked into the tornado.

Tony was 11 years old. He had been sleeping, but sat up suddenly, sweaty and breathing hard. The dream had shaken him to his core. Tony was finally able to bring himself to look at the time and couldn't believe how long he had been sleeping, "Shit, I'm late. She's going to kill me." He managed to get his right foot into the pants leg of his jeans and tried to balance himself while getting the other leg into his pants. It didn't work. He jumped up, zipped up the jeans, and slipped on his running shoes. Next was his T-shirt . . . it was a hot summer night and he had a long run to make to the other side of town. He would have to make his trek to the old abandoned power station, just north of town, in record time or there would be hell to pay.

He managed to climb out the window and he ran like the wind. Pine Lake was a small southern town of 900 people, give or take. Nothing really happened there and everyone knew everyone else. Just sneeze and it would make the front page news. The biggest event since the union troops and ridden into town was when they got their first traffic light . . . the one and only traffic light.

Tony was out of breath by the time he reached the old power station, which was a large complex with several building that had been long forgotten when a new, and bigger, station had been built further north. It had been taken over by a group of homeless kids that had made themselves into a kind of 'family', and the station was their home.

One day, when Tony had been playing in the park, he met a lovely girl by the name of Ashley Moore. They had just happened to run into each other and at first, it seemed like they were going to become very good friends. Tony had never had a girlfriend before . . . she was his first. He found the whole thing very interesting, and boy did she smell good. She was older than him . . . by two years, with medium-length long black hair. Tony had realized that the world around him was changing and somehow he found that he was looking at girls differently.

Tony enjoyed the time talking with Ashley. She was funny and her smile . . . let's just say her smile did something to him . . . it confused him. She had started telling him stories about her father who was an Air Force combat pilot. Tony was fascinated. She had told him to meet her at the power station, and she would tell him more stories.

The only problem with Ashley Moore was that she belonged to the leader of the gang. They had become almost like a mother and father to all the kids, so Tony was definitely taking a chance coming to this place but he was excited . . . taking chances gave him a little spice in life. It was better than sitting at home all the time.

Tony had managed to get near the center of the main building by keeping in the darkness and not being spotted. He was standing just outside the main club room where everyone was asleep. The room was lit by fires in old oil drums. The sun was just breaking the horizon when Tony jumped as a hand touched him from behind, or should one say that he almost wet his pants. He tried to calm himself. "You scared the crap out of me, Ashley," he said as she snickered at him. She grabbed him by the hand and led him away from the room.

On the second floor, the two found what looked like it might have been an office at one time. The room was a wreck with trash on the floor, broken furniture and a balcony that might have been glass enclosed at some time. The sun was just coming up and was providing the light in the room. They found a little corner and sat on the floor together. Ashley continued her stories from where she had left off the other day. Then, with only one thought on her mind, and not giving him any sign or warning, she kissed Tony. He pushed her away from him and jumped to his feet. "What are you doing?" He asked.

"It's called a kiss, Tony. There is nothing wrong with a kiss." She sat there, looking up at him.

"I thought we were friends . . . I thought you understood me."

Ashley knew by the tone of his voice that he was upset and stood up to face him. "It was just a kiss . . . that's all." She couldn't understand his reaction to what had happened.

"I don't think I should see you anymore." Right on cue, on his last word, Glenn and an army of kids completely loyal to him, charged into the room and surrounded Tony. This is what Tony had worried would happen.

Glenn marched up to Ashley and slapped her, enraging Tony. He wanted nothing more than to beat the crap out of Glen, but he was being held in place by some of the kids. Glenn went to face Tony. He looked him over and didn't like what he saw. "And who are you?" Glenn asked.

"Fuck you," was all Tony said in response.

"You think you're really something, don't you. Sneaking in here and making out with my girl."

"Glenn, nothing happened," Ashley countered.

Glenn snapped his head around to look at her. "Shut up, Woman. You're in enough trouble as it is," he said with a voice that sent a chill up her spine.

And then Tony shouted out, "A ZOMBIE . . ." Yes, it was the oldest trick in the book, and they knew it, but had to look anyway. Ashley had to laugh at Tony for having the guts to pull it off and make his escape. He was climbing down the fire escape as Glenn yelled for his boys to go get him. The group scurried out of the room, using the same fire escape.

Tony was fast on his feet. There weren't many kids that could keep up with him when he was running the way he was down Main Street. As he ran past the old buildings, he looked behind him to see where his pursuers were. Most of the kids had stopped but Glenn and two others were beginning to close in on him. Suddenly, Tony ran into a woman coming from one of the shops, and knocked her to the sidewalk. He helped the woman to her feet, apologizing to her. It was probably a good thing to do, but not the best idea, since it allowed Glenn and his friends to shorten the gap.

Tony left Main Street and headed for a line of trees that lined the lake. A short time later he emerged from the trees and continued running down the shoreline, his feet pounding hard into the sand.

Annie Roberson was one of four Roberson children and she was the youngest of the bunch. She was 10 years old, with fair skin, grass green eyes and long blond hair that was blowing from the breeze from the lake. With her fair skin, she sunburned very easily. She always wondered why her mother always put a sun block on her that had a rating power enough to withstand a burst of radiation and let the wearer live to tell about it. She was spending the morning at the beach with her mother and while her mother was sunbathing, Annie was building a sandcastle. She loved building sandcastles and then taking pictures of them before the tide washed them away. The castle she was building was her best one yet. It had towers, a moat and windows . . . even brickwork. She could just imagine everyone's reaction when she showed them the pictures. It was obvious where Annie got her beauty, she was almost a carbon copy of her mother. Nancy started to gather the things around her. "Annie, it's time to go!" Annie was kneeling beside her castle . . . she was almost finished.

"Please, Mother . . . just a few more seconds . . . I'm almost done."

"All right, Sweetie. But when I get back we will have to go."

"All right, Mother . . . thank you." She went back to work . . . just a couple more things to do before time to take the pictures.

Tony was running by a couple of women sunning themselves. He couldn't take his eyes off them. Yes, they were older, but soooo pretty. He just couldn't understand his sudden fascination with the female of the species. It was really confusing him, and he had been embarrassed to talk to his parents about it. Still eyeing the women, he wasn't watching where he was going and plowed right into the sandcastle that Annie was getting ready to photograph. Tony found himself lying on his back looking up at a 10-year old female that looked like an evil dragon ready to devour him for lunch . . . he could have sworn he saw fire coming from her nose.

# CHAPTER ONE

*"Tony, I have to say this to you, because you worry me."*

ANNIE WAS NOW on top of Tony, ready to teach him a lesson he wouldn't soon forget. "Do you know what you have done?" She said angrily.

"I'm sorry, I was not paying attention." Tony was wondering what was going to happen. His father had always told him to respect and honor a woman and, most of all, not to hit them. So no matter what happened, all he could do is to try to protect himself.

"I have been working on that all morning and you come along and destroy it in seconds!"

"You look familiar to me." He started looking at her oddly. Before she was able to respond they were interrupted.

"Little girl, he belongs to us; but we thank you for your help."

If there was one thing that Annie disliked it was to be called, 'little girl'. That's what had made her beat up boys in school, more than once, actually. Those two words irritated her to no end. Annie snapped her head to the three boys standing nearby and she had a look of destruction on her face.

"What did you call me?"

"You heard me." Annie slowly stood up as she grabbed the shovel that was sticking out of the ground. Annie had been taking martial arts training, Tae Kwon Do, to be exact for a couple of years. She had already gotten her black belt. She swung the shovel over her head like a helicopter and swinging it behind her back, she dropped into a fighting stance, extending her free arm out in front of her, palm up.

"Who wants to be first?" She asked. There wasn't much that Annie feared. OK . . . maybe the occasional thunder storm would make her hide in a closet, but when it came to facing the opposite sex, well, she could stand her ground with the best of them. She had to, with three older brothers to contend with. She waited for one of the guys to make the first move, and when Tony started to get up Annie put her foot down on his chest, keeping him pinned to the sand. All he could do was lay there and watch what was going to happen.

Glenn ordered the boy on his right to engage the girl, but that boy shook his head and ran off. Then without saying anything to the boy on the left, he pushed him toward Annie, wanting him to fight her. As that boy nervously faced Annie, found found himself wishing he was anywhere but there. He took what looked like a boxer's fighting stance.

Before the boy could make a move, Annie swung the shovel over her head and brought it down crashing into the side of his leg. The boy went down, looking up at her and finding the end of the shovel at the base of his throat. She then looked at Glenn who stood there, shocked.

"Now, what about you?"

Glenn didn't say a word, he just took off running, as the boy on the ground pushed the shovel away, got to his feet and ran after him. "Just as I figured . . . . yellow." Annie said and looked back at Tony.

"Who are you?" Tony said as he looked up at her with amazement. She looked down at him, swinging the shovel over her head again and slammed it back into the sand. She grabbed Tony by the front of his shirt and pulled him to his feet. He was taller than her, but she didn't seem to care.

"Now, what about you?" She asked Tony.

At first he was a little scared to say anything, afraid that he might get his face punched in by this little powerhouse and then something strange happened to him. Something he had no control over . . . it just came out.

"You have the prettiest eyes I have ever seen."

"If you think your smooth-talking is going to get you out of this, you're sadly mistaken."

"I'm sorry . . . I don't know what made me say that. It just came out." And then something else happened . . . he couldn't stop it . . . . he leaned over and kissed her . . . just a little peck on the lips. She pushed him away, still holding onto his shirt. It was her first kiss from a boy.

"What do you think you are doing?" She asked, not sure how to feel or what to do.

"I'm sorry . . . my brain must be broken, or something." Annie looked back over her shoulder and saw her mother coming toward them.

"ANNIE! LET THE BOY GO!" Nancy shouted at her. She came alongside her daughter, taking hold of her hand and the shovel. "Come on, Annie. We have to go," she told her as she pulled her away from Tony. Annie looked over her shoulder at him as she was being pulled away and waved to him, watching as Tony waved back. He dropped back into the sand, thinking about what he had just done. He touched this lips, trying to figure out why this kiss was affecting him more than the one he received from Ashley, his hand covering his mouth. What was happening to him?

The blue Honda CRV belonging to the Roberson family was slowly traveling down Pine Lake's Main Street. They were heading home so they could get cleaned up before opening the restaurant for the noon rush. The restaurant was located on the southern end of the town and had become very popular because of the fine cooking. Several other restaurants were in the town, a pizza place, a night club and another fine restaurant called the Pasta Imperial, run by the Cross family. Annie had not said anything since they left the beach and couldn't understand why this boy had kissed her. She didn't know why it affected her so much. She touched her lips and then looked at her mother who was concentrating on her driving.

"Mother, do I have pretty eyes?"

Nancy felt like she had been slapped in the face, forgot where she was for a second, and slammed on the brakes, causing the vehicle to skid to a stop. One of the vehicles behind her also had to slam on the brakes to keep from hitting her, and began blowing his horn at her. Nancy finally moved the CRV to the side of the road and parked. She ran both hands through her long hair, tucking it behind her ears. She finally turned to her daughter. "Who said that to you?"

"That boy." Annie wasn't one to dish out full information on a subject or event.

"What boy?"

"The one on the beach. The one you told me to let go. Come on, Mom, get with it!"

Nancy almost snorted out a laugh. She knew there was more to this story, after all Annie's three older brothers had led her and her husband on a merry chase. "You're not telling me the whole story, are you?"

"He kissed me."

Nancy lowered her head for a second and then fell back against her seat and looked at Annie again. "Where did he kiss you?"

"On the beach."

Somehow Nancy knew that was coming. She had a tight grip on the steering wheel and was twisting her hands back and forth as if she wanted to rip the wheel apart. "What part of your body did this boy kiss?"

"My lips."

Again Nancy lowered her head and thought to herself. "Oh God, Mom said there would be payback for all the years she had . . . ."

Annie cut her off . . . "Are you all right, Mother?" She looked at her mother strangely. "Do you want me to drive?"

That really hit Nancy. "NO!"

Annie looked disappointed. She knew she was not old enough to drive, but she had figured it wouldn't hurt to ask, then Nancy continued her line of questioning.

"How did this kiss make you feel?"

"Kind of strange, really. But I enjoyed it. There is something else, Mom, lately I find I can't concentrate on my studies, what's wrong with me?"

"Oh, Dear God, what do I do now?" Nancy said as she looked out onto the street. Once the traffic cleared, she pulled away and headed toward home. Nothing more was said between the two of them. Nancy couldn't really be upset with Annie, she remembered how she was at that age. Just the same. She had had sex for the first time when she was fifteen . . . and that boy turned out to be her husband now. But she sure remembered the mood swings. Thank God things had worked out the way they did and she could remember her mother saying, "Things have a habit of going full circle. One day you will understand." Annie had been a good kid, well most of the time, but her comment today had taken her by surprise. She just wasn't ready for the events that took place today.

Tony was in the kitchen of his family's restaurant. He loved to cook . . . it was in his blood. After all, his parents had been cooking for as long as he could remember. He loves the times that he would spend with his father in the kitchen, helping with the cooking. This was Sunday, and the Cross's restaurant was not due to open until later that afternoon. He was cooking his favorite afternoon snack . . . mac and cheese. He didn't go all out on the dish . . . it was plain and simple. He preheated the oven, combined the cheddar sauce, water, chilies, tomatoes and cheese in a bowl, and stirred in the uncooked macaroni then spooned the mixture into a casserole bowl, covered it with aluminum foil and put it in the oven to bake. Forty-five minutes later he removed the casserole from the oven, removed the foil and sprinkled the top with the remaining cheese, then put it back into the oven for five more minutes.

When it was ready he grabbed a bowl and fork and went into the dining room to a booth by the window. He had grabbed a root beer, his favorite soda to drink. He had also grabbed his sketchbook . . . he had not drawn anything for a long time.

He sat down in the booth, scooped some of the mac and cheese into the bowl and got ready to chow down. Instead of eating he found his hand gliding over a blank page in the sketch book and a face began to form. Annie Roberson's face. He could swear that she was sitting there modeling for him, as the picture came to life in seconds. He picked up the pad and sat back, smiling as he looked at what he had done. He hadn't noticed his mother, Angela, had come and sat down in the booth across from him until she put her finger on top of the pad and pulled it down so he could see her. "Hi, Mom. How long have you been there?"

Angela thought about it. "Oh . . . about an hour."

Tony didn't believe her, as she took the pad from him and looked at the picture. "You haven't drawn in a long time, Sweetheart. Who is this? She's pretty." She laid the pad back down on the table. "You should concentrate on your artwork rather than your cooking . . . you're very good."

"I don't know who she is. I just met her on the beach today."

Angela scooped some of the mac and cheese into a bowl and took a bite, then looked at the picture again "You know, she looks like Annie Roberson."

A surprised look formed on Tony's face. "The little girl that tried to beat me up last week. Damn, I thought she looked familiar."

Angela took another bite of the mac and cheese, savoring every taste. "Ummmm. We've got to talk your father into putting this dish of yours on the menu." She looked at Tony. "I have to say this to you, because you worry me."

Now his full attention was on his mother . . . he wasn't sure what she was going to say . . . . had he done something wrong? "I don't understand, Mother."

"Your father and I are concerned that if you don't straighten up, we may have to send you away to a military school."

Tony was shocked. He felt like someone had hit him with a sledgehammer. "You can't do that!"

"You have been hanging out with the group at the power station. You're always getting into some kind of trouble. You have to change before something happens to you."

"Mother, please . . . don't send me away, I need to be here with you and father . . . cooking."

She saw the fear in his eyes. "You really love cooking, don't you?"

"Yes, Mother."

"Well, tell you what . . . if you behave and show improvement in your schoolwork, we can see if your father will let you continue to cook." Angela couldn't help but smile at her son's reaction. The gleam in his eyes even got to her.

"Oh, Mother . . . . I want to be the best chef possible."

She just leaned back and shook her head in disbelief. "Well, you're going to have to study hard. Becoming a great chef is not an easy task."

"I just want to make you and Father proud of me."

"We are honey, we always have been." There was a tap on the glass window, interrupting their conversation. They looked up to see two men standing by the window, wanting to come inside. Angela let them in and showed them to a booth. "I had to disappoint you gentlemen, but the chef is not in yet."

The two men looked at each other, then back at her. Mr. Smith was the first one to talk. "We have been on the road for a long time. Could you please allow us some time to rest?"

"Of course. Would you like something to drink?"

"We would like some beer, tap please."

"Very good," Angela said and went to get them a beer while they talked between themselves. Angela slipped the pitcher under the faucet and pulled the large brass handle. When the pitcher was full, she sat it on a tray with a couple of glasses as Tony came up to her.

"Mother, let me cook for them."

"They are willing to wait for your father, Tony."

"Please, Mom. I can do this. I know I can."

"All right . . . we'll give it a try."

Tony ran to the kitchen to get things ready while Angela returned to the men with their beer. She sat the tray down, "You're in luck, gentlemen, our assistant chef has just reported in." The news seemed to make the two men very happy, so they began looking at the menu again. When Angela came into the kitchen, she was surprised to see her son hard at work, cooking something. She had no idea what it was. She had to smile at the eagerness she saw in her son and realized that he really did belong in the kitchen. She gave him the order and he seemed to understand, so she left to let her son do his work without interference. Tony was in the process of making something called Black Bean and Couscous Salad.

Tony brought the chicken broth to a boil and stirred in the couscous. He then covered the pot, removed it from the heat and let it stand while he grabbed a large bowl and mixed in the olive oil, lime juice, vinegar, cumin, green onions, reed pepper, cilantro, corn and beans. He then fluffed the couscous to break up any chunks and added it to the vegetables and mixed them well, seasoned everything with salt and pepper and it was ready to serve.

A few minutes after Angela left the kitchen she heard the bell signaling that an order was ready. "Tony, this is not what they ordered."

He looked at her . . . "It's something I've wanted to try . . . . it's something new . . . and on the house."

"I hope you know what you're doing."

"Trust me, Mother." She stood there for a second, then took the dishes to the booth. They looked at her strangely as she sat the dishes down in front of them.

"This is a new dish the chef wanted to try. He said to tell you that it's on the house." They both looked at each other, then at her, then tasted the food and from their reaction, they liked it.

In the kitchen, Tony had gone to work on the order his mother had given him, Baked Salmon with Tomatoes, Spinach & Mushrooms. He place the fish fillets skin-side down in a baking dish, sprayed them with cooking spray, then combined the remaining ingredients, spooned them over the fish and let it bake until the fish flaked easily with a fork. When he was finished he hit the bell again.

When she came back into the kitchen, Angela saw that Tony was already cleaning up after his work. She looked the food over and took a deep breath, inhaling the aroma. The two men were still talking over the food they were already enjoying, but stopped when Angela brought them their main dish. She sat the plates down in front of them and moved away so she could see their reaction, hoping she would not have a lot of explaining to do. Tony was standing at the portal window, also watching the men's reaction to his cooking. This was the first time he had prepared the main dish for a meal, he usually only did the side dishes while his father cooked the main dishes.

Mr. Jones got Angela's attention and motioned for her to come to their booth. At first she was hesitant, but quickly went to see what they needed. They asked her if they could talk with the chef and were surprised when Tony came over to them. "You are the chef here?" Mr. Smith said, surprised at Tony's age.

"Actually, Sir, my father is the chef, I just help out the best I can."

The two men looked at each other for a second, then back at Tony and Mr. Smith continued, "It was your father that prepared these dishes then?"

"No, Sir. I did. My father is not here right now." Smith looked over his shoulder at Angela who was standing nearby, not sure what to do.

"These dishes are amazing, Son," Mr. Jones said. "We are publishing a cooking book that should be out next year. We have been traveling the country trying different styles of cooking and are planning to put a lot of the recipes we gather in the book. We would love to put these dishes of yours in that book."

Tony glanced over his shoulder at his mother, who had a hand covering her mouth. He looked back at the gentlemen. "It would be an honor, Sirs. Just leave me your email address and I will send them to you tonight. Thank you both, very much."

"No, Son. Thank you."

Tony went to stand with his mother, who patted him on the back, and they walked back toward the kitchen as the men finished eating. Tony had to tell someone. He wanted to call his dad, so Angela handed over her cell phone and Tony went into the kitchen to talk while his mother picked up a coffee pot to refill the men's coffee cups.

# CHAPTER TWO

*"I had to, you would have put me in the hospital."*

TONY STOOD HELPLESS and powerless, watching as the tornado continued on a collision course with his home. He knew by the monstrous size of the tornado that there would be nothing left of his home. He stood there as the massive force of destruction devoured his home, tearing it apart like it was made of toothpicks. He turned just in time to see Annie sitting at her computer desk, still working at her computer as she flew through the air, sucked up into the tornado.

Tony suddenly sat up, looking around his room. He was breathing hard and he was sweaty. He didn't understand the dreams he had been having and finding that he couldn't go back to sleep, he went to his computer to look up the Roberson family. Way before the sun came up, Tony found their restaurant, but of course in a small town like theirs, nothing was hard to find. He sat down on the sidewalk and leaned against the building as he pulled his knees up against his chest and wrapped his arms around them, then rested his head on his knees. For some reason he needed to see Annie Roberson. Not just the fact that the dream had upset him, but he wanted to tell someone outside the family what happened. Maybe he would see her pretty smile again.

Tony didn't know how long he had been asleep until he heard the CRV belonging to the Robersons pull to a stop. He hopped to his feet and smiled when he saw Annie get out of the truck. He went to her and took her by the hand, surprising Annie, but she didn't remove the hand.

"What are you doing here?" She asked him.

"I had to come see you," he said as she smiled at him.

"I don't even know your name," she said.

"Cross . . . Tony Cross."

"Tony Cross . . . I like that name."

Nancy was surprised to see Tony standing there holding Annie's hand, but she did know him . . . his mother was her best friend.

"Well, Mr. Cross, what brings you here? Nancy said as she folded her arms in front of her and looked at the two.

"Hello, Mrs. Roberson, it is good to see you. I need to talk to your daughter about something, if it is OK? Can I borrow her for a moment?"

"Of course, Tony, take your time," Nancy stood there watching as Tony took her daughter toward the alley, but first he turned to face Nancy.

"I just wanted to say, Mrs. Roberson, that I now see where your daughter gets her beauty from."

Nancy's eyebrow went up on that one. Angela had told her what a flirt her son was, and Annie was giggling as the two disappeared into the alley.

Mark Roberson was the oldest of the Roberson sons at the age of 16. He came walking into the restaurant calling out for his mom. Nancy always believed that Mark looked more like her husband than the other two boys. She came from the back room carrying a large box. Mark took the box from her and sat it on the counter. "Hey, Handsome, what's up?" Nancy asked him as she started taking the cans from the box and putting them on the shelf behind her.

"Where's Annie? We were going to the beach today?"

"She's with her boyfriend."

Mark looked at her, stunned. "Boyfriend?"

"Our little Annie is growing up, Mark," she said, still working with the cans.

"Who is he, Mother?"

"Does it matter?"

"Mother!"

"Well, since you must know, it is Tony Cross."

That really surprised Mark . . . he knew the boy from school. "Cross?"

"Yes, Mark, is there a problem with that?" She began wondering about the over-excited expression on her son's face as she began breaking down the box to take it to the dumpster.

"Oh come on, mother. You know what kind of boy he is . . . always in trouble with the law. Hell, he could be a killer, or a masked rapist."

"Mark . . . he's only 11 years old."

"Remember the movie, 'Sunrise'?" Nancy nodded her head. "I rest my case. Where are they now?"

"In the alley."

"By herself?"

"No . . . with Tony." Mark started for the door but Nancy intercepted him. "Don't bother them, Mark . . . . leave them alone."

"But, Mother. She is supposed to clear any boyfriends through me . . . we've talked about this."

"Oh . . . I see. You're more upset that she found someone without getting your approval first."

"Mother, I'm not that way."

"Could have fooled, me."

"I have to go save her."

"From Tony?" She couldn't stop him, as Mark stormed out of the restaurant just in time to see the youngest of his brothers dismount his bike. Ethan was 12 years old and almost worshipped his oldest brother.

"What's up, Dude?" Ethan asked as he walked over to Mark.

"Annie is in trouble." That was all he had to say. The Roberson brothers were very protective of Annie . . . at least they thought they had to be.

Tony and Annie had been standing with their backs to the stone wall of the restaurant. Tony had blabbed away, telling Annie about the dreams and what had happened at his own place with the two men that had come in to dine. He found himself really opening up to her, finding it very easy to talk to her and she had been listening with such interest. That was new to him . . . Annie kept smiling at this boy who had taken an interest in her. She had never known anyone like him that could talk so much. But she had to admit that she really enjoyed spending this time with him and couldn't help laughing at the things he said. Somehow her hand found his and they intertwined their fingers . . . it felt so nice to be holding hands with someone like him.

Mark looked at his younger brother when they saw the two holding hands and they marched right up to them and Mark forcefully broke the hand hold, surprising Annie to no end. "Mark, what are you doing!?" She said as Mark pushed Tony against the wall.

"What are you intentions toward our sister?" Mark asked.

"Wait . . . you're her brother?"

Ethan had to make himself known . . . . "Me too, bro . . ." Ethan said as he slammed his fists together, ready to do battle with anyone who made a move on his sister. Then it hit Tony was Mark had just said.

"Intentions . . . . what intentions? We just met."

Before Mark could do anything else, Annie kicked him in the shin and took hold of Tony's hand, pulling him away as Mark jumped up and down in pain.

"You are not to touch him. I like him!" Annie said as she left the alley with Tony in tow. Tony kind of gave the brothers a half salute as he disappeared around the corner of the building.

"I don't know, but I can tell you one thing," Mark said to Ethan, "we will watch that bro." And again Ethan slammed his fists together.

"Yeah, watch," Ethan said.

Nancy was leaning on the counter watching her daughter with this boy and could not believe how Annie was acting. It looked as if she was star struck with him. Nancy smiled as her own love came into the place. He was Ryan Roberson, a tall man and according to Nancy damn good looking, and even after so many years together, he could still get her motor running.

"What's the Cross kid doing with Annie?" Ryan asked as he slipped his arm around his wife's waist. She looked up at him, then back at the two kids.

"Annie's got a boyfriend."

Ryan looked at her, shocked. "Tony Cross?" Nancy nodded as Ryan continued, "She got into trouble for beating him up in school last week." Again Nancy nodded.

"Look at them, Darling, she looks so happy."

"Well . . . I guess it will be all right, after all, you beat me up a time or two," Ryan said as he smiled at Nancy.

"But you still married me."

"I had to. You would have put me in the hospital."

"I love you," Nancy said, making him kiss her.

"And I, you." It was time for Tony to head home, and he stood just outside the restaurant with Annie, still holding his hand.

"Would you like to get some ice cream tomorrow?" Tony asked, hoping she would say 'yes'.

"I would like that, Tony." She had to smile at the excitement on his face.

"Me too . . . great . . . I'll pick you up tomorrow." Mark and Ethan came up behind Annie. Mark pointed to his eyes with his fingers, then at Tony. Ethan slammed his fists together. Tony had seen them and said his goodbyes and ran off.

"You are not going to go out with that boy." Mark said as he made her turn to face him and saw the anger in her eyes.

"Why Mark? Because he got drafted into the basketball team and you didn't?"

Ethan looked at Mark. "She's got you there, bro."

Annie left her brothers and went inside.

# CHAPTER THREE

*"It would be better to take a shower with water."*

THE NEXT DAY, at the ice cream parlor located in a small strip mall on the south end of town, Annie and Tony sat across from each other at a window booth. They were sharing a big bowl of ice cream with different flavors that was in front of them. Several other couples in the parlor were doing the same thing. The parlor was small, with a white tile floor, several drop fixtures, a glass enclosed case showing all of the ice cream flavors. "Here's an easy one." Tony said, then continued, "Captain Kirk or Captain Picard?"

"That's an easy one. Kirk. Going into unknown territory, I would much rather have a warrior than a diplomat." She said.

"That's my girl." The two did a high five over the table, and then it was Annie's turn.

"OK, I got it . . . . Dr. Smith or Dr. McCoy?"

Tony gave her a funny look as he scooped up some ice cream. "No contest. McCoy . . . I wouldn't trust Smith as far as I could throw him." They both snickered.

"I've got something to show you," Tony said as he reached into his backpack and pulled out his scratch pad, opened it and sat it on the table so that Annie could see the drawing he did of her. She was surprised and dropped her spoon so she could pick up the pad and look at the picture. Then she looked at him.

"You did this?"

Tony nodded. "After I had met you at the beach?"

"This is very good, Tony."

"Thanks." He looked up when he heard someone come in the door and couldn't believe who he saw. "Your brothers are here."

Annie looked over her shoulder and was not happy to see them. She doubted that they were there by chance. Mark sat across from Ethan at the next booth. He acted surprised when he saw Annie come up to them.

"Annie . . . what a surprise."

She was standing there looking at them with her arms folding and looking very much like the dragon Tony had imagined when he first met her. "What are you doing here?" She asked.

"We've come for some ice cream . . . it's hot outside."

"Yeah, hot," Ethan said as Mark looked in Tony's direction.

"Are you here with Tony?" Mark said, trying to act innocent, but wasn't doing very well. "Why don't you two join us?" Annie didn't say anything to the two. She looked at their sodas that they had gotten before Tony saw them. She picked up Mark's glass and poured it over his head. Ethan started laughing at his brother, then yelled as the same thing happened to him. Annie went back to Tony, taking him by the hand and not giving him much of a chance to gather his things.

"Come on," she said as she pulled him from the booth.

Tony couldn't help saying something as he walked by the two boys. "It would be better to take a shower with water." He continued laughing as Annie pulled him from the building.

"I don't like him," Mark said.

"Yeah . . . don't like him," Ethan said, slamming his fists together.

As they headed back to their house on their bikes, it started to rain. They ducked into the Pine Lake Book Store to wait it out. Annie was giggling as the two entered the shop. "Well, your brothers won't have to worry about taking a shower now," Tony said as he watched the rain come down even harder.

"Brothers can sure be assholes sometimes," Annie said.

"He just loves you, Annie, that's all."

"He chases all the boys away."

"Really," Tony said as she nodded. "You've been interested in other boys?"

"Yes. Remember Paul Tuckerman?"

Tony nodded. "I have heard of him."

"Mark beat him up because he said something he didn't like to me."

Tony found that interesting. "What did he say?"

Annie whispered in his ear and an odd look came over Tony.

"Really?" After hearing what that boy had said, Tony felt that he would have done the same thing to him.

"So, what kind of books do you like to read?" Annie asked as she looked around the fully-stocked bookstore. She looked toward the window as there was a bright flash of lightning and clap of thunder.

"I like action adventure," Tony said then continued. "It allows me to go some other place, but I have been reading a lot on cooking."

She smiled at him. "You like cooking?" She said as the power in the store flickered.

"Yes . . . . I want to be a great chef like my father is."

"Me too . . . maybe some day we can cook something together."

Tony smiled at the idea of the two of them cooking side-by-side in a kitchen . . . it would most definitely be interesting. There was a huge clap of thunder and the power went out. Annie jumped at the sound of the thunder and buried her face into Tony's shoulder. She hated thunderstorms. If she was home right now, she would be hiding in a closet until it was over. Tony didn't mind . . . he would hold her like that for as long as she wanted. He found he liked holding her.

A squad of fire trucks sped by with sirens and lights flashing. The sun was returning and the rain started to let up as Annie realized she was still in Tony's arms. She bashfully pushed herself away from him.

"Sorry . . . I hate thunderstorms."

'Never apologize for that."

She looked at him for a second . . . "what's wrong?"

"Come on, we better get back." Tony took her by the hand and they left the store and couldn't believe their eyes when they saw Tony's family restaurant fully engulfed in flames.

# CHAPTER FOUR

*"No, Sir. I'm going to remain a happy bachelor."*

PINE LAKE HOSPITAL was small, but efficient. Tony and Annie were running down one of the hallways when they finally saw both of their families. Annie ran into the waiting arms of her mother as Tony stood to face his mother.

"It was a lightning strike, Tony," Angela explained.

"Is Dad all right?" Tony was worried and scared.

"He's fine, Tony. He managed to get out. Aside from some minor burns, he's going to be all right."

"What about our place?" Tony said as he sat down.

"We will rebuild . . . make it even better."

Annie went over and sat down next to Tony. "It's OK, Tony. I'm here."

\*   \*   \*

That night, Annie found she couldn't sleep, thinking about Tony and what had happened to his family had her mind pretty active. She was pacing back and forth in her pajamas and finally decided to look for her mom . . . she would know what was wrong.

Nancy was in the kitchen, sitting at the table. She had a cup of coffee and was reading a book that she found she could not put down called "Love So True". She looked up when her daughter came in and sat down at the table with her. "Can't sleep, Sweetie?" She said as she sat the book down.

"I want to talk about boys."

Nancy was taking a sip of coffee but it didn't go down all the way and came out in a sloppy spray. She wiped her face with a napkin. She had a funny feeling something was going to happen, especially after the conversation in the truck while they were coming back from the beach. But she was just really not ready to have the talk about the birds and bees yet.

Annie continued, "I've been watching HBO, but I am still confused about things."

'You know, Honey, I think you should talk to your father about this." Annie stood up, more frustrated than ever.

"I don't want to talk to him. He's a boy. Besides, what does he know about it?" She couldn't figure out why her mother would want her to do that.

"He knows a lot more than you think, Dear."

Annie left her mother as she tried to figure out why nobody wanted to talk about the sex thing. She couldn't understand it as she took the steps to the second level.

Ryan had been pretty proud of himself when he decided to have an office at home so he could spend more time with his family and watch the kids grow up. It gave him a place to escape from the business, and sometimes when the kids were off doing whatever kids do, and the wife was running the business, the place was nice and quiet. He was so happy that his best friend Sam Cross was all right and when he got himself together, they would have to go and have a beer or two, after all they had known each other since kindergarten. In fact, Ryan had introduced Sam to Angela. He had no idea back then that the two would make a hell of a couple, and he was happy for them when Tony came along. By that time, Nancy had given birth to Ethan followed shortly by Annie. Nancy had difficulties with Annie's birth so the doctor had cut off the pipeline, which was all right by him. He didn't want anything to happen to his wife and he was happy with the kids they had. After all, Mark, Tyler, Ethan and Annie were proving to be an army of trouble.

Ryan looked up and was surprised to see his daughter sitting at his desk. He sat forward resting his hands on the desk. "You look like a person who has a lot of questions."

Annie looked at him. "I want to talk about boys." There's nothing like having someone drop a bomb in your lap.

"I really think you should talk to your mother." He saw the frustration in her eyes and watched as she stood up.

"She told ME to come talk to YOU!"

"She did, did she?"

"Yes."

"Well, perhaps you should watch some of the programming on HBO."

"I already do, Father. Why is it so hard to talk about the subject?"

Ryan had to snicker a bit as she stormed out of the office almost running into Mark. "What do you know about it?" She said to Mark who just stood there confused as she marched back to her room.

Ryan had just leaned back in his chair and tried to relax when he opened his eyes and saw his oldest son standing there. Again he leaned forward. "You look like a person who has a lot of questions."

"I'm worried about Annie." Now that interested Ryan, considering that she had just left him with a problem.

"And why are you worried about your sister?"

"Ever since this Cross kid came into her life, she's been acting strange and I don't like it."

Ryan could see that it was bothering his son.

"Mark, there may not be anything we can do about it."

"You mean you approve of their relationship?" Mark couldn't understand why he was the only one worried about Annie. "Do you know what kind of person Cross is?"

Ryan leaned back in his chair. "I do know Tony Cross. I remember him when he came into the world. He comes from a very reputable and famous family."

"That may be so, Dad, but he's none of that."

"I do know his reputation, Mark. Tony is a good kid. Annie might be just what he needs to change him and I think you may find he loves her as much as she does him."

"Love . . . . isn't that some kind of disease?"

Ryan could help but chuckle at that. "No, Mark. It is not a disease."

"Well it should be classified as one, the way it has affected Annie."

Ryan chuckled again. Mark, one day you will understand what she is going through . . . just wiat until you find that one special person."

"No Sir, I am not going to get affected in a way that I can't see beyond my own nose."

"Mark." Ryan couldn't believe the way his son was acting.

"No, Sir. I'm going to remain a happy bachelor." Mark left the room and Ryan decided to go back to dreaming about those hula girls. But it didn't last long when he jumped as Nancy came into the room and slammed the door.

"We have to talk about our daughter." She said, crossing her arms in front of her. It was then that Ryan figured that he was not going to get any rest until his entire family had reported in regarding Annie.

# CHAPTER FIVE

*"Happy Birthday, Kiddo."*

THE SCHOOL SEASON had started and the Cross's restaurant was finished and open and doing very well. Everything was new and even nicer than before. Tony was playing basketball and was also working part time at the garage, changing oil and filters. He seemed to enjoy it, although he might have been a little young for the job. The garage owner was a friend of the family and knew Tony very well. Tony had spent a lot of time in the garage with Joe and had always been eager to help out. Joe liked Tony and Tony's young age didn't concern him. He knew that Tony was different from the other boys his age, so with his studies, and basketball and cooking, he still found time for Annie.

Annie was good for him. Everyone could see the differences in Tony since he had met her, and it seemed like he was good for her. Mark still believed he was wrong for his little sister, and still tried to make trouble for them. It was November and Annie's birthday . . . she was turning eleven and her family had given her a hell of a party even though she had told them she didn't want it. Tony managed to get Annie away from the party so that the two could spend some time alone, so they were walking along the beach, holding hands.

They stopped and turned to look at each other. "I have something for you." Tony said as he reached into the cargo pocket of his pants.

"Tony, you don't have to get me anything," she said, watching him unfold a bag and pull out a gold flower pendant. She covered her mouth with her hand as he moved to put the pendant around her neck. She turned to face him.

"I love you," she said to him. She knew that those three words might not mean anything to Tony at his age, but she was happy with him. She loved being in his arms, and she loved his smile and the gleam in his eyes. Just being with him did something to her that she couldn't explain. She didn't know what, but she wanted him to know and when she just said that to him his face lit up like the sun . . . it just sat her inside on fire.

He gently touched her cheek, making her close her eyes at his touch. "Happy Birthday, Kiddo." He took her hand. "Come on    we'd better get back." The two walked back to the house.

After the party was over, Annie and Tony had found themselves at the Cross's place. They were in the kitchen, cooking a special dinner for themselves. They moved around the room with ease, it was almost like watching someone dancing. Tony was working on a pasta dish.

Tony started his dish by melting butter and added garlic in a medium saucepan. He then added flour, stirred, and added broth and milk, stirring frequently until it came to a boil and thickened. Then he added parsley, salt, pepper and cheese, stirring until the cheese melted. He then added his cooked pasta and mixed everything together.

While he was doing that, Annie had started working on an apple and pecan salad. She soaked farro in cold water then let it drain. She brought salted water to a boil and added the faro and simmered until it was tender. She drained the farro, rinsed it under cold water and transferred it to a large bowl which she covered and the put in the refrigerator to cool. She started heating cooking oil in a large skillet and added onions. Letting it cook for a few minutes, she added apples and stirred until the apples were slightly softened. She then transferred that mixture to the farro mixture and added thyme, vinegar and more oil, pecans, salt and pepper and tossed gently. The two then sat across from each other in a booth to enjoy the dishes and each other.

\*　　\*　　\*

The high school gym was packed with an overexcited crowd cheering for the home team as they moved about the court. Both teams had done very well when it came to racking up the score. Annie and her family, along with the Crosses were sitting on the first row of the bleachers. Annie had been cheering for Tony every time he got the ball. Tony had the ball and was setting up for his shot. His jump shot went into the basket, but as he came down, he landed wrong and he fell to the floor, clutching his ankle.

After the game, Annie barged into the locker room full of half-naked boys. When they saw her they tried to cover themselves . . . shocked that a girl would come in there. Annie didn't care. She had one target in mind and that was Tony. She marched up to the table where he was lying as the trainer checked him out. His ankle had been wrapped. "Jesus, Annie, do you know where you are?"

"I live with three big brothers . . . no big thing. Why did you do that?" She demanded an answer.

"I won the game, didn't I?" When the trainer finished, Tony swung his feet around and sat on the edge of the table.

"You told me you couldn't do that shot, and yet you did it. Why do boys have to be so macho?"

"Come here," Tony said.

"No!" Tony pulled her to him and planted a kiss right on her lips as a ton of towels came flying at them.

The next day, Annie went to her locker and when she opened the door two paper snakes came flying out at her, scaring the crap out of her. She leaned her back against the door. "I'll kill him." Was all she said. Tony had worked late that night and when he came home he ran up the steps to his room, opened the door and ended up with a bucket of water on his head.

Annie was in her bed and had rolled over laughing. She knew that Tony had to be home by now and had walked into the trap. She had to thank Mark again for setting the trap for her.

Even though it was chilly, Tony and Annie still liked to walk on the beach. It was their spot since they had first met there. The sky was clear and the stars were out and the moon lit the earth with a romantic white glow. The two were able to sneak away from their families and were holding hands. They stopped walking and turned to face each other. "You know, I never knew what love was all about until you came into my life," Tony said to her. "But now that you are in my life, I see things differently. I'm looking up to see the sun and moon. I'm looking around to see how alive the world really is. I feel complete, now, not alone."

"As long as I am at your side Tony, you will never feel alone. I know they say people our age are not supposed to feel love, to want to feel needed. I went online and found stories about other people our age that fell in love. The point is Tony Cross, I love you. I don't know how or when it happened, but it did . . . . it did. Call it crazy if you want, the fact is it's true. I know that all my life I have been on the edge, causing trouble, getting into fights and people called me wild and untamable. Maybe I was, maybe I am . . . . I don't know . . . . oh hell!" Annie kissed him on the lips and held it. However, they were interrupted by the sound of several motorcycles surrounding them. Annie stayed right next to Tony, holding onto his arm. Yes, she could take care of herself, and yes, she had a black belt in karate, but even her training taught her that when the odds are against you, it was better to be a diplomat than a warrior. But, if needed, she was damn ready to fight if she had to when it came to her Tony.

Once Glenn had dismounted his bike, he walked over to face Tony. "I want to talk to you," he said as Tony glanced at Annie then looked back at Glenn.

"Not with her here." Glenn thought about and and looked at Ashley.

"Ashley, take her home."

Tony removed Annie's hand from his arm and pushed her toward Ashley. "Go with her, Annie."

"No. I want to stay with you," Annie said, scared.

"Annie . . . please go home." Annie looked at both men with hesitation in her eyes, but turned to Ashley and got on the bike behind her. Once she was onboard, the bike drove away and Tony turned to Glen. "OK . . . what the hell do you want?"

Ashley and Annie arrived in front of Annie's restaurant and she got off the bike. "Tony told me about you," Annie said as Ashley smiled at the news.

"How does that make you feel?" Ashley asked her.

"I don't care who Tony saw, or what he did in the past. I know the kind of man he is now and that is what matters. But I do want to know one thing." Annie crossed her arms in front of her.

"Sure," Ashley said.

Annie found it hard to ask, but, "Did you two have sex?"

Ashley snickered. "No . . . I wanted to, but he turned me down. Good luck with him, he's all yours." Ashley then spun the bike around and took off.

"I've been watching your business. You have been very busy this week. I also know that your parents have not gone to the bank yet."

Tony figured out what Glenn was getting at . . . "You want me to steal from my parents?"

"You are a smart one, aren't you?" Glen said.

Without thinking about it, Tony answered, "No . . . I will not, could not, and how dare you even think about asking me?"

"Well . . . you know there's always Annie."

Tony grabbed Glenn by the front of his shirt. "You touch her, and so help me I'll . . ." The sound of Ashley's bike returning got their attention and Tony released Glenn.

"You won't do it?" Glenn asked.

"You know the answer."

Glen was afraid that Tony would go to the law and pulled out his switchblade and without warning jabbed it into Tony's stomach.

# CHAPTER SIX

*"This is not going to stop me from seeing him."*

ANNIE WAS SITTING at the restaurant doing her homework. She looked up when an over-excited Mark came running into the place. "Annie . . . it's Tony. He's in the hospital." That was all that he had to say (and he didn't like Tony . . . yeah . . . right.)

Annie was heading for the operating room that was blocked by two swinging doors that had a sign reading, "Hospital Personnel Only". That wasn't going to stop her. She was going to Tony. As she reached the door, her father intercepted her and scooped her up in his arms. "Let me go!" She cried out, struggling against her father's strong arms as he managed to carry her to a nearby waiting room.

"You can't go in there . . . he's being operated on."

"He needs me," she said, still fighting Ryan.

"Will you calm down?" Annie finally looked at both mothers who were standing near her brothers. She went to Mark.

"This is not going to stop me from seeing him."

"Annie, I . . ."

She didn't let Mark finish as she went to her mother and put her arms around her. "What happened to him?"

"We don't know all the facts yet, but a Good Samaritan found him on the beach. He had been stabbed. Annie, he's lost a lot of blood . . . they've been in there for a long time. We just have to hope and pray that he will come through this."

"I can't lose him . . . . not now."

Nancy took her daughter to one of the chairs and sat down with her and tucked a stray strand of hair behind Annie's ear.

"Mother, I love him."

"Annie, are you sure it's not just puppy love?"

Annie couldn't believe her mother would say that and stood up.

"I am not a child, Mother. I am 11 years old." She went to stand in front of Angela. "Mrs. Cross, I do love your son."

When the doctor came in, Annie almost ran him down. "How is he, Doctor?"

The doctor stood there for a moment, slightly confused. "It's OK, Doctor . . . she's his girlfriend." Angela told him.

Understanding, the doctor said, "It was touch and go for awhile, but he's going to pull through."

"Can I see him?" Annie said, not wanting to wait to be at his side.

"He's in ICU right now. I will allow two people at a time to see him." Angela took Annie's hand and the two followed the doctor out of the room. Shortly they stood at Tony's bed. He was still sleeping and there were IVs hooked up to him and an EKG monitor, showing a strong reading. Annie kissed Tony on the cheek and sat down next to him, taking hold of his hand. Tony slowly opened his eyes, but was verrrry groggy.

"Annie . . . . is that you?"

"Yes, Tony. I won't leave you."

"I love . . . ." Tony started to say, but fell back under the influence of the medication. Angela put a hand on Annie's shoulder.

"He's sleeping, Annie . . . . we need to let him rest."

"No . . . I need to be here, Mrs. Cross. Believe me when I say I love him. I'm not some school girl with a crush on him. My feelings are real . . . you must understand that."

Angela nodded . . . "I understand now."

"Hi, Mom . . ." Tony said waking up again. "Watch Annie . . . . he . . . he wants to harm her." He closed his eyes, but forced them open again. "They wanted me to steal from you . . . . I need to see Mark. Please, let me see Mark."

Angela left the room and a few seconds later Mark was standing next to Tony's bed.

"I'm here, Bro." Mark said.

Tony was fighting the grogginess, "Promise me . . . . protect . . . ." Suddenly the EKG monitor alarm sounded as it showed a flat line. Seconds later the crash cart team came in and Annie and Mark were taken from the room.

# CHAPTER SEVEN

*"Annie, have you been here all night?"*

A FEW DAYS LATER, Tony had gotten stronger. The doctor could not explain what had happened. Tony was now in a shared room with an elderly man that he had come to know as Henry. He found the old man to be very funny and he made him laugh all the time, even though it sometimes hurt when he laughed. Henry had told him that laughter was the best kind of medicine, other than love, of course.

Annie wasn't going to allow Tony to eat hospital food. She had told him that she wouldn't feed that stuff to her cat, if she had one. So, with approval from Tony's doctor, Annie decided she was going to bring Tony home cooking that would make the hospital chef envious.

The first of her many dishes was a good bowl of chicken soup. What else would you give to a recovering patient? She put the chicken and the vegetables into a large soup pot and covered them with cold water. She let them simmer, uncovered, until the chicken meat was falling off the bones (skimming the foam off every so often). She took everything out of the pot, strained the broth, picked the meat from the bones, and chopped the vegetables. She then seasoned the broth with salt, pepper and chicken bouillon to taste. She returned all the ingredients to the pot and stirred.

Nancy came into the restaurant, surprised to see her daughter slumped over in a chair, head resting on her arm. It appeared that she was sleeping. It was a good thing that it was the weekend, with no homework and no school to worry about. She knew that Annie would not stay away from Tony, not now, and most likely not ever. It seemed that her little girl had found the one she wanted.

Nancy went to her daughter and shook her shoulder to wake her. Annie opened her eyes and looked up. "Mom?" She said . . . surprised to see her.

"Annie, have you been here all night?"

"Shit, the soup!" Annie jumped to her feet and made a mad dash for the kitchen. She checked the soup and was satisfied that nothing had happened to it. She grabbed a thermos and poured the soup into it.

Nancy and Annie were soon at Tony's bedside, feeding Tony like he was a small child. Tony wasn't exactly happy about it at first, but decided there wasn't anything he could do, or say, to make her stop. Besides, the soup was some of the best he had ever had.

Henry inquired about the wonderful aroma that was making it's way through the room. He wanted some of the soup after Nancy explained what it was, but she had to check with the doctor to make sure it was all right. When the doctor gave Nancy the OK she got a bowl and gave Henry some of the soup. He sighed deeply, as he happily devoured the soup. Unfortunately, on Tony's birthday he turned 12 years old and was still in the hospital. Annie had prepared him a hell of a cake, and of course, Henry participated in the activity. With all the fine cooking and attention, Henry was released from the hospital with a clean bill of health. He left the hospital stating that he would miss that fine cooking . . . it was the best he had in ages.

Tony was also soon cleared to leave, but with orders to rest and no basketball or work for awhile. Well, he didn't play basketball, but he did help Joe out at the garage as much as he could. He didn't feel right about just sitting around watching TV when there was so much for him to do at Joe's place.

As time marched on, Tony got stronger and stronger and their feelings for each other, well, let's just say Pine Lake had not seen a relationship like those two in centuries. Annie convinced him to take up the martial arts. She was already at the school and warming up and wondering where Tony was. He was late, but when he was working at the garage he sometimes seemed to forget time, he loved it so much. Sometimes she wondered if he loved working there more than he loved her.

The Ann Phillips Martial Arts School was the only martial arts school in the area. People came there to train so they could defend themselves and keep in shape. Ann, co-owner of the school, was a fourth degree black belt and her husband was a fifth degree black belt, and martial arts master. He could launch a series of lightning speed kicks at an opponent while blindfolded, and not touch them. He could also send a person into next week in the wink of an eye. Most people came to the school because of the friendship offered by the two artists. They offered not only help with training, but a very good shoulder to cry on, if needed.

There was nothing special about the school. It was big, and had all of the equipment need to teach many of the martial arts styles, and the master knew them all.

Annie was paying more attention to the front door than her master and when she saw Tony enter the school, she jumped up and ran to him, and kissed him. Two of the mothers waiting for the class to finish started talking about them. "Annie, let Tony go," Nancy, who was sitting nearby, said, surprised that her daughter would act like that. The disturbance brought Ann Phillips from the office. She was tall, slender, with long black hair that she always had pulled back into a ponytail, and she was dressed in the school uniform.

"Miss Roberson, would you please explain your behavior?" Ann said as she stood there with her arms crossed.

"Ms. Phillips, this is Tony Cross, my boyfriend," Annie explained as she brought him to face Ann.

"That much I figured out," Ann said as she looked at them.

"He wishes to learn the martial arts, Ma'am."

"Do you have any experience in the martial arts?"

"No, Ma'am. I was just put in the hospital by a guy with a knife. I think I need to know how to defend myself if the situation comes up again."

"I see. Well, Ms. Roberson, take Mr. Cross to the locker room so he can put his things away and join the class. You will help him get started." Annie bowed, and when Tony didn't, she smacked him behind the head, making him bow, then the two moved off. Tony found he liked taking the class and decided to continue the training.

That night, after class, Annie went to the restaurant. There were some things she needed to take care of and was about to unlock the door when she was hit from behind, causing her to black out.

A winter storm had rolled into the region and it had started snowing pretty hard when Tony ran into the restaurant. Both families were there, along with the police. Tony rushed up to Nancy who stood to face him. "Where is she?" He demanded to know. He had just changed into his grease-monkey jumpsuit to work on a car when he got the word that something had happened to Annie.

"She was taken."

Tony was confused. "What do you mean, 'taken'?"

Looking at the note in her hand, Nancy handed the paper to Tony.

"DAMN IT!" That got everyone's attention and Ryan stood up. "I know where she is," Tony told them.

"How could you possibly know where she is?" Ryan asked.

"This is about me, not her."

Ryan took a few steps toward his son. "What do you mean? Help us to understand."

"You don't have to." Tony started for the door, but a tall, muscular African American man in a business suit stepped in front of him. Tony looked up at him.

"Where are you going, Son?" Keon Johnson asked him.

"My name is Tony Cross. I am not your son. Now get out of my way."

"All right, Mr. Cross," Keon said. "You want to tell me about it?"

"Get out of my way. I have to go save Annie." Tony started to move around Keon, but was stopped when Keon grabbed his arm.

"I can't let you do that."

The delay in action was bugging the hell out of Tony. He could have been at Annie's side by now and bringing her home. His next action surprised everyone, including Keon, who was suddenly slammed back against the door. "You don't love her. I do." Tony said as he shoved Keon aside and stormed out of the building, while Keon started yelling at him. Several police officers, with guns drawn, suddenly blocked Tony's path. Keon had given orders not to let him leave. As the snow came down, Tony turned to face Keon.

"I am a police detective, Mr. Cross. My name is Keon Johnson. I will only allow this action one time. Do it again and I will arrest you."

Surprised, Tony stepped back. "I'm not the bad guy here."

"I'm not saying you are, but you are a man in love, and I have seen what that can do to a man. You must remain calm or it will tear you apart, as well as cloud your judgment."

Tony couldn't believe what he had just heard. "Remain calm! How can you say that? Have you ever had a loved one in this situation?"

"No, I have not, but I do understand what you are going through."

"How can you say you understand if you haven't been there yourself? He's going to kill her if I don't show up!"

"We can help, Mr. Cross. We have been trying to get those kids in the power station for months. Problem is, it's like a fortress and they spot us every time. I have a SWAT team standing by, ready to move as soon as I give the order. Do you know a way in without being spotted?"

Tony nodded. "Yes, there is a series of drainage tunnels running under the station."

"You know how to get to these tunnels without being spotted?"

"Yes."

"Will you show us how to get in there?"

"Only if I come with you."

"You can't. It would be too dangerous."

Tony started to leave, but Keon stopped him again.

"Let go of me!"

"Why?"

"Because I love her, that's why!"

"All right . . . you can go, but if shooting starts, you have to take cover."

"Look Detective, my only concern is for Annie."

Keon nodded. "Now, can we go back inside? I'm freezing my ass off."

Tony laughed and they went back inside to plan their attack.

\* \* \*

Some cold water was thrown on Annie, shocking her back to consciousness. She looked around the room and found that Glenn was standing in front of her. Her arms and legs were tied to a chair. "You!" She said with anger and disgust.

Glenn started to walk around her, looking her over. "Sorry for the discomfort, but I know what kind of fighter you are." He stopped when came around to face her again.

"Oh, you have no idea what I can do."

Glenn thought that statement was interesting. "It would be interesting to put you into a contest with some of my best fighters."

"Why wait? Untie me and I'll give you a first hand demonstration."

"I don't think so."

"Then let me go."

"Sorry, I can't"

"What do you want with me?"

"I'm using you as bait."

Annie didn't like the sound of that, at all. "You're what?"

"I made a mistake with Tony Cross the last time. I didn't realize how strong he was. But without you, he is pathetic and weak. With you, he is as strong as any man could be. He cares about you a lot."

"I'm going to make you eat those words." There was a gleam in Annie's eyes that even got to him.

"Perhaps one day, but not today." He grabbed her cheeks with his hand and planted a kiss right on her lips . . . she couldn't fight him. When he released her, she spit it out.

"You taste like sandpaper."

He left her there, laughing as he walked away.

\* \* \*

It was still snowing when Tony and the police arrived at one of the drainage tunnels and moved into the darkness of the tunnel. With guns ready and flashlights to show the way, they waded through the ankle-deep water. They had travelled pretty deep into the tunnel when they came to a ladder. They climbed the ladder and quietly moved into the building. When the attack came, it was quick and without a shot fired. If Keon had know it would be this easy, he wouldn't have brought such an army.

Tony began to panic when he couldn't find Annie or Glen anywhere. Tony was standing by the police bus, watching the prisoners board it, one by one. Ashley came to stand in front of Tony, before getting onto the bus. She was not happy. "I trusted you," she said to him.

"Sorry Ashley, but my heart belongs to Annie." She just looked at him for a second longer before an officer took her by the arm and led her onto the bus.

"TONY CROSS!"

His name seemed to echo through the station, getting everyone's attention. He couldn't believe it . . . . Glenn had Annie on the water tower, the tallest structure in the complex. When Tony saw the condition that Annie was in, he couldn't believe his eyes. She looked drugged, even from where he was standing.

"COME FACE ME OR THE GIRL DIES!"

Keon brought Tony a bullhorn so he could respond to Glenn. "RELEASE ANNIE AND I WILL FACE YOU. BUT SHE NEEDS HELP . . . LET LT. KEON COME AND GET HER."

"I'll DEAL WITH YOU FIRST . . . THEN THE LIEUTENANT CAN HAVE HER."

"AGREED!" Tony handed the bullhorn to an officer and he and Keon ran to the ladder leading to the top of the tower.

Before Tony started his climb, he looked over his shoulder at Keon. "If I don't survive this, will you tell Annie that I love her?" Keon didn't like the sound of that, he was beginning to like the kid. Keon had a rope and repelling equipment with him. His plan was to repel off the tower with Annie in his arms.

"Why don't you tell her yourself?"

Tony smiled and started his climb as the snow continued to fall. He soon stood in front of Glenn and Annie. Glenn was holding Annie at knifepoint, with his arm around her.

"Oh, hi, Tony . . . you know . . . I can see my house from here," Annie said.

"What did you give her?" Tony asked Glenn.

"Just something to calm her. I know what kind of fighter she is."

Tony looked over the railing. "OK, Lieutenant!" Keon made the climb in record time. When he reached the two, he began to secure the line then dropped it over the edge. Tony helped Keon with Annie after he secured himself to the rope.

"Good luck, Cross," Keon said.

"Take care of Annie."

Keon nodded and launched himself off the platform. "Wheeee . . . I'm flying," Annie said as they sped to the ground and Tony turned to face Glenn.

"Up the ladder to the top." Glenn ordered and the two climbed to the roof of the tower. There was a slight curve to the roof and a layer of snow. "This is how it's going to be," Glen said, then went on to explain the rules. "We fight. The one left standing is the winner. No holds barred . . . we go at it hard and fast . . . understood?"

"It doesn't have to be like this," Tony said.

"You took everything from me . . . Ashley, my family, and now this place. We are going to fight and we are going to do it now." He let out something that sound like a battlecry and launched his attack on Tony. As medics were attending to Annie, Keon tried to see what was happening on the tower. Sometimes he could see the two men, then they disappeared from sight.

The fight went on, long and fierce. Glen was definitely the better fighter. Tony had just started his climb in the martial arts. He had learned things well, but it was the lower level of the arts, and Glenn was getting the better of him and seemed to be enjoying the fact that things seemed to be going his way for a change. As they fought, the snow kept falling and getting deeper . . . and was becoming very slippery. One mistake and someone would go over the edge . . . . just then both of them screamed as they lost their footing and went over the edge.

# CHAPTER EIGHT

*"I can see why you were anxious to get here."*

KEON AND A group of officers came running around the tower where they believed that Tony had fallen. At first they couldn't find him, but suddenly a hand appeared out of a dumpster full of trash and took hold of the rim. Keon just stood there shaking his head in disbelief as the watched his men pull Tony from the dumpster. Somehow Glen had missed the dumpster and lay face down on the pavement, very dead.

Annie came running up to Tony and threw her arms around him, hugging him so tight he had trouble breathing, but who cared. Keon came up to him. "You just used one of your nine lives, Son . . . I don't know how you did it."

"Detective, this is Annie Roberson." Annie wasn't about to let go, not even for a handshake.

"I can see why you were anxious to get here." Keon smiled at the two, he could see the bond they had.

"I am destined to be here, just like this," Tony said. Keon nodded and put a friendly hand on Tony's shoulder, then moved away. Tony and Annie followed him, still holding onto each other.

\*　　\*　　\*

That night Annie and Tony were sitting on the couch in the Roberson's living room. Nancy had made some hot cocoa and cookies for the two to enjoy while they watched a movie on TV. Annie was feeling like her old self again, and was snuggled to Tony as close as she could. "When I saw you scream out, my heart went right to my gut. I feared the worst . . . that I would never see you again. I never want to feel that way again."

"I'm sorry I put you through that," Tony said as she smiled at him.

The snow that had hit that October turned out to be a freak storm that had come right up from the south and with a cold mass in place, the rain storm had become a snow event. A group of people had recently bought the power station and was turning it into something useful . . . at least for the season . . . . it was becoming a haunted house attraction. And since it had been a power station, they had decided on a radioactive theme. They had mutants running around, as well as zombies and a mad scientist. The owners were surprised at how the idea had taken off and the lines of people waiting were getting longer and longer. They soon had to get more help and came up with a pre-show to help keep the masses outside entertained. There were now monsters of all kinds running about, scaring the innocents.

Annie and her older brother were in line. She knew that Tony had taken a part-time job here, but she had no idea what he was doing. She became very interested in watching as a mutant was scaring some pretty girls with a chainsaw. Annie was holding Mark's hand, but would have preferred that Tony had been the one at her side. She looked at Mark, wanting to say something to him, but realized it was not Mark's hand she was holding. It belonged to a one-eyed zombie. She let out a yipe, patting her chest. The zombie took hold of her cheeks and planted a kiss right on her lips. "I love you," the zombie said then ran off.

"Tony Cross, you come back here!" Annie started to run after him, but Mark stopped her. She turned to face her brother. "You knew what he was doing, didn't you?" Annie punched him in the arm. The mutant with the chainsaw started it up and came toward her, trying to scare her. "You are not going to scare me, Tony Cross." The mutant didn't know what to do when Annie started to beat up on him. That had never happened before. Finally Mark had to pull Annie from the monster so that it could get away. Mark couldn't help but laugh at the situation. "What's so funny?" She asked him.

"That wasn't Tony."

Surprised, she looked at Mark. "What?"

"He's over there, chasing those pretty girls around." Annie looked in the direction that Mark was pointing and, sure enough, Tony the zombie was chasing some very pretty young girls around the parking lot.

"Oh, I am going to kill him," she said to herself as she watched him spanking the girls on the butt, making them scream and laugh.

\*    \*    \*

The next Monday, at school, Annie was marching down one of the busy hallways at a pretty fast pace. Tony had to basically run after her as he tried to explain that what he had been doing was part of his job. Problem was, she wasn't listening to him. Finally, Tony had enough and grabbed her by the arm and pulled her into an empty teachers' lounge and put her back to the wall. "Why wouldn't you talk to me?" He asked her. She wouldn't look at him, even when he was that close.

"Just because," was all she would say.

"Because what?" Then it hit him . . . he realized what had gotten Annie all fired up. "You saw me playing around with those girls, didn't you?"

"I wouldn't have minded you playing around with them, but you kept hitting them on the butt and goosing them. Just leave me alone for awhile, OK?" Annie said as she tried to get around him, but he took hold of her arm and pushed her against the wall again and planted a kiss on her lips. She struggled for a few seconds but finally succumbed to the power of the kiss. "I hate you," she said when they finally broke the kiss.

"You know you love me," Tony said.

She put her hands on his chest. "Why do you have such control over me?" She asked as they touched foreheads.

"What is going on here?"

Suddenly they realized one of the teachers was standing behind them with her hands on her hips.

"Oh, hi, Mrs. Jones," Annie said. "We're sorry . . ."

"Oh, it's you two . . . . look, I can understand your relationship and how you feel about each other, but don't you think you can control yourselves a little while you're in school?"

"We will try, Mrs. Jones," Annie said as she took Tony's hand and pulled him from the room, then kissed him on the cheek. "I'll see you after school," she said and ran off.

"ANNIE . . . DON'T OPEN YOUR LOCKER!"

Annie didn't hear him in time and screamed when a dozen fake bats flew at her.

# CHAPTER NINE

*"She's everything I want in a companion."*

TONY HAD BEEN cautious . . . expecting Annie's retaliation at every door and every corner, but nothing had happened. He just couldn't believe that Annie would let what happened to her at school just slide, but it seemed like she had. The lockers at the martial arts school were assigned to the students, just like the lockers at school, everyone had a private locker.

Annie was already in class when Tony arrived. He had been working late at the garage and came directly to the school after he had cleaned up. He reached his locker and opened it. He wasn't expecting Annie's retaliation to come at the school. As soon as he door opened, a boxing glove on a spring loaded apparatus came flying at him, punching him in the face . . . not hard, but he felt it. The other students in the locker room burst out laughing. Annie had gotten Tony, big time and unexpectedly. He went into the training area and took his place next to Annie, who was snickering at him as the class finished their stretching exercises. "You are dead meat," Tony said as he jumped right into the exercise.

"This is fight night, Sweetheart," Annie whispered back to him.

"You don't intimidate me, Annie." The two were now doing a series of back leg roundhouse kicks on both legs.

"It is not my intention to intimidate you, Darling . . . I love you," Annie said as they started doing the back leg snap kicks. The class was soon ready for the sparring segment, and, as always, even 'though Tony was a lower belt, he was teamed with Annie. He was getting beter with his fighting and this time, he seemed to be holding his ground.

\*    \*    \*

Thanksgiving and Christmas had come and gone. The Robersons and the Crosses had spent the holidays with each other alternating between the homes. This was how they intended it to be as long as Tony and Annie were in love and seeing each other. They had become one big, happy family.

Winter left and Spring rolled right in behind it. Tony was running for dear life down Main Street of Pine Lake. A hand reached out to grab him and pulled him into the alley, with his back against the wall. A huge kiss was planted on his lips. Annie ran by the alley not realizing that Tony was there. The kiss was broken. "Ashley," Tony said, not happy to see her there in front of him. "How did you get out of jail?"

"It's amazing what a woman's body can do," Ashley said as Tony shook his head. "You disapprove?"

"Yes, I do . . . . I thought you were better than that."

"It got me out of jail, didn't it?"

"How many of the guards did you sleep with?" Tony asked as he took hold of her shoulders.

"Does it matter?"

"How many!!?

"Five, I guess, more or less."

"Ashley! How could you?"

"Don't look at me like that. I don't need your pity."

"Look Ashley, I can't see you any more."

"Why, because of Annie Roberson?"

"Yes . . ."

"I've been watching the two of you. You look very happy together."

"She's everything I want in a companion."

Ashley slapped him. "You bastard! If only you had given me the amount of attention you have given her, I might have turned out differently."

"Don't go blaming me for your troubles." She started to slap Tony again, but he intercepted it. "You are a special person, Ashley. I just hope you see that before it's too late." He turned to leave.

"Don't you dare walk away from me!"

Tony stood there for a second, not even looking back at her, then walked away. Ashley slid down to the alley pavement and started crying.

"Annie is going to be hurt when I tell her about this." Mark said, standing there leaning on the building with his arms and legs crossed. Tony took a few steps toward him.

"What do you want, Mark?"

"I don't like you, Cross. Never have. Even if everyone else has gone star crazy over you, I still believe you are wrong for Annie."

"Well, I happen to think that Annie should be allowed to make up her own mind. And if you haven't noticed, she is a big girl now." Their conversation was cut off by a loud scream.

"TONY CROSS . . . . YOU'RE A DEAD MAN!!!!"

The two boys looked up to see Annie charging at them.

"Got to run, 'bro," Tony said as he took off running.

"MR. ROBERSON . . . . DON'T MOVE!" Mark didn't understand why Annie was targeting him, but he wasn't going to stick around and find out. He took off running, following Tony.

\*       \*       \*

The two boys sat together on the beach. "You put a bunch of rubber bats in Annie's locker?" Mark couldn't believe what Tony had done. "I must say, Bro, you've got guts."

"Mark, I know we've not seen eye to eye, but you really don't have to worry about Annie and me. I love her."

Mark couldn't help smiling. "I know."

"Then why have you been against us?"

Mark took a deep breath before he answered. "It's not that I am against you guys. Before you came along, Annie and I were like buddies, the best that a brother and sister could be. Then suddenly she was hanging with you and I didn't see her."

"I'm not trying to take Annie away from you. Look . . . she is the most incredible person I've ever known."

"You act like you want to marry her?"

Tony thought about it for a second. "Perhaps, one day, when we're older."

"You think it's safe to head back to town?" Mark said, looking around. Out of nowhere a bucket of wet sand is dumped on both of them. Annie started laughing and took off running as Tony jumped to his feet.

"You come here, you little butt-breath!"

Mark came to stand beside Tony. "I can't believe you just said that," he said as they took off running after Annie.

Tony and Mark were hiding behind a building and Tony was holding a hose. "Are you sure this is a good idea?" Mark asked him.

"She's a good sport, Mark."

"I don't know, Bro . . . ." Tony smiled when he saw Annie walking down the street, heading their way. He suddenly let out a yell and jumped from his hiding place, letting loose with the hose. Problem was, Annie wasn't the only one that got drenched. Tony froze as he saw the very wet, very disgruntled police officer that had just come out of the building and walked right into the stream from the hose.

# CHAPTER TEN

*"I know that. Do you think I'm some kind of dumb blond?"*

T HE TWO BOYS found themselves in a holding cell at the Pine Lake police station. Mark was pacing back and forth, madder than hell that he had gotten caught up in all that. He had let his guard down for just a second and ended up in jail next to a person he didn't like before, and now disliked even more. How could he possibly have believed he could be friends with that dude? Another thing he couldn't understand was where his parents were. The two boys were sitting on a bench, but jumped to their feet when they saw Annie walking up to them. And, no mistaking it, she was madder than a wet hen. She stood there with her arms crossed, just looking at them. An officer unlocked the cell door to allow only Mark to leave. He looked at Tony then stuck his tongue out at him. Annie saw what he did and punched him in the arm, and not lightly . . . . it hurt.

"Hey, Annie. What about me?"

"What about you? I've been told that I can leave you here for at least a week."

Tony was suddenly worried that she might do just that. "Annie, it was just a few rubber bats . . . from Halloween . . . remember?"

"I know that. Do you think I'm some kind of dumb blond?"

"No . . . no . . . . never. You know that."

Annie rested her chin in her hand, thinking for a minute or so.

"All right, Tony. I'll make a deal with you.

"Anything . . ."

Annie started to pace back and forth as Tony watched her, trying to read her but couldn't.

"For one week, you are to be my slave, without arguments. You will do my nails, brush out my hair, perhaps a back and leg massage. Even cook me a steak dinner. If you agree, you can come out of there now. If not, you can stay for a week, or at least until your parents decide to come and get you."

"All right . . . I'll do it. But I have no idea how to do nails."

"There's always the internet."

"Come on, Annie." Annie once again didn't say anything and turned as if she was going to leave.

"Will you stop that?!!"

She turned back to him. "Well . . . . ?"

"I'll do it."

"OFFICER!"

For the next week, Tony did everything she told him to do: her nails, her hair, a steak dinner, and during that time he found himself falling more and more in love with her. Annie was lying flat down on her bed with nothing on but a towel covering her butt. Tony was using a hand lotion and rubbing it on her back and the back of her legs. All she could do was the lay there motionless and enjoy the sensations. Tony removed the towel and started to massage her butt cheeks and soon she was completely lost to his touch and fell into a sound sleep. When he finished, he covered her with a sheet and left the room.

Nancy walked by him and started to say something, but he put his finger to his lips and they moved off and went to the kitchen. Tony sat at the kitchen table watching Nancy fix a pot of coffee. "You like it black, Tony?"

"Yes, Ma'am."

Once she had fixed the coffee, she went to the table and handed Tony a cup, then sat down across from him. "You are one grade up from Annie, aren't you?" She asked him.

"Yes, Ma'am."

"What are your plans after high school?"

"I want to attend the culinary school at Timber City University," Tony said, taking a sip of the coffee.

"Interesting choice, Tony. Why there not, say, Washington, DC?"

"Well, Timber City is a hop, skip, and jump from here. I will be able to come home on weekends and spend time with my family and Annie.

"You really do care for her, don't you?"

Tony nodded as he took another sip of coffee. It's more than just care for her, Ms. Roberson. I am in love with your daughter."

That was nothing new to her, in fact, their relationship reminded Nancy of her and her husband. When they met and fell in love, they made it known to the world that they were an item. And when they were going hot and heavy, they didn't care where they were. Ryan was not the bashful type and she could see that same quality in Tony. "I have to admit, Tony, at first I was very skeptical about the two of you. I thought it might be just a fling and you would disappear on her. But now, the way she is with you, I have never seen her so happy." Nancy saw the excitement on Tony's face when Annie came into the kitchen wearing a bathrobe. She walked over to Tony, leaned down and kissed him on the cheek, then took the chair next to him.

"Honey, are you all right?" Nancy asked.

"I had the most incredible experience, Mother."

Nancy looked at both of them, wondering what her daughter meant by that. "Would you like to explain that statement?"

"Tony has the most amazing hands."

Nancy's eyebrow went up. Annie had to snicker when she realized what she had said. "It's not like that, Mother." Now Tony gave her a surprised look as she glanced at him. "Tony, help me out here."

"You're doing just fine . . . just keep digging the hole you're going to find yourself in."

Nancy gave up and started laughing.

*　　*　　*

Tony rose through the martial arts training, learning very fast, and was now getting ready to test for his black belt. He had already become well respected in the martial arts community. Tony and Annie had been horseback riding for most of the day. Tony was now 16 years old and Annie was 15. They were holding hands as they walked their horses and Annie glanced at him for a second.

"You've been very quiet today, Tony. Is something wrong?" She said as they stopped and faced each other.

"You know I test for my black belt next week?"

"I know and I am so proud of you. You went through the belts very quickly, and I just found out I will be testing for my second degree belt."

"I may have to fight you," Tony said, "and that is not something I want to do." She touched his cheek, trying to make him feel better with her bright smile.

"Oh, we may not have a choice, but there's something more, isn't there?"

"I've been accepted into the culinary school at Timber City University next year."

Annie was excited to no end and threw her arms around him. "That's great, Tony. It's what you've always wanted."

Tony nodded kissing the top of her head. "Joe wants to retire and sell me the garage. He said I have the right to own his business. I don't know what to do, Annie. I don't want to work on cars all my life. My dream is to become a great chef, like my father, but I don't want to hurt, or disappoint Joe, he has been so kind to me."

"I know you'll do what you feel is right, Tony. Remember, I am behind you all the way." Tony smiled at her.

"I love you." They kissed.

# CHAPTER ELEVEN

*"All right, Tony, I will do it . . . it will seal us together, forever."*

IT WAS TESTING night at the martial arts school and it seemed like everyone in Pine Lake had shown up to watch Tony Cross and Annie Roberson. The two had almost become as popular as actors. Most of the couples living in Pine Lake could only dream of what Tony and Annie had. They had found that they couldn't even walk down main street without being stopped by someone to talk or have passers-by in vehicles blowing their horns and waving at them.

Testing night went smoothly. They were tested on everything they had learned from day one until their most recent class. Every candidate performed flawlessly, each demonstrating the moves that they had learned. They had to demonstrate the kicking, forms and breaking, then the sparring. It was as Tony had feared, he was teamed up with Annie. According to the master of the school, no one ever knows what or who they will face in the street. Tony was put in a circle with 20 other students ranging from yellow belt to 4th degree black belt and Tony had to fight each one. It could be one at a time or two, three or more students, whoever the master call out to go into the ring. The fight began and Tony did a hell of a job fighting. He fought the best the school had, giving and receiving blows. He took care of his opponents with ease. The then master ordered everyone to the side of the room except Tony and Annie. He ordered them to face each other. "I don't want to do this, Annie," Tony said as the master ordered the two to take their fighting stances, but they both did as they were told.

"We don't have a choice," she said to him.

"Just remember, I love you."

"Of course," she said as the master ordered them to begin. The whole room grew quiet as they watched what might be the battle of the century as the two put on quite a show. Neither of them held back and went full force. As they continued to block each other's kicks and blows it seemed that they were reading each other and then Annie did the unexpected and flipped Tony to the floor. He found himself looking up at her as she extended her hand down to him to help him up, but Tony surprised her and tripped Annie and they went down to the mat and wrestled back and forth. Soon Annie was on top of Tony. "God, I love you," she said to him then kissed him and everyone erupted in laughter.

Then came the belting ceremony and the reception afterwards. There was food and drink for everyone. Tony wanted to talk to Annie in private so they went out back to do so. "There is something I want us to do together," he told her, making her wonder what could possibly be on his mind.

"I don't understand, Tony," she said as she watched him reach into his backpack and pull out a piece of paper. He sat the pack down and showed her the paper that had a heart shaped drawing with the letters T or A. She looked at the paper then at Tony. "What is this?"

"It is a tattoo, Annie." She didn't know what to say. She had never even considered having a tattoo on her body.

"The T is for Tony and the A is for Annie. You have the T and I will have the A. It can be very small and on our ankles." Annie turned away from him and Tony came up behind her and put his arms around her.

"I don't know, Tony."

"I have a friend that owns a tattoo shop. Since he is my friend, he will do these tattoos for free, besides I did some work on his car."

Annie knew this was something that Tony really wanted to do, she could see it in his eyes and hear it in his voice. She turned to him as he kept his arms around her.

"Will it hurt?"

"He assured me it will not," Tony said.

"All right, Tony, I will do it . . . it will seal us together forever."

"Forever," he said as they kissed.

"Jesus, will you two stop that!" Mark said as he stood in the doorway to the school, his hands on his hips. "Everyone is waiting for you . . . out front . . . let's go."

The party at the Cross's restaurant was something to remember. After all, they had two black belts in the family. Tony with his first degree belt and Annie with her second. There was music, lots of food, drinks and everyone enjoyed just spending time with each other. Even though both families were in the same business, it didn't bother them . . . they were as close as any two families could be.

Annie could never understand why her mother always had a camera with her, taking pictures of everything the family did. She had said that one day, time would separate them and everyone would have their own lives to lead and go their separate ways. Nancy wanted to remember these times so when she was missing her children, she could like back on the pictures.

Tony was standing behind Annie, his arms around her, her arms resting on his and his head resting on top of Annie's head. It was the time in Tony's life when he started to sprout and it looked as if he was going to get his height from his father, who was a very tall man that could have been a basketball player rather than a man being in construction before he opened the restaurant. The funds he had made in the construction business had enabled him to buy his restaurant. Nancy had to take a picture of the two, not because they were together, but they were glowing so bright that they could have been a lighthouse beacon. What she wasn't expecting when she took the picture was the rabbit ears fingers that appeared behind Tony.

\*　　\*　　\*

The next day the two were at the Pine Lake tattoo shop located off the main street. Annie was sitting on a table, watching the young man work on her ankle, and Tony was right about one thing, it didn't hurt. She was so fascinated with what he was doing that she never looked away. She was dressed in flip-flops, shorts and a bright colored tank top, and her hair was hanging loosed around her shoulders. She was holding one side of her hair with her hand as she watched the man work. Then it was Tony's turn.

Later that night, at the garage, Tony was working on the engine compartment of a 2014 Corvette Stingray Coupe 1LT when, without warning, a thick black stream of oil shot out at Tony's face. He stood there wrapping his face with a towel. It wasn't helping, it only made it worse. "Annie Roberson . . . . ," he said to the car as if it would talk back to him. Tony went to the workbench and opened a can of oil. He was going to track down the culprit and knew he would have far to look. He knew where she was, and that was at home.

Tony barged into the Roberson's home on a mission. Mark was sitting on the couch watching TV and burst out laughing when he saw the condition that Tony was in. Tony marched right up to Mark, and using a small brush, painted Mark's face with the oil, then went on to find his next target.

Annie was sitting at her computer, surfing on the internet and jumped up when the door opened. She almost burst out laughing when she saw what Tony looked like, however, a worried look came over her when she saw the oilcan in his hand. Tony slowly approached her as she retreated back against the wall. "Now, Tony, we can talk about this," she said, almost with a plea in her voice.

Tony had a devilish grin on his face that Annie wasn't sure how to read. Nancy appeared at the door to the bedroom and was surprised to see the shape Tony was in. Somehow, she knew Annie was somehow behind it. "Annie, what is going on here?"

Tony looked over his shoulder at Nancy and that gave Annie the chance to make her escape, and escape she did. She flew down the steps with Tony in hot pursuit.

The two flew from the house. Annie didn't know where she was going, she just knew that if he caught up with her that stuff would be all over her, and she could only imagine how hard it would be to wash it out of her hair. She could become a permanent brunette. Tyler Roberson pulled up to the house in his pickup truck, blocking Annie's escape. She backed up against the truck. "Tony, don't you dare!" She said to him.

Tyler had hopped out of the truck and ran around to the two. "What's going on here?"

"If you love me, Tyler, you will help me," she said to him.

"Help you . . . against him? He fixed my truck, Annie," Tyler told her and started laughing as Tony let go with the oil can and poured the contents over her head.

"I'm going to kill him," Annie said under her breath.

# CHAPTER TWELVE

*"So, Annie West Roberson, when you turn 21 will you marry me?"*

IT WAS TONY'S graduation day. He was now 17 and Annie was now 16. Since Pine Lake had a small population, the graduation class was also small. There were about 100 graduates that day, considering that several local communities were represented in the schools. It was a rainy day and looked like it would continue into the night. With the thunder and heavy winds, the ceremony was moved into the school gymnasium.

The ceremony continued smoothly, even with the occasional power flicker. Since Tony's last name was Cross, he didn't have long to wait until his name was called and he had made a prior arrangement with the school principal to interrupt the ceremony for a few moments. Tony received his diploma, then went to the podium. "Hi, you all know me as Tony Cross, and you must already know my relationship with Annie Roberson, and how the two of us feel about each other." There was a flash of lighting and a crack of thunder and the power flickered again. "My heart went out to her the day I ran into her sandcastle and she was about to punch in my face. Since then I have not been able to look at any other woman. She locked up my heart and eyes for only her." Again a crack of thunder and this time the power went out and the emergency lighting came on as everyone laughed at the timing. The power came back on and Tony continued, "It amazes me that we live in a very advanced country, after all, we have put a man on the moon, why can't we develop a descent power grid?" Again the lights flickered. "I'd better hurry up and get this done so we can get on with the ceremony. Can Annie Roberson please come up to the stage, please?"

Annie was sitting with her family and after her mother kissed her on the cheek, she ran across the floor to the stage. Tony took her hand and helped her up so she could face him. "You mean the world to me, Annie. You are my life force. Without out you, my life is not worth living. I want to marry you Annie Roberson. I know we can't get married now . . ." He reached into his pocket and pulled out a small black box and knelt down on one knee. He opened the box to reveal a beautiful gold engagement ring, with one beautiful diamond set in the center of the band. "So, Annie West Roberson, when you turn 21, will you marry me?"

She nodded vigorously as both of her hands were shaking so hard that Tony had to take hold of the hand while he slipped the ring onto the ring finger and the entire place erupted with approval.

Tony stood up and kissed Annie and they left the stage to be with their families. Tony's mother and father gave their son a huge hug and congratulated him on graduating from high school and the proposal, then congratulated Annie.

There was a party that night at the Roberson's house and Annie had stepped outside onto the porch and stood at the railing, looking out at the night. The storm had passed and the stars were beginning to finally appear. A can of Diet Coke appeared in front of her and she took it and popped it open, taking a sip. Tony leaned back against the railing next to her. "Happy?" He asked, as he held his own soda in his hand.

"I'm very happy Tony. I just wish we could marry right now."

"I know, but the law wouldn't be kind to us if we did that right now."

"But to wait six years. You might lose interest in me and find someone else," Annie said to a surprised Tony.

"I love you, Annie. There can be no one else for me." They moved to each other and kissed as she took hold of the back of his neck. This was the first long, passionate kiss they had experienced. They broke the kiss and then something else surprised Tony.

"I want to take you to bed," Annie said to him.

Tony turned from her to face out into the night. "We can't, Annie. In the eyes of the law you're too young. If anyone found out it could be very bad for us . . . for both our families. I'm sorry, but we have to wait until we can get married."

She nodded. "That is what I love about you, Tony, you have a lot of respect and honor in your heart. It is full of love and your eyes are kind. I love you, Tony, I always have, and always will, no matter what happens to us, know that my love for you is genuine and true . . . there will be no other." She touched his cheek with her right hand, then they slowly moved in for a second kiss . . .

"GOT YOU!" Nancy said as the flashbulb went off. She made a mad dash back into the house.

"MOTHER!" Annie yelled out and ran back into the house after her. Tony stood there for a moment and found himself giggling, then it turned into full blown laughter.

The next day, Saturday, Annie and Tony managed to set some time to themselves and wanted to cook a good dinner together. They found themselves at the Cross's restaurant, working in the kitchen. Tony had gone to work on the steak while Annie started on the side dishes. Tony heated the oil in a large skillet while he coated the cube steak pieces with flour. After shaking off the excess he dropped the pieces into the hot oil and let them brown. He then removed them from the pan and sat them aside. He mixed onion soup mix with some flour and sprinkled it into the skillet and let it start to brown. He gradually mixed in the water to make a gravy then returned the cube steaks into the pan, added seasoning, covered and let it simmer.

Annie had been working on a dish called Fresh Corn and Zucchini Sauté. She had heated butter in a skillet until it had lightly browned and added onions until they were translucent. She added zucchini and corn and stirred until the zucchini was tender, then added the seasoning. She had also been working on a second dish call Provincial Tomatoes. She preheated the broiler, placed the tomato slices in a single layer on a baking sheet, seasoned with a little salt, pepper and olive oil, then mixed together the Parmesan cheese, Asiago cheese, bread crumbs and parsley. She sprinkled the mixture over the tomato slices, drizzled a little more olive oil over the top and broiled until golden and toasty.

When they were finished and happy with their dishes, they sat in a booth across from each other. The only light source in the restaurant were two candles flickering away. They laughed and enjoyed each other's company as they ate and talked. Tony surprised Annie by pulling out a boom box and switched it to some slow dance music. Annie looked up at Tony who offered her his hand. She took it and he pulled her to him, placing a hand on her back, taking hold of her hand, the two started to sway to the music, slow dancing around the room. She looked at Tony with such a star-struck gleam in her eyes that at the time, she probably couldn't have remembered her name.

Later, the two stood facing each other just outside her home. "Thank you, Tony, for a wonderful evening."

Out of nowhere there was a flash of light. "GOT YOU!!"

"MOTHER!!!" Annie rushed into the house, stopped to think for a second, rushed back and kissed Tony, then ran back to find her mother.

Annie and her mother had come from the supermarket when Annie spotted Tony and his father walking to the market across the street. Annie told her mother to go ahead and that she would catch up with her later. There were two brick columns at the entrance of the market, and Annie was hiding behind one of them. She could hear Tony and his father discussing something about the business when she grabbed Tony by the hand and pulled him away from his father, who went into the building and saw a friend and began talking with him, not realizing that Tony had disappeared.

Tony's back was to the wall and he found himself in the middle of a kissing frenzy. Yes, he wanted to wait until they were married, but this girl was so horny that he was wondering how long it would be until they crossed that fine line. They both were in the midst of devouring each others' mouths. Tasting and sucking each others' lips and tongues, forgetting where they were as they got lost in the passion of ecstasy. The only reason they stopped was that someone was trying to get their attention and it took them a few tries to get their attention. When they finally turned, they saw a police officer standing there with his arms folded. "Oh, it's you two," he said as he watched them try to compose themselves. They turned to face the officer, still holding hands. "Look, you really must try to control yourselves in public." They both apologized to the office and the same time.

"It's just that I can't get enough of him," Annie told the officer.

"I know, I know about your relationship . . . hell the whole town knows. But you must contain yourselves . . . . there are decency laws, you know. Have you two had sex yet?" He knew that was a personal question, but he was thinking they if they hadn't, it might help calm them down a bit.

"No, Sir, we're waiting until after we get married." Tony told him.

The officer was happy to hear that. "See, you two are being reasonable. I had almost lost hope in the youth of today. Just be careful . . . . OK?"

They both agreed that they would try as the officer disappeared into the market. "What am I going to do with you?" Tony asked Annie as he made her turn to face him.

"I can't help it Tony, I just can't." He ran his hand through her hair and touched her cheek as he smiled at her.

"Whenever we do have sex, it's going to be wild," he finally said. "Hungry?" Annie nodded. "Let's go have some pizza, but I've got to tell Dad first, OK?" Again she nodded as he took her hand and they went into the building.

# CHAPTER THIRTEEN

*"Come on, Tony. We know we're just playing, right?"*

IT HAD BEEN a while since Tony's night had been plagued by the nightmare of the tornado. It was a nightmare that he had never understood, since that area had never seen such an event. But his mind had been so occupied with Annie and their relationship that he must have pushed it away somehow. Tonight was different . . . the tornado was back and just as confusing as ever. It was like some unseen force was trying to warn him of a disaster, but he didn't know what to do. Everyone in his family and Annie's were all healthy. He woke up once again from that nightmare, scared, breathing hard and sweaty. He grabbed his cell phone and called Annie. He knew that it was late and that she would be sound asleep, but he needed to hear the sound of her voice.

Annie was lying on her side in bed, when her cell phone started to ring. She rolled over, complaining. She had been having a wonderful dream about Tony and her on a tropical island . . . naked and enjoying each other to the fullest. "This had better be good," she said as she grabbed her phone, then sat straight up when she realized who it was. "Tony . . . what's wrong? Are you all right?" She was in her pajamas and didn't seem to care as she flew off the bed and down the steps. She didn't like the way he sounded.

Tony was sitting on the porch swing and stood up when Annie came out of the house. "Tony, what's wrong?"

He threw his arms around her, pulling her in tight as he could. "Don't leave me . . . please don't leave me."

Annie didn't like the way he was acting and took hold of his cheeks with her hands. "Tony . . . I am not leaving you, I promise. I would never do that. Please, you have to calm down."

"I can't live without you . . . I need you . . ." Tony kept babbling.

"I know, Baby, I know . . . . please calm down."

"I saw you die . . . you were taken away from me. It was so real . . . ."

"Tony, you're not making sense."

"Annie . . . . I love you so much, I . . ." he suddenly passed out and collapsed at her feet. Annie screamed out and rushed into the house, calling for anyone that would hear her.

\*     \*     \*

Tony was lying on the couch, covered up with a blanket, with Annie sitting on the floor next to him. Nancy had brought a bow of cold water and a towel and was gently using it to wipe Tony's forehead and face, trying to cool him down. "He's been working late at the garage, trying to get Mr. Johnson's car done for him. Mr. Johnson wanted to take his car to a show next month." Annie explained.

"I just talked to his mother, she'll be here first thing this morning," Nancy told her.

"He scared me, Mom. He's been having these horrible dreams about something always happening to me, that I am taken away from him. I don't want to leave him, Mother, I love him."

Nancy smiled at her daughter who was so madly in love. She could see a change in her daughter, and in Tony. Their relationship was good for both of them.

"You'll never leave him, Annie. I have never known two people who belong together more than you two. You have something special . . . you need each other."

"Oh, I do love him, Mother. I never dreamt that someone could have the power over me that he does."

"Remember when you first met him in kindergarten?"

Annie snickered . . . "Do I . . ."

\*     \*     \*

*"Come on, Tony, be a sport. We will both give you ten bucks if you put this frog in her desk." The blonde haired boy said.*

*"I don't know." Tony was very nervous about the whole thing. "She might beat me up into next week. You saw what happened to Billy Jones last week." He looked at both boys and the brown paper bag that one of them was holding, and in that bag was a large frog.*

*"So you are chicken," the black haired boy said.*

*"I am not."*

*"The whole school will know if you don't do this." The blonde haired boy said.*

*"Tony snapped the bag from the boy. "OK, I'll do it." That evening after everyone had left the school Tony sneaked into Annie's classroom, lifted up the top part of the desk and slipped the frog into it. Tony turned to see Annie standing at the entrance of the classroom with her hands on her hips.*

*"What are you doing, Mr. Cross?"*

*Tony had to think fast, "I     I forgot my book." He quickly picked up a book on a nearby desk.*

*"You too? I forgot my backpack," Annie said as she grabbed her pack hanging on the back of the chair at her desk. "I'll see you later, OK?" She said as she left the room, knowing that her mother was waiting for her.*

*"I have no doubt," Tony said as he left the room after her.*

*The next day, Annie sat down at her desk and lifted the top of the desk and the frog jumped out, scaring her, and caused everyone in the class to laugh at her. Tony was at his locker when he heard, "TONY CROSS, YOU'RE A DEAD MAN!!" Tony took off running, with Annie close behind him. He ducked into the boy's restroom hoping to hide until it was safe to some out. But, instead, Annie came into the room and as she approached him, he stepped backward until he found the wall. She smiled at him and put the same frog down the front of his shirt.*

\*     \*     \*

"Did you know that was Tony when you saw him on the on the beach that day?" Nancy wondered.

"I wasn't sure if it was him or not," Annie said. "Since the frog incident, he'd been avoiding me." The two then noticed Tony coming up to, still groggy.

"They made me do it. I stayed away from you because I knew you would beat me up. Annie . . . I love you," Tony said, then fell back asleep

Annie looked at her mother. "Was I really a little terror back then?"

Nancy folded her arms in front of her. "Why do you think all the boys ran from you when you approached them?"

"Is that why little Timmy refused to go to the dance with me?" Nancy nodded, not saying anything.

Early the next morning, after everyone had left the house, Annie was in the kitchen cooking some breakfast for Tony, knowing that when he woke up he was going to be hungry. The aroma coming from the kitchen was what woke him up.

Annie smiled when Tony came in and sat down at the table. She knew he liked his eggs, sunny side up. "How do you feel?" She asked as she sat down across from him.

"I'm sorry for the way I acted," he told her.

"There's nothing to be sorry for. You've been working way too hard on Mr. Johnson's car . . . work that he should have been doing himself."

"He just didn't have the time, Annie. He's very busy."

"And you're not?" She took a sip of coffee as Tony just looked at her and leaned back in his chair.

"Perhaps you're right. You know what I would like to do tomorrow?"

"What?"

"Let's go riding up to the outlook and have a picnic lunch."

A bright smile came over Annie's face. She loved the idea. "I'll fix lunch, oh, and I have something for you." She jumped up and got a small, brightly colored box that was sitting on the counter behind her. She brought it back and handed it to Tony, who nervously took it from her.

"You didn't have to get me anything."

"It's nothing, really. I just wanted to," she said as she stepped away.

Tony opened the box and jumped to his feet as a frog leaped out at him, scaring the crap out of him. Annie laughed and ran for her life up the steps to her room. "I'm going to get you!" Tony said, running after her.

She was planning to get to her bedroom and lock the door, but she wasn't fast enough, as Tony jumped through the door, just in time. Annie found her back to the wall as Tony came face to face with her. "Come on, Tony. We know we were just playing . . . right? Besides . . . you had it coming." Tony didn't say anything, he just grabbed her shoulders. "What are you going to do?"

He planted a kiss right on her lips and the longer he held it, the faster she fell under his spell. Her hands slid up his back to grip his shoulders. She loved the way he kissed her and could not wait to see what he would do to her in bed.

# CHAPTER FOURTEEN

*"No, Tony those are Crazy Jim's"*

SHORTLY AFTER NOONTIME on Sunday, Annie and Tony were horseback riding and it was looking like it was going to be a gorgeous day for riding in the woods with all the oak and pine trees. Especially with the pines giving off their scent that seemed to be soothing to one's senses. That was one thing Tony liked about going up there . . . . the sounds and the smell were so different from those in town.

There was something strange about the woods that day. Somehow things were different . . . he suddenly had an awful feeling and he dropped back, allowing Annie to ride ahead of him. When Annie realized that he was not beside her any longer, she looked over her shoulder and didn't like the way he looked. She turned her horse and rode back to him. "What's wrong?"

At first Tony didn't say anything. "It's just a feeling," he finally said.

"It's the nightmare, isn't it?"

He looked up at the sky that was beginning to darken. He nodded as the wind started to pick up and the horses were showing signs of nervousness. "We'd better head back." The horses weren't the only ones getting nervous.

"No, it's coming in too fast, we'll be caught up in the middle of it."

"Then what do we do?"

There are some log cabins up at the overlook, we'll be safe there. Come on, we'd better make tracks." The two had the horses at a full gallop as the sky became even darker and they were starting to hear the thunder and see the bolts of lightning.

They reached the cabins to find them locked and boarded up. There was no way in and it was starting to rain. "What now, Tony? I'm getting scared."

"There are some caves nearby, we'll be safe there." He mounted his horse again and they two rode off. Annie didn't want to go into the cave when she realized where they were.

Tony was at the entrance of the cave, but Annie was still on her horse. "No, Tony. Those are Crazy Jim's caves."

"Come on, Annie. That is just something the Park Police say to keep kids from going in there." He went to help her down from her horse.

They led their horses into the cave and took them to the back, where Tony removed the saddles, then tied the reins to a rock. "Everything is going to be all right, Annie," he said as he saw the fear in her eyes.

"I want to go home."

"After the storm, Annie. These things blow over faster than they start . . . . you'll see." The rain was coming down even harder and the thunder and lightning seemed to be all around them. Tony gathered some wood that was in the cave and started to build a fire. There was a large flash and even bigger clap of thunder and Annie screamed out when a figure appeared at the entrance to the cave.

A big man with a full beard and ragged clothing stood there. He had a dead deer draped over his shoulders and was holding a bloody hatched and a pistol at his side. He let the deer drop to the ground as a crunching noise could be heard outside the cave. The wind was now shooting into the cave like a wind tunnel, carrying all kinds of debris with it. The man known as Crazy Jim moved to the two, and even though Annie could most likely defend herself, Tony felt that since he was the man, he had to protect her. He jumped in front of Annie and yelled, "YOU CAN'T HAVE HER!"

Suddenly a loud, bone chilling sound that resembled a locomotive started to shake the cave. Rocks and dirt began falling from the walls and ceiling. Annie was knocked to the cave floor as the horses began to panic. Tony jumped onto Annie to protect her from the falling debris. He kissed her and tried to maintain the kiss as a way of keeping her under control. Then everything went black.

# CHAPTER FIFTEEN

*"I would give the world to her if she asked."*

ANNIE SLOWLY REGAINED consciousness to find Tony out cold. She began to panic that something terrible had happened to him. She managed to get him off her and then touched his neck with her fingers, trying to find a pulse. "No, you can't go . . . I need you." She took hold of his shirt and shook him, hoping that would bring him around. She was now crying. "Come on, Tony . . . please . . . . this isn't funny." Annie heard Jim moaning in pain as he also began to come around. She gently laid Tony's head in her lap. Jim found that he couldn't put any weight on his leg, and it was bleeding. He slid over to her. "Don't touch him," Annie said angrily.

Jim ignored her and touched Tony side. "He's alive. He should be coming around soon." Jim tried to adjust himself so he could lean back against the cave wall, but let out a yelp of pain. Annie suddenly realized the condition of Jim's leg.

"Your leg . . . . it looks bad."

Jim looked at her for a second, trying to contain the pain that he was in. "Don't you worry your pretty little head. I've had a lot worse happen to me." Tony slowly started to wake up and Annie started to pat him on both cheeks, trying to make him wake up faster. Soon Tony opened his eyes.

"Annie?"

"Yes, I'm here."

"Stop hitting me, OK? I'm awake now." Annie help him sit up as he looked around the cave, surprised that they had survived whatever it was that hit them.

"What was that?" Tony said, touching his forehead which was cut and bleeding.

"It was a tornado, Son, and a good sized one at that," Jim explained. Annie went to retrieve the small, but well stocked first aid kit in one of the saddlebags, and a canteen. She returned to Tony and started to work on the cut. She cleaned the cut with water then applied the Betadine that was in the kit and put a bandage over the cut.

Tony tried to slap her hands away. "That stings."

"Why do men have to be such babies?" She said, then looked at Jim who had just groaned. She and Tony went to look at Jim's leg. Tony used a knife in the kit to cut away the pants' leg and Annie gasped at what she saw. "Tony, we need to get him to a hospital."

"That will take too long . . . I will have to fix it for him, now." Tony went to work building a fire and within seconds he had one blazing away. He shoved the knife blade into the fire. "Jim, do you have any whiskey on you?" Jim reached into his jacket and pulled out a fresh bottle that a friend in town had given him. He was going to to drink it with his dinner that night. Jim handed the bottle to Tony who opened it.

"Is that for sterilization?" Annie asked him.

"Tony looked at the bottle. "This . . . hell no, it's for my nerves, they're shot to hell." Annie was surprised when Tony took a swig from the bottle then started to hand it back to Jim, but Annie intercepted it as the men looked at her.

"What . . . ? My nerves are shot too." The burning from the whiskey got to her throat and she started to cough, then handed the bottle back to Jim and wiped her lips with her hand.

Jim laughed at them. "You two drink well." He said and took a swig from the bottle. Tony was turning the knife in the fire. "Do you know how to do this, Boy?" Jim asked.

"Saw it done once in a movie," Tony said and removed the knife from the fire. Jim yelled out in agony as Tony began to work on the leg.

\*     \*     \*

Late that night, both Jim and Tony sat with their backs to the cave wall, enjoying the bottle of whiskey. Annie was napping on the other side of the fire, lying on the blanket they were going to use for the picnic. They had shared their food with Jim, who told them it was the best eating he had done in a long time. "She's a good woman, Tony."

Tony took the bottle from Jim. "You have no idea, Jim." He took a sip and handed it back to Jim.

"You love her, don't you, Boy?"

Tony nodded. "I would give the world to her if she asked." Jim nodded, understanding. "I don't know about you, but I think I can use that nap," Tony said as he got up and move to Annie. He sat down and gently laid her head in his lap.

\*     \*     \*

It was after dark and Mark was out in the front yard of their home. They were some of the lucky ones, with only minor damage. Part of the second floor had been hit by a tree and now had a large tarp draped over the opening. Luckily Annie's room and the master bedroom had been spared. The power and water had not come back on yet, and it was reported it could be several days before that might happen.

Their front yard was full of debris and the CRV was missing. Who knew where it had ended up. Mark was scanning the darkness with a flashlight, hoping that he would spot Annie coming home. They had been worried sick about her. "Where could she be?" Mark asked.

"We can only hope that she is with Tony and he is taking care of her," Nancy said as she came up behind him.

"Tony Cross . . . one would think that you believe that he is God's gift to Annie."

"Can't you see how good he is for her? How happy she is with him? Mark, they're going to be married one day."

"I swear, Mom, if he ever hurts her, I will kill him. Hell, he's probably having sex with her right now."

"Come on, Mark, if they are, don't you think that's their own business?"

"Not when it comes to my Annie." Suddenly, an over excited Ethan got their attention as he came running around the corner of the house.

"MOM . . . MOM . . . IT'S THE CROSS'S . . . THEY'RE GONE!!!" Nancy took her younger son's shoulders as the yelling brought Ryan and Tyler out of the house. Ethan was almost in shock.

"What are you talking about?" She asked him.

"Their house . . . it's completely gone . . . there's nothing, don't you understand." With that, they went running to where the Cross's house had stood. They all stood there in shock as Mark scanned the wreckage with his flashlight and an eerie quietness surrounded them. There was nothing but darkness.

"ANNIE!" Mark cried out as he started to run to the wreckage, but his father stopped him. "Let me go, she could be in that."

"No, Mark, stop . . ." Ryan told him as Mark dropped to his knees.

"I love you, Annie."

Ryan pulled his son up and wrapped him in his arm to let him cry it out. "I would trade places with her right now, if it would bring her back," Mark cried.

"We don't know if she was there, Mark. They were going riding . . . . or they could be in town. We don't even know if the Cross's were at home."

"Come on, Dad . . . we don't even know if the town is still standing."

"We will look for them in the morning . . . there's nothing we can do until daylight. It would be too dangerous to start searching with only flashlights," Ryan said as the group slowly walked back to their house. "What I want to know is where the rescue teams are." He tried to make a call on his cell phone, but there was no service . . . not even the emergency lines were working. They saw several National Guard trucks rolling into the area with troops aboard. Seeing them rolling toward the town made the situation even more surreal. It did happen . . . . they were not dreaming. The Cross's were gone, their dear friends . . . and Annie and Tony were missing. How could something like this happen? These storms just didn't hit in that area. None of them were really sure what they were going to see in the true light of day. It suddenly occurred to Ryan that maybe the rescue teams hadn't shown up because there was too much destruction in town . . . or maybe there was no rescue equipment that had survived.

*     *     *

Way before Jim or Annie woke up to the morning sun, Tony had been up and clearing the entrance of the cave so they could get out into the fresh air. It was beginning to get kind of stuffy in there. Tony had taken care of the horses, fed them and got the saddles ready for the ride back to town. They needed to get home, that was if they had a home left. He looked around at the devastated trees and realized that the wildlife was slowly returning.

The dreams that had disturbed his nights were only half right. There was a tornado of destructive power, but Annie was alive and unharmed and still with him. He made a promise to himself that if everything was gone, and it was just the two of them left, he would take care of Annie, no matter what.

Annie and Jim were standing at the cave entrance watching Tony cinching the saddles. "Jim, how did you come to live here?" Annie asked as she looked up at him.

"I was married to a wonderful woman at one time . . . at least I thought she was. My work took me away from her a lot, I spent a lot of time travelling overseas and our relationship began to fall apart. One day I came home early from a long trip and found her in bed with another man. We had a huge fight. After a while I couldn't blame her for what she did . . . I understood a woman's need for companionship . . . . something I was not able to give her. After we split, I took to the bottle, lost my job and the rest of my family and friends. I had no one to turn to so I came here. It's not so bad, really, I like the solitude, but sometimes I do get lonely."

"You're not alone any more, Jim. You have us. Why do people call you Crazy Jim, anyway?"

"What people don't understand, they try to give it a name."

Annie smiled at him. "I don't think you're crazy . . . I think you're sweet." Even though he had the thick beard, she could see that he was blushing.

"Annie, we have to go," Tony told her. Annie rubbed Jim's arm and then went to her horse. She thought about it for a second, then ran back to Jim, threw her arms around him and gave him a huge hug. That was it. Jim started to cry. Annie ran back to her horse, mounted and the two rode off. She turned and waved to Jim, who waved back at them.

\*       \*       \*

Annie and Tony were walking with their horses. They arrived at their neighborhood and didn't know how to feel or what to say as they walked through the wreckage. They could not believe how some of the buildings were completely destroyed while others only received minor damage. The debris field was enormous . . . it covered everything. Several people were out trying to see what was left of their property . . . and for some, not a lot.

They stopped at a corner lot, where Mr. Thomson lived. He was an army captain and would tell them all kinds of war stories, whether they believed them or not was something else, but he was a sweet man. They next house they stopped at was where the Hinson brothers lived. Annie had beaten both of them up a time or two. Suddenly Tony froze as his heart hit his gut. He dropped the reins of his horse and slowly walked away from Annie, leaving his horse with her. He slowly approached what had been his home. His quick walk became a run, leaving Annie behind as he began calling out for his parents.

The Robersons had just gotten back to the Cross's house when they saw Annie and Tony coming toward them. Annie spotted her family, and from what she could see everyone looked good. She ran to them, throwing her arms around her mother. Tyler took the horses from Annie as Tony started calling out for his parents as he searched the wreckage for any sign of them. Annie couldn't bear to hear, or see Tony in this agony and buried her face into her mother's side. Emergency vehicles had finally started to arrive in their area and Ryan sent Mark to get help.

Nancy told her husband to get Tony, but before he got to him, Tony found the bloodied hand that belonged to his mother, and dropped to his knees. He didn't know if he should cry, yell or what . . . he just didn't know. "Tony, you must come with us." Tony didn't even look up.

"What happened? Why didn't someone help her?"

"The emergency sirens sounded too late, Tony. There was no time. The tornado was on us in seconds. We barely made it to the basement. I doubt if your parents even knew what hit them."

"And that's supposed to make me feel better?" Tony just sat there, trying to take it all in as the fire department personnel arrived and started trying to get to his mother. Ryan pulled Tony to his feet as the paramedics started to examine his mother. One of them looked at Ryan and shook his head. "This is all I had," Tony said. "I have nothing left."

"That's not true, Tony, you have us . . . and Annie. "We'll always be here for you. You have to come with us and let these men do their work." Ryan looked at the engine captain and gave him their address. "We'll take him home with us. Please let us know when we can start making some arrangements." The captain nodded as Ryan led Tony away from the site.

# CHAPTER SIXTEEN

*"You don't love me anymore, do you?*

A WEEK LATER, AFTER the dead had been buried, and the massive cleanup had begun, the people of Pine Lake were not about to let something like the tornado take away their way of life. Pine Lake was a beautiful place to raise a family and even though that had been a loss of life, those living in Pine Lake would go on.

Annie had finally gotten fed up with Tony's moping around. She had not seen him since he locked himself up in the guest room. He ate, when he wanted to, in his room. Annie finally snap-kicked the door open but Tony didn't even flinch as it swung back and hit the wall. He just continued looking out the window.

"Go away," was all he said, with deep sadness still in his voice. Annie stood there at the door with her arms crossed in front of her.

"What do you think you're doing?" She asked him.

"Just go away. I don't want to talk to, or see anyone right now." He didn't even turn to look at her, just kept staring out the window.

"So that's it, huh?" Annie said as she went over and grabbed his shoulder and turned him to face her.

"What are you talking about?"

"You don't love me anymore, do you?"

"You know better than that, Annie."

"Do I? You haven't talked to me in a week."

"I just need some time."

"No . . . . you've had enough time. Damn it, you are going to spend some time with me. But first . . . you have to take a shower . . . you smell like a pig." She took him by the hand and led him to the bathroom. "Now take your clothes off and I'll wash them for you." Annie didn't mind it when he took his shirt off, but when he started to unbuckle his belt, she shoved him into the bathroom.

"I thought you wanted to see me naked?" Tony shouted through the door.

"I do, but not when you smell like that!" Annie said as the jeans and underwear were thrown out the door and landed at her feet.

"You know, you could come in and wash my back."

"I am your fiancé . . . not your slave," Annie said as she scooped up the clothing. "Now shower, then we will get something to eat and take a walk on the beach."

"Don't I have any say in this at all?"

"None whatsoever. And tomorrow night, we're going to see a movie."

Annie started walking away from the door when she heard, "I know who's going to wear the pants in this family."

"Damn right," she shouted back at him and continued walking away.

"Damn, she's got ears everywhere," Tony said as he turned on the shower.

Annie was in the utility room in the basement of the house, and had just thrown Tony's clothing into the washer, and was bitching to herself about their relationship. "Wash his back, he said. He loves me, he said. Wants to marry me, he said. AND YES I AM GOING TO BE THE BOSS!" She shouted out that part as she slammed the hatch of the washer down.

Mark and Nancy were sitting at the kitchen table. "Why is Annie yelling at the washer?" Mark asked.

"One day, when you are involved with someone, you will understand. I remember when . . . ." Nancy stopped at thought for a minute about the interlude that she and Ryan had on the washer that time . . . . They had been arguing for days and finally Ryan had enough and picked Nancy up sat her on the washer and did her right there. "No, on second thought, maybe you shouldn't know about that," she finally said to Mark.

"Come on, Mom, you can tell me," Mark said as Nancy could not help but wonder if Mark had finally started coming into the adult world.

"No, Mark . . . there are some things that should never be talked about." Nancy took a sip of coffee as they heard a commotion coming from the living room. Mark went to investigate and saw Annie going through her brothers' clothing. "What are you doing?" He asked her as she started going through another storage box, where she found a jersey.

"I'm looking for clothing for Tony to wear." Annie was surprised when Mark snatched the jersey from her.

"You are NOT going to give him that!"

"You have so many jerseys, what one more, or less."

"Not this one." Annie shrugged and started going through the clothing again and found a T-shirt with a horse on it. "You can give him that one," Mark said as Annie gathered up the clothing, put it back in the box and stormed back up the steps. She found Tony sitting on the edge of the bed with a towel wrapped around his hips. He watched as she put the clothing on the bed beside him.

"Put them on," she demanded as Tony stood up and let the towel fall to the floor. Annie gasped and turned her back to him, but found herself looking into the mirror and could still see him in all his glory. It wasn't a bad sight at all.

A short time later, Annie had fixed them both some dinner, and before the sun sat, they found themselves walking on the beach. They were surprised at the amount of damage that had been left by the storm, and how much was still left to be cleaned up. But, then again, the whole town had been grieving. There had been more important things that needed to be done and the beach was the last thing on anyone's mind, at least for the time being. Even with everything, the lake and the seagulls overhead still marched on with life as if nothing had happened. The two decided to take a rest before heading back home and sat down on a fallen tree. Tony had not said much since they left the house. Annie smiled at him and reached into her pocket and pulled out a penny, holding it in her fingers so that he could see it. "What is that for?" Tony asked.

"Penny for your thoughts," she said as Tony looked out at the lake, taking in the breeze that was blowing in from the water.

"Just thinking," he finally said.

"About what?"

"My future . . . our future."

"I don't understand," Annie said.

"I may have to leave."

A shock came over her face. "No! . . . Why?"

"Annie, I know the situation with your parents. They are financially strained. The repairs on both the house and the restaurant . . . there is only so much insurance will pay. They need to support you and your brothers . . . and now me? I don't want to be a burden on them, Annie. It's wrong for me to stay here."

"Tony, you belong with me . . . with us."

Tony closed his eyes and shook his head slightly. "I heard your mother and father talking about me. I'm a headache for them."

"No, Tony . . . I don't believe that . . . they love you. You must have misunderstood what they said." She looked at him for a moment. "You've made up your mind, haven't you?"

"When I'm 18 I will come back for you. You must believe that."

"Tony, I love you."

"I know . . . I love you too."

"When are you leaving?"

"In a couple of days."

Annie lowered her head in sadness, then looked up at him. "That's not much time. Tony, I want to do something for you . . . for us. Something to remind us of what we are when we're together."

Tony couldn't believe what she did next and that was to take off her shirt and let it drop to the sand. "Annie . . . someone might see you."

"We're the only ones here, Tony. I wanted to wait until they were bigger to show you, but since you have decided to leave, I'm not sure when I will see you again. This is the best time to show you as any." She blushed as she saw the way he was looking at her. "Don't they please you?"

"They're awesome," Tony told her.

"Then they are yours to do with as you wish." She moved to kiss him and when they did they fell behind the tree, out of sight.

"ANNIE!"

# CHAPTER SEVENTEEN

*"No, Mother. We made love."*

ETHAN CAME RUNNING out of the house. "Don't go in there," he shouted to Annie and Tony who looked at each other, not understanding the excitement in her brother.

"Ethan . . . what are you talking about?" Annie asked him.

"There's a woman talking to mom and dad. She's from the child welfare agency. She wants to take Tony away."

Annie couldn't believe what she just heard coming from her brother. She charged into the house to find her parents talking with a strange woman. They had been sitting around the table and stood when she rushed into the kitchen. "You can't have him!" Annie shouted.

"Ms. Cooper, this is my daughter, Annie." Nancy explained.

Ms. Cooper was a tall, slender, African American female. She smiled at Annie. "It's nice to meet you, Annie," she said as she extended her hand but Annie wouldn't take it.

"Forgive me if I don't shake hands with you" Annie said defiantly, surprising her mother.

"Annie."

"It's all right, Mrs. Roberson," Ms. Cooper said as she looked at Nancy for a second. "I understand."

"No, you don't," Annie exclaimed, "I love him . . . he belongs to me . . . with us."

"Annie West Roberson, you will be polite to our guest," Nancy said, beginning to get more than a little upset with Annie. The four of them heard the front door slam and Annie knew it was Tony.

"Tony, NO!" Annie shouted as she ran from the kitchen. She spotted Tony making a run for the woods and called out to him, then started running after him. Nancy came from the house, ordering her boys to go after them and bring them back. The boys had been working on the yard and finally had it beginning to look decent again. They dropped their tools and started running after Annie and Tony. Tony had already disappeared into the woods followed by Ethan and Mark. Mark managed to catch up to Annie and tackled her to the ground. The wrestled back and forth and Annie was screaming for Mark to let her go, but he didn't.

"I can't do that, Annie."

"He's running away, Mark . . . I'll never see him again," she said, still struggling.

"No, Annie . . . he loves you . . . . he'll be back."

"He told me he was leaving."

"Annie, you're not making sense."

She finally got Mark off her and jumped to her feet and started to make another run for the woods, only to have Mark grab her arm and swing her around to face him. She responded by slapping him.

"Leave me alone, Mark." She turned and ran into the arms of Tyler. She fought him, but his hold on her was too strong. "Let me go!"

"We lost him," Tyler said. "First light tomorrow, we will continue the search."

"No! We look for him now," Annie said.

"We can't, Annie. It's getting dark."

"You have to let me go!"

"Annie, stop it!"

"You stop it. Let me go!"

Tyler slapped her. He hated what he did. He had never hit his sister for anything . . . but he had to do something to get through to her. She held her cheek as tears began to flow. "I'm sorry, Annie. Believe me, I am." He told her as he put his arms around her and they slowly walked her back to the house.

The three adults were standing at the open door as Annie went to face Ms. Cooper. At first Annie didn't say anything, then, "I hope you satisfied. He's gone and I'll probably never see him again. I hope you know what you've done. Yes, he's only 17, but this was the only home he had left . . . the only connection to his parents. I hope you can all sleep tonight." Annie couldn't take it any longer and disappeared into the house.

Tyler went to stand in front of Ms. Cooper. "I don't understand how the government works, or politics, or any of that stuff. But I do know that this was wrong!" He followed Annie into the house as Ethan came up to her.

"If you weren't a woman, you wouldn't be standing right now," he said as he slammed his fists together.

On cue, Mark walked up to her. "I may not like Tony very much, but Annie is in love with him. I have seen what they are together . . . hell the whole town knows. If you had just spent some time with them . . . . oh hell . . . forget it, you wouldn't understand anyway!" He followed the others into the house.

"Sorry about that," Nancy said. "My boys all grew up with Tony and we love him as if he was our own."

"I think I do. I know how my report will read. Goodbye, Mrs. Roberson, Mr. Roberson." They all shook hands and Nancy and Ryan watched as Ms. Cooper got into her car and drove away.

"What now, Ryan?" Nancy asked as he came up behind her and put his arms around her.

"I don't know, Baby. We we will look for him tomorrow."

"What if we don't find him . . . what about our little girl?"

"She's not a little girl anymore, Nancy. She's a young woman . . . and in love. She'll have to learn how to deal with this before it eats her up. She will need our support and love, now, more than ever."

Nancy turned to face him. "And if she can't, Ryan . . . what then?"

"What would you have done, if this had happened to us?" He asked her.

"I know my heart would have been crushed. It would have taken a long time for me to recover . . . if at all. I love you, Sweetheart. I fell in love with you the day I gave you that black eye."

"How can I forget that one?"

"Oh, Ryan, I do love you," Nancy said as Ryan bent his head and kissed her.

\*     \*     \*

Tony was running . . . he wasn't sure how long he had been running, all he knew was that he could not hear the shouts of the Roberson brothers any more . . . they must have given up their pursuit. He knew that they would come looking for him at first light, and maybe with the police. He had to keep running . . . to where he didn't know, or care. He just had to get somewhere far away from there. He suddenly let out a scream as he ran into the arms of Crazy Jim.

"Where's the fire, Boy?" Jim wanted to know.

"They're looking for me. Please, you have to help me."

"Come on, this way, Boy." The two ran off, toward the cave. Jim could tell how upset Tony was by the way he was acting. It wasn't the same boy that he had met a few days ago. He acted like he had been betrayed. Jim wasn't sure where the anger was directed, but it was there, and Jim was worried for him. He had seen this in himself a long time ago.

Tony spent a long time with Jim, telling him what had happened since they had left him that day. They were sitting on the cave floor with their backs to the wall, sharing a bottle of whiskey. Jim had figured that Tony needed it more than him. "Jim, can I stay here until I am 18 . . . then I can go back and they can't send me to some orphanage, or worse."

"No, Boy . . . you can't," Jim said, not happy about the situation.

"I won't be here long, just a few months."

"No, Boy, no. Sometimes you don't eat . . . you're all alone, and this is the only thing that helps me to sleep," he said, showing him the bottle. "This is the only friend I have."

"Then what am I going to do?"

"Run, and stay alive. Then when you are ready, return and claim what is yours. You're a smart boy, you can do this."

"What will I do, where will I go?"

"Anywhere far away. You must be free and alive. But you must remember that Annie is your woman. Never betray the love and trust you have with her. Keep her close to your heart and she will always be with you. You two love each other. I saw it when you were here."

"I'm scared, Jim."

"You have the right to be."

"All right, Jim, if you think that is best."

"It is for you. I will take you down to the railroad tracks, but after that, you're on your own." Tony didn't like it, but he understood.

\*　　\*　　\*

There was a soft knock at the door. Nancy was concerned for her daughter and all she got in response was, "GO AWAY!!!"

"Annie, please open the door." She didn't like talking to a door, but a few moments later, it opened and Nancy went inside to find her daughter standing at the window, looking out.

Annie didn't even look at her. "He trusted me, us. How could we do this to him?"

"I didn't call them, Annie, Ms. Cooper just showed up about an hour before you did. I would never hurt Tony. You must believe that."

"I'm never going to see him again, Mother."

"He loves you, Annie. He'll be back, you'll see." Annie took a couple of steps toward Nancy.

"You don't understand . . . we said our goodbyes to each other," Annie said as she ran her fingers through her hair.

"What do you mean, Annie?"

"I think he must have heard you and Dad talking. He thought he was a burden on us. He said he would have to leave. I made out with him, Mother."

"As in . . . kissing?" Nancy was hoping that's what she meant.

"No, Mother. We made love." Annie moved to sit on the edge of the bed, burying her face in her hands. Nancy didn't know what to say, her heart had dropped to her stomach as she went and sat down next to her daughter.

"Did he . . . ?"

Annie cut her off. "No, Mother, I did."

"Oh, God," Nancy said under her breath. "Thank, God, you were on the pill."

"No, Mother, I was not." A sick look came over Nancy.

"What do you mean?"

"I had to stop taking it. It was making me sick."

"I didn't know," Nancy responded.

"I didn't want you to know. I didn't want you to worry." Nancy pulled Annie into her arms to hold her. "What am I going to do? I love him so much, so very much." Nancy just let her cry in her arms as long as she wanted.

# CHAPTER EIGHTEEN

*"You mean you're the Tony Cross that has this girl so beside herself."*

IT WAS A clear, sunny day and Tony and Jim stood next to the train tracks. They could hear a train coming, but couldn't see it yet. "Now, she'll have to slow down. There's a series of turns up ahead that she will have to maneuver through. That will be your time to board her," Jim told him. They could see the train in the distance, but it was closing fast. Tony had retrieved his backpack and black belt from the wreckage of his home. He unzipped the pack and pulled out his black belt. "This is important to me, Jim. Please make sure Annie gets it and tell her that I love her, and I will be back for her." He handed the belt to Jim, and he slowly took it from Tony.

"Don't worry, Boy. I will take care of it."

"I'm going to miss you," Tony said as he threw his arms around Jim to hug him.

"And I you. Make me proud. Stay alive . . . and free." The mile-long train was now upon them and passed with such force, the wind almost blew them off their feet. The sound of the trains' brakes was almost ear-piercing, indicating that it was slowing down.

"This is your chance, Boy . . . now go."

A string of boxcars was passing them.

'Don't forget, OK?"

"Don't worry, Boy . . . go." One of the doors on one of the cars was open and Tony took off running. The training was now moving slowly enough for Tony to keep pace. He took off his backpack, threw it inside. It took several tries, but Tony was able to grab the ladder that ran alongside the car and climbed up and swung into the car. He looked to see if he could see Jim, but he was out of sight. Tony went to the front corner of the car and slid to the floor and pulled out a photo of Annie. He just looked at it for a while and smiled.

She was the most amazing woman he had ever known . . . that wasn't saying much since he had only really known one other girl, but since they had made love, he loved her more than ever. He doubted that he would ever be able to have a relationship with another woman. He touched her photo with his finger as if he was actually touching her, but the sudden movement of the train brought him back to reality.

The train was stopping but he didn't know why. He pushed himself from the floor to look out the door but saw a group of state troopers searching the train. He didn't know what they were looking for, but he wasn't going to let them find him . . . he promised Jim he would live, and be, free.

Tony slipped on his backpack and was ready to jump from the train when he heard, "Don't move, Son." Tony slowly turned to see a huge frame of a man, holding a gun on him. The state trooper's name tag said, 'J. Smith'. "I want you to take off your backpack and drop it on the ground, jump down here, and put your hands over your head."

Tony did slip the pack off, but didn't drop it. "Don't you know it's against the law to hitch a ride on a train?" He was asked.

"I would love to stay and talk with you, Sir, but I made a promise to someone to stay free." With that said, Tony took a flying leap out of the car and started running. The trooper got on his radio, alerting the others. Tony saw the troopers start coming after him. He took off running in the opposite direction. He didn't get far when he saw some of the troopers jump from the car in front of him and he was suddenly surrounded. He had nowhere to go. He was ordered to drop to his knees and put his hands behind his head. He did what he was told and a trooper cuffed his hands behind him.

*     *     *

Smith was on his cruiser's radio, talking to headquarters and a female voice responded. "We didn't find the escaped prisoners, but we did find a boy that had hitched a ride in one of the boxcars. I need a want and warrant on 17 year old Tony Cross." Smith waited for a few seconds then got his response.

"No wants or warrants on a Tony Cross."

"Thank you, we will bring him in shortly." He threw the mike down on the seat and moved around to the front of the car. He was still looking at Tony's wallet and the school information card. "According to this, you're from Pine Lake."

"It's not against the law to be from there, is it?" Tony asked.

"Why were you on the train?"

"I was running away from a situation that could have been dangerous."

"For who?"

"For me . . . . does it matter?"

Smith was now looking through the backpack and found the picture of Annie.

"Put that back . . . that's mine," Tony demanded.

"She's very pretty. Who is she?"

"Annie Roberson . . . my fiancé."

"I know a Nancy and Ryan Roberson . . ."

"She's their daughter."

"You mean, you're the Tony Cross that has this girl so beside herself?"

"I guess you could say that. Look officer, I can't go back there?"

Smith put the photo back into the backpack. "Why not?" He leaned against the car, waiting to hear Tony's story.

"I just can't . . . that's all."

"Well, Son, you're in a lot of trouble. Running away from home . . . riding a train . . . I'm afraid I'll have to take you in."

"You're just trying to scare me, Officer," Tony said.

"Perhaps, but, nevertheless, you will be spending the night in jail. Damn, it's a hot one today. You know, going to an orphanage might not be so bad, in fact they would probably just find a foster home until you turn 18." Tony had a terrible vision of Annie coming to see him in jail, but it would be the only time. And going to an orphanage, or foster home would be worse. He had heard the terrible things that go in an orphanage, and even if it would only be a short time, he just knew it would be bad for him. At least the police didn't know about his fighting skills and his proficiency in the martial arts. If he could just get a chance . . . Tony watched the officer, who was leaning back against the car. It looked like he was getting sleepy. Tony figured that if he fell asleep that would be the time to make his move. Tony did a jump snap kick, striking the officer, causing him to go over the hood of the car and land hard on the ground. Tony dropped to his butt and moved his handcuffed hands to his front. He ran to the unconscious officer and grabbed the keys from his belt and freed his hands. He knew he was in for it . . . striking an officer . . . he had to get out of there and fast. He just couldn't go to jail, or to a orphanage. He just couldn't. He also knew that Annie would be pissed as hell at him and turn into that fire-breathing dragon he believed her to be when he first met her. He looked into the car and saw the keys still in the ignition. He jumped in, started the car, and sped away.

The officers still searching the train could not believe it when they saw one of their own cruisers coming at them at high speed. They leaped out of the way and started to fire at the vehicle, but, by that time, it was out of range. The chase began. Tony glanced over his shoulder to see several police cars chasing him, and even though he had the accelerator to the floor, they were closing in on him. He was amazed that he was able to keep all four on the dirt road that ran along the tracks. He was scared . . . he didn't know what he was doing, or where he was going . . . he had nowhere to go. Annie was the only person he loved, or loved him, and he just had to get away so he could go back to her someday. He knew this whole situation was going to turn out bad for him, but he was in too deep. What was he doing? He realized that there was a news helicopter over the area, reporting on the high-speed chase.

Annie was trying to forget what had happened to her Tony, but their love-making was so strong in her mind that her heart still ached for him. She wanted to hold him, touch him . . . be with him. How could all of this happen so fast? She was scared. She just knew something was going to happen to him. There was a knock at her door and Mark stuck his head in. "Annie, you'd better come down to the living room . . . it's on the TV . . . it's about Tony." That was all her brother had to say as she flew from her room and down the steps. Everyone was watching the news report of the high speed chase. Annie covered her mouth with her hand as she saw who was in the speeding police car. Her legs almost gave out as both hands now had a death-grip on the back of the couch.

Tony couldn't believe what he was seeing . . . the bridge he was on was blocked off by more police. The roadblock was close and he had to slam on the brakes and stopped within a few yards of the barricade. He looked out the back window to see the other cars coming to a stop. He was surrounded . . . there was nowhere to go and the bridge was over Grant's river was at least fifty feet above the water. Officer Smith got out of the car he was in and spoke through the PA system. "Mr. Cross . . . exit the car with your hands up and surrender." Tony noticed the radio in his vehicle and switch on his radio.

"No way. As soon as I get out you will blast me."

"We wouldn't do that. Nobody wants to see you get hurt."

"I'm not going anywhere, Officer Smith . . . not until I see Annie Roberson."

"The one in the photo?"

"Yes, I want her brought her now."

"All right . . . but it will take some time."

"I'm not going anywhere . . ." Tony said as he replaced the microphone on the clamp.

Nancy ran to the phone and after she answered, she covered the phone with her hand and called to Annie. Annie rushed to the phone and brought it to her ear. "Yes, this is Annie Roberson. All right . . . I'll be waiting." She hung up the phone and looked at Nancy. "Mother, we have to go."

"Go where?"

Annie pointed to the TV. "There." A few moments later the house shook as a low flying police helicopter flew over and landed in the vacant lot across the street. The co-pilot hopped out and opened the side hatch. He offered his hand as he helped the two ladies inside. Once they were all onboard, the chopper took off. "I'm scared, Mother. I have a bad feeling about this."

"Do you think you can talk him into surrendering?" Nancy asked her.

"I don't know, Mother. He's running scared. He's not with me and most likely afraid he will lose me. How could you do this to him?"

"He didn't hear the whole story Annie, and neither did you, for that matter. We didn't call social services, they just came to check on him. Even if they had wanted to take him, it would only have been for a short time, maybe a month or so; just until we could support him when the restaurant is back on its feet. Now that the house is done, the construction crew is going to be there tomorrow to finish clearing debris and start repairs."

"He's heard horror stories about orphanages. He's terrified of them. Oh, Mother, what have we done? Annie buried her face in her hands and started crying.

*   *   *

The helicopter soon landed at the bridge and the co-pilot hopped out and opened the side door for Annie and Nancy to get out. They were taken to where Officer Smith was standing beside the car. "I'm Annie Roberson," she said to him.

"Right now, Ms. Roberson, he is one scared puppy. You must calm him down and get him to surrender. We're not going to hurt him."

"I will try my best, Sir," Annie said as the officer showed her how to operate the mike. "Hey, Tony . . . it's me, Baby . . . your Annie."

Tony glanced over his shoulder and smiled when he saw her waving her hand. "God, she's gorgeous," he thought. "I'm sorry, Annie, so very sorry," he said into his mike.

"It's all a big misunderstanding, Tony . . . you can stay with me. Please come to me. Nobody is going to hurt you."

Tony had started crying. She could hear it and glanced at her mother for a second. "I'm sorry, I'm sorry," was all that Tony was saying. "I'm scared, Annie . . . I love you so much."

"I know, Sweetie, I love you too. Please come to me now, so we can go back to the beach."

He was really crying hard by then. "I can't . . . . I can't."

"Yes, you can. Yes, we can." Annie looked at Nancy, who was standing just behind her. "He's going to kill himself, Mother." Annie had a gut feeling about the situation and turned her attention back to Tony. Nancy covered her mouth with both hands, realizing that Annie was right.

"I'm sorry, Annie. I can't come to you . . ."

"Please, Tony, I need you. I can't live without you."

"I'm sorry, Annie, but it's time for me to go."

"NO, TONY!!! PLEASE DON'T." Annie screamed as Tony jumped from the car, grabbed the railing of the bridge and flung himself over the edge.

Annie fainted.

# CHAPTER NINETEEN

*"I thought you were bringing home fish . . . not a white boy."*

RAY BROWN WAS a former US Marine Captain. He retired when he met his lovely wife, but had lost her a few years before. He was a 55 year old African-American with dark skin and balding head. He was whistling a happy tune as he planned to end the day at his favorite fishing spot on the banks of Grant's River. He had a folded wooden chair tucked under his arm, his fishing pole was resting on his shoulder and he was carrying a bucket of worms. Whatever he caught was going to be dinner for him and his daughter. He opened the chair, sat it down, sat the bucket on the ground beside him and baited the hook. He cast the line out into the river and waited. He liked these times . . . he could clear his mind, and sometimes, just sometimes he could hear his wife talking to him. He missed her greatly. They say time heals the soul, but for some reason, his love for her had just gotten stronger. As he got comfortable, he spotted something floating near the shoreline, amongst the cattails and other water plants. He went to investigate and couldn't believe what he found. A white boy, face up, just floating, motionless. He went and fished the boy out, and began CPR. He wasn't sure if it would do any good, the boy looked like he had been in the water for quite some time. As he did a quick check, he found that there was a faint heartbeat. Then, the boy started to upchuck everything. Ray rolled him onto his side and let him get all of the 'gunk' out of his stomach.

After a few minutes, when the boy had relaxed a little, Ray asked, "What's your name, Boy?" He watched as the young man seemed to try to think.

"I don't know."

"Where are you from?"

Again the boy had to think . . . "I, I don't know."

Ray thought about it for a minute. "Did you just come through the rapids?"

"I don't know."

"Can you stand up?"

At the same time they both said, "I don't know." Ray slowly helped the boy to his feet, but to the boy, the whole world seemed to tilt and he passed out.

"Damn, it" Ray said as he flung the boy over his shoulders like a sack of potatoes and headed back to his place. The Brown Farm was small, but had several structures, included a barn for the horses and cows, a chicken coop, a garage, a pig pen with two happy pigs, a windmill and the main house that looked as if it had seen better days. It was a two level structure with wood sides, a screen porch, and slanted roof with a chimney.

Jackie Brown, Ray's daughter, was a tall, slender, 16 year old, with brown skin, brown hair and brown eyes. She wore no shoes, ragged short jeans, and a T-shirt that was cut just above the belly-button. Her long hair was pulled into a ponytail. She was feeding the chickens when she saw her father coming back . . . not with fish, but with someone draped across his shoulders. "I thought you were bringing home fish . . . not a white boy." Jackie said, as she stood there with her hands on her hips. She was not fond of white boys, or men.

"Stop your bitching, woman and help me get him into the house." Ray said as he passed her and headed for the house. She followed him and they went up the rickety steps. The inside of the house looked no better than the outside. The paint was peeling from the walls, the furniture and appliances were modern and it seemed that was where Ray had put his money.

They took the staircase and headed for the guest room. Jackie held the door open for her father as he took the boy and placed him on the bed. The room was small, with a double bed with a wood frame. There was also a dresser, desk and chairs and the window was open, allowing the warm summer breeze to enter the room. The floor was wood and the walls were plaster and one drop fixture hung from the ceiling.

Jackie was standing at the side of the bed with her arms crossed in front of her. "Pa, he is good looking."

Ray glanced at his daughter. "I thought you didn't like white boys?"

"He's handsome, who is he?"

"He doesn't know."

"What do you mean he doesn't know? How could he not know?"

"I'm guessing he's been in some sort of accident. It's probably amnesia."

"Where did you find him?"

"Floating face up in Grant's River. Look, we've got to get these wet clothes off him. Wait outside."

"I can help, you know."

"How old are you?" Of course Ray knew how old she was, he just wanted her to acknowledge it.

"Sixteen."

"Then wait outside."

"Oh, Pa," Jackie said as she left the room. A few minutes later her father called her back into the room. He had put their guest into fresh pajamas and had tucked him under the covers of the bed.

"Now, we need to call Doc Summers," Ray said as he went to the door, then turned to his daughter. "You are not to touch him, Girl." Ray left the room.

"He don't know me very well, do he?" Jackie said as she stepped toward the bed.

Ray stuck his head back into the room. "The point is, I do know yah," he said, then left.

*　　*　　*

A black RV pulled up in front of the Browns' home and Ray ran to the driver's side of the vehicle. Doc Summers got out and they shook hands. Doc was a middle aged man with silver hair and dark skin, not black, just tanned. He was casually dressed in a plaid shirt and jeans. "I'm glad you could come, Doc."

Summers reached into the back seat and grabbed his medical bag.

"So, who is he?"

"Don't know. Found him floating in the river. He woke up for a couple of minutes . . . said he didn't know who he was or where he came from."

"All right. Let's take a look."

The two men went into the house and Ray showed him where their guest was. "All right," Doc said, "you two let me do my job." Ray patted Summers on the back and started to leave the room, but hesitated when he realized that Jackie wasn't moving.

"I can help you, Doc," she said.

"How old are you?

"Sixteen," Jackie said with disappointment, then followed her dad out of the room.

An hour later, Doc Summers walked down the staircase and both Jackie and her father stood up. "How is he, Doc?" Ray asked.

"He is strong, and very healthy," the doctor answered. "I am troubled by his amnesia."

"Do you think he will ever remember?" Jackie asked.

"It's hard to say. It could be tomorrow, next week, next year, or never. Amnesia is funny that way."

"Is there anything we can do to help him?" Jackie asked, fascinated with the whole situation.

"No. Not really. Just make him comfortable until he is ready to face the world. But don't force him to try to remember. That could just make things worse. I will be back in a couple of days to check up on him."

The two men shook hands. "Thank you, Doctor. I will walk you to your car." They left the house and Jackie ran back up the steps to the guest room and found the boy sitting up in the bed. He smiled at her as she approached him and sat down in the chair beside the bed.

"Is it true you don't know who you are?"

"Yeah . . . I'm afraid so."

"Well . . . we can't just keep calling you 'Boy.'" Jackie brought her hand to her chin to think.

"My favorite uncle's name was Troy and my best friend's last name is Witt. So . . . how about Troy Witt?"

Troy thought about it for a minute. "I like it."

"All right, Mr. Witt, are you hungry?"

He didn't have to think about that one. "Yes, very hungry."

"Then, I will get you something to eat." She started to leave, but Troy grabbed her by the arm and pulled her down to him. They were close . . . almost touching noses.

"Mr. Witt . . . please." She told him.

"You just said my name was 'Troy', didn't you?"

"Please, Troy . . . my Pa may come in and see us like this."

"You are very beautiful."

"You're making me blush."

"Why do you keep your hair up?"

"It's easier to work when it's like this," she responded, even as Troy reached behind her head and untied the leather strap that was holding her hair in a ponytail and let it fall to her shoulders.

"You have such lovely hair, you should want to show it off."

"Who are you?" Jackie asked.

Troy touched her lips to silence her. "Shhhh." He pulled her even closer and they kissed. As they held the kiss she felt like she was about to blast off to the moon. She had NEVER been kissed like that. "Has anyone told you that you have pretty eyes?"

She tried to swallow, but couldn't. "Let me go get your dinner," she said as she was finally able to push his hand from her arm and stand up.

"What is your name?" Troy asked her.

"Jackie, Jackie Brown. My father, Ray, is the one that fished you out of the river." She went to the door but turned when he called out to her.

"Jackie . . . . thank you." She flashed him a smile and left the room, and she leaned back against the wall, trying to compose herself.

"Wow," was all she could say. She bounced down the staircase and headed for the kitchen where her father was at the table, reading the newspaper. He lowered the paper so he could see his daughter and was surprised to see her with her hair down. She never let it hang loose for anyone.

"What the hell did you do to your hair, Child?" He said, watching her go to the refrigerator and grab the leftover chicken. She slipped it into the microwave, pushed the keypad and then went over and kissed her father on the cheek. Something she had never done before.

"Thank you, Father. He's a dream." She went back to the microwave, got the food and a beer. She smiled at her father and left the room.

"A pretty smile and she gets all flustered . . . did she just call me 'Father'?"

Troy watched as Jackie sat the tray of food on the bedside table and go to his side. "Do you need help to sit up?" She asked.

He shook his head, but she did steady him as he stood up, then sat down in the chair. "I'll check with you later," she said and turned to leave, but Troy stopped her.

"Please stay."

She thought about it, smiled and grabbed another chair and moved to sit down next to him.

# CHAPTER TWENTY

*"He's not dead, Mark."*

NANCY WAS OUT in the hallway with the doctor, who was telling her about his findings that day. Annie was in a private room that could have been a suite at the Marriott. The door was slightly open and they looked inside to see Annie sitting up and crying into her hands. They looked at each other then quickly entered the room. Annie reached for her mother as Nancy sat down on the bed beside her. "He's gone, Mother. He's gone. I'll never see him again." Nancy didn't say anything, just held her daughter. After a few moments she pulled away from Annie to allow the doctor to examine her. When the doctor was ready to leave Annie asked him to stay so she could talk to him in private. Nancy thought it was strange, but went out to the hallway to wait.

"Doctor, I need you to check something for me," Annie said to him.

Concerned, he asked her, "What's wrong?"

"I had unprotected sex with Tony the night before all this happened. I had been on the pill for sometime, but it made me sick and I stopped taking it."

"It's too soon to check right now, but after you've been home for a week or so, come to my office and I'll run some tests, OK?"

Annie nodded her head. He left the room and walked over to Nancy who was waiting to go back in.

"Is something wrong, Doctor?"

"She's doing just fine. There's nothing to worry about, in fact, she will probably be able to go home in a couple of days," he said as he watched Nancy release the breath she had been holding. "She really did love this Mr. Cross, didn't she?"

"More than anyone could know," Nancy replied.

"She's going to need help, whether she believes it or not. I can have the hospital psychiatrist come in and talk to her. She's a very nice lady."

Nancy had to think for a minute, wondering what Annie would say about it. "I'll think about it, Doctor. Thank you."

"I'll check back with her tonight," the doctor said, then turned and walked away as Nancy went back into the room.

"How do you feel, Sweetheart?" Nancy asked as she sat down on the side of the bed and pushed a stray lock of hair from Annie's face.

"I'm drained, Mother. I feel empty inside, like my soul has been ripped from me." Nancy took hold of her hand. "Mother, they say when someone close to you dies, you will know it."

"And do you?"

"I feel that he's alive somewhere. Maybe cooking in some restaurant, doing what he loved to do. Is that so wrong?"

"No, Honey, I know how much you love him. If something happened to your father, I don't know what I would do to keep my sanity. But, Honey, you must know that he's gone."

"Do I? Did they ever find a body."

"No, but Annie, please . . . you can't do this to yourself."

"Do what? Hold on to him . . . I will never let him go. He's out there somewhere and I will find him again."

There was a knock at the door and Mark came into the room holding what looked like Tony's backpack . . . it was still wet.

"We didn't like the police report, so we have been searching the river for any sign that Tony might have lived. We found this." He handed the backpack to Annie. She took it and a tear started to fall as she searched the pack to find something that she could hold onto . . . she found the picture. The photo was the one that her mother had taken of the two at their graduation party after the black belt testing. Tony was standing behind her with his arms around her, and the two were looking as bright as the sun itself.

Annie brought the picture to her chest and began crying again. How was she going to do this without him? Nancy put an arm around her daughter, trying to make her feel better. Annie looked at Mark. "His black belt, Mark, he kept it here in this pack."

"I'm sorry, Annie, that was all we found." She extended her hand out to him. He took it and the three of them cried together.

\*　　\*　　\*

Annie was sent home a couple of days after that. It was hard for her to go in the house, but with the help of family, she built up enough courage to go inside. The cleanup in the town was almost finished and the rebuilding had begun. Her father had completed the repairs on the house . . . it was as if it had never happened.

Early the next morning, before anyone was up, Annie had walked to the lot where Tony's home had once stood. Now, it was just a bare lot. Annie walked to the center of the lot, rubbing her bare arms as if she was cold. She just stood there, lost in thought and didn't even notice her brother come up behind her until he put his arms around her. "You OK?" Mark asked. He didn't like seeing his sister like this.

"He's not dead, Mark."

That statement hit Mark in the gut. "Annie, the police found no sign of him. We didn't find anything . . . except the backpack."

"Precisely. I won't believe he's gone until I see the body."

"Annie, you can't keep doing this to yourself."

She turned to him. "Do what, Mark? Keep loving a man I can't hold or touch . . . I love him, Mark, don't you understand?"

"In time you will forget and move on. Perhaps you will find someone else."

She slapped him. "Never, Mark." Annie turned and started walking back to their house.

"Annie, I didn't mean it," he shouted and watched her turn and run back to him and she threw her arms around him.

"I'm sorry, Mark."

"For what?"

"For hitting you." Mark put his finger under her chin and made her look up at him.

"You can use me for a punching bag anytime you want."

Annie wasn't quite sure what to say, but she knew she had to tell someone. "Mark . . . I . . . we made love."

Stunned, Mark said, "Excuse me?"

"Tony and I made love just a little while before he left."

"Did he force himself on you?"

"No, Mark. If anything, I was the one that 'forced' the issue."

"Oh, Annie. Are you . . . ?"

"No, I don't think so."

"Thank, God."

"Mark, I would have the baby. It would help me live without Tony . . . I would still have had a part of him."

"You have to tell Mom."

"I did, Tony. Just don't tell anyone else . . . please?"

"OK. What can I do for you?"

She thought for a minute. "Take me to the park and push me on the swing like you used to do."

Mark smiled. He always enjoyed the time he had with his sister. He loved her and would take care of her, no matter what. "Sure . . . let's go."

# CHAPTER TWENTY-ONE

*"He's the man that is going to take you apart."*

TROY WAS FEELING better as the days passed. In fact, he was up and about helping with chores for the family that had been so kind to him. It was something that he would never forget . . . and there was something else . . . he was falling in love with Jackie Brown. She had qualities that shook him to his core. He was standing at the open window, watching as Jackie hung the wash on the clothesline. She knew that he was watching her, and she was making sure he saw every movement she made.

Troy was sitting at the table, drinking a cup of coffee and dressed in some of the clothes that Ray had given him. He was wearing a pair of ragged jeans and blue-checked shirt that was open to reveal his blue T-shirt underneath. He seemed happy that he had been given a second chance at life. He still had no idea why he had been floating in the river, or what his life had been before waking up here. But he was happy. He planned to stay with the Browns and maybe, someday, he would ask Jackie to marry him. There was one thing that bugged him . . . the tattoo on his ankle. A heart with the letter "A" in it. It had been on his mind since he first saw it and he just wished he knew what it meant. There were also the images that plagued his dreams at night. Just flashes of people, places and events that he should know, but he just couldn't hold onto them. He also wondered what he would do if he did remember. Would he leave Jackie and go back to the life he had before . . . what if that life had been bad? There were so many questions, and no answers.

A worried look came over him when he heard the sound of Harley Davidson motorcycles. There was no mistaking that sound.

Jackie was still pinning some of the clothes to the line and froze when those motorcycles formed a circle around her. There were six of them . . . muscle-bound buffoons dressed in Harley Davidson gear from head to toe. The leader of the group was Dylan Crest. He was the worst-looking of the group with dark skin, tattoos all over his body and a scar on his cheek. He was the only one that didn't have a shirt on underneath the vest he was wearing. Jackie shivered in fear when Dylan came up behind her and moved one side of her had behind her shoulder. "I like it when you wear your hair down, Girl," he said as he studied her neck that seemed to be begging for his kisses.

"You didn't come all this way just to tell me that," she said with disgust. And he disgusted her to no end.

"You know what I want, Jackie . . . and you know what my boss wants. Why does your father fight us?"

"Because you're nothing but low-life worms," she answered as the men around them laughed. He started to kiss her neck and cheek but she swung around and slapped him . . . hard. The men found that funny too. "Don't you dare touch me again!"

He ignored her, grabbed her and pulled her to him and began to have his way with her as she tried to fight back.

"LET HER GO!!!"

Everyone looked to see who had called out to them and turned to see Troy standing there. "Now who the hell is that?" Dylan said into her ear."

"He's the man that is going to take you apart." She replied.

Dylan grabbed his knife that he kept in his boot and brought it to her neck as he held her close.

"It doesn't matter who I am," Troy said. "But if you don't let her go, you won't leave this property standing."

"GET HIM!" The battle began as Dylan took Jackie to the barn to have his way with her. She was fighting him, but he was too strong. Troy may not have remembered who he was, but he had not forgotten his training. It was just like riding a bike as he took care of the men one by one.

Dylan got Jackie into the barn and found an empty stall full of hay. He threw her down onto the hay, took off his vest and dropped down next to her. She was still trying to fight him but he slapped her, hard, stunning her enough to get her under control.

The war outside was taking its toll as one of the men went flying through the air and crashed into the pigpen, where even the pigs sounded like they were laughing at him. Dylan laughed, thinking that it was the stranger that had landed with the pigs. He was now on top of Jackie, kissing her lips and neck and his hand was playing with her breast.

Another of Dylan's men landed in the mud with the pigs as Dylan used his knife to cut open Jackie's shirt. She wasn't wearing a bra, which delighted him to no end. Now, two more of Dylan's men joined their friends in the mud bath. Dylan was in the process of trying to get Jackie's shorts off, but her struggling was making it difficult for him.

A hand suddenly appeared on Dylan's shoulder and he was pulled off Jackie. Troy saw Dylan slowly get to his feet with his knife in his hand. He was going to slice up this boy so bad that Jackie wouldn't want to look at him. Troy made his move and, using a jump spin back leg hook kick, knocked the knife from Dylan's hand and then said, "Never touch . . ." He hit Dylan in the chest with a back leg side kick and sent him crashing through the wall of the barn . . . "her again."

Dylan and his group of Neanderthal throwbacks were just leaving the property when Ray pulled up in his rusty old Ford pickup. It skidded to a stop when he saw the condition his daughter was in. She was now wearing Tony's shirt and was holding it closed with one hand while his arm was around her shoulder. Ray ran to his daughter. "Are you all right?" He asked and she nodded her head.

"Troy saved me, Father . . . he was incredible."

"Come on . . . let's get her inside."

\*     \*     \*

There was a knock at Annie door. Nancy came into the room. "Mark said you wanted to see me." Annie could have kicked Mark's butt for this. She was not ready for the conversation she was about to have.

"My period has been off lately. That's why I talked with the doctor at the hospital. He said it was a little early to tell, but he wanted me to come back and see him in a couple of weeks to test again."

"We'll go to the doctor tomorrow," Nancy said to her.

"If I am pregnant . . . I want the baby . . . I want it bad. I will take care of it and love it as no one else could. I need it."

Nancy was now stroking the back of Annie's head. "Shhh . . . everything is going to be all right, Baby."

"Why, Mother? Why was he taken from me?"

"God decided it was his time to go."

'How could God be so cruel?" She said as she went back to look out the window again.

"Annie West Roberson! I am shocked at you!"

Annie looked over her shoulder at her mother. "Doesn't he know what he has done to me? Taking the only person I ever cared about . . . loved. I miss him so much it actually hurts."

"You are not the first one to lose someone close to you. You'll see, Sweetheart, with a little time, this will all pass."

"I guess that depends on whether I'm pregnant or not, doesn't it? If I am, at least I will have a part of him."

Nancy moved to her daughter and pulled her into her arms again.

"The family is behind you, Annie. We all love you."

"Will the family accept the baby?"

"Of course. You know we will. You know that Mark would want to be a part of the baby's life, don't you?"

This was the first time that Annie had even come close to laughing and it was more like a snicker.

"Mark . . . he's such a jerk. I know he will be a part of the baby's life. I don't think I will be able to keep him away from it."

"When you were born, I never saw you that much. Mark had you in his room and was playing with dolls on the floor with you, pushing you on the swing in the park, he even changed your diapers."

Annie blushed.

*   *   *

Blake Carter was an angry man. Angry at the man who was supposed to be the best. Carter was a tall, good looking man of 34. He wore the best suits that fit like a glove. He had pearl white hair and dark blue eyes. He got up and moved around the desk to face Dylan Crest, who stood there with his head lowered in shame. "I hired you because you came highly recommended by my brother. Now you come back with some story about someone who was like Jackie Chan?"

"He was incredible, Sir. My men never laid a hand on him."

"Who is he? Where did he come from?" Carter sneered with disgust.

"I don't know, Sir. He did seem to care about the Browns."

"Is he someone I can buy off?"

"I don't think so, Sir." Dylan watched Carter walk around him and go to a table displaying a 3D model of a building complex.

"Do you know what this is, Crest?"

"Yes, Sir, I do."

"It is my dream. A huge entertainment complex that would draw the tourist trade tenfold to this dormant area of the country."

"And add money to your pockets."

"This complex includes a shopping mall, a hotel and casino, multiplex movie house, and condos. Anything one would need during their stay in the area.'"

"And add money to your pockets."

"Now, I have approached the Browns with a reasonable offer for their property, but they refused. I don't like to be turned down."

"I know, Sir. Maybe you should look at another location, Sir."

Carter turned to him. "That piece of land is the biggest in the area. It will easily handle this complex. No, Dylan, I need the Brown's place and I need it now!"

"All I'm saying, Sir, is that it might be difficult with this new person in the picture right now."

Carter took a few steps to Dylan. "If you can't do this, Dylan, I will get someone who can." Dylan nodded and didn't understand when Carter pulled out his wallet and removed twenty dollars and handed it to him.

"For God's sake, go buy a shirt."

Dylan nodded and started toward the door. "Not that way, the back door," Carter told him. "I don't want anyone to see you leave here. Dylan turned and went to the back door, opened it and left. Carter went to his desk and picked up the phone. "Get me Lee Du-Ho, Korea. I don't care about the time difference; just get him on the phone." Carter slammed the phone down and went to the window and looked out. "Ray Brown, if you think this newcomer will be able to keep me from what I want, you are sadly mistaken . . . I will kill him first."

# CHAPTER TWENTY-TWO

*"They did have something special."*

THE DOCTOR STEPPED into the small examination room. Annie was dressed in a hospital gown and sitting on the examination table while Nancy stood by her side. The doctor hesitated for a moment, then approached the two. "I have some good news for you, Ms. Roberson. You are not pregnant." A sad look came over Annie as she glanced at her mother, then back at the doctor.

"It has to be a mistake . . . run the test again," she told him.

"Annie!" Her mother said, angrily.

"It has to be wrong, Doctor. My period has been off, and I've been feeling sick."

"You have been under a lot of stress, young lady. And from what I have been told you have not been eating or sleeping well." He watched as her eyes gathered with tears. "I'm sorry if the results did not meet with your approval. I am surprised. Most young, unmarried women would be happy that they were not pregnant."

"Doctor, can I talk to you outside?" Nancy asked him and both of them stepped out of the room.

"I don't understand," the doctor told her.

"My daughter loved Tony Cross, Doctor, very much."

"I am very aware of that, Mrs. Roberson. I hear the gossip on the streets, in the coffee shop, in the grocery stores. It appears that the two of them had become something like celebrities."

"Yes. This whole area has been fascinated with the two of them. I don't know how my daughter will be able to handle all the attention. I feel it may drive her insane. Doctor, my daughter wanted this baby so badly; it was the last thing in her life that she had to remind her of Tony."

"I understand, Mrs. Roberson, but I strongly suggest that she see a psychiatrist. It could help and I can recommend one to you."

"I don't know if she would agree to something like that." Nancy turned as Annie came out of the small room, dressed and ready to go.

"Can we go home now?" She asked.

"I'll send you that information," the doctor said as he left the two women. Annie put her arm around her mother.

"Let's go grab some lunch . . . I'm starved." Annie said as they walked away.

\*   \*   \*

A bad storm rolled into the region that night with thunder and lightning so fierce that it lit the room like day, and the thunder actually seemed to shake the walls. Annie sat up, calling Tony's name. She looked around the room as a flash of lightning made her cower under the blankets. She didn't stay there long before she jumped up and ran to the bathroom to wash her face. It was one o'clock in the morning. She found she couldn't go back to sleep, so she sat at her desk and began typing on her laptop. She had decided to make a journal of her daily feelings from this point on and she was now happy that her mother had taken all of those pictures of the two of them together.

*"This is the first log in my journal. I have been without Tony Cross for weeks and I feel empty without him. I walk the streets of town and can hear the talk, the blame, and the finger-pointing. Pine Lake adored the Cross family and their son. Sam Cross had built the school and shopping plaza which had increased the population of the town. My father had constructed the hospital and the library. This whole place was supportive when Tony got drafted onto the basketball team and the popularity of that team shot through the roof. Joe, at the garage where Tony worked, closed down. He felt he could no longer keep it open without Tony at his side. Ethan is making noise about being a police officer when he comes of age, so he has started taking the social studies and government courses in preparation for high school graduation and getting into the local college. Tyler has been accepted into a very well-known culinary school in Washington, DC and Mark has gone to Timber City University to take up accounting so he can help his father with the paperwork from the business and me . . . I find I miss my brothers. But, Tony, I miss you so and love you now, more than ever. I know you are dead and gone, but I have the strangest feeling that you are alive out there somewhere. I don't understand these feelings and I can't explain them, but they're there."*

She shutdown the laptop and closed it then buried her face in her hands and began to cry.

The next day, the storm had passed and it was already proving to be hot and humid. Nancy was at her daughter's bedroom door and knocked. "Annie, we're heading out to the restaurant, you coming?" There was no answer so Nancy opened the door and was surprised to see that Annie was not in her room. She checked the bathroom, then called out for her husband who came running in.

"What's wrong, Nancy?"

"Annie's not here . . . she's missing." Ryan couldn't believe it and pulled out his cell phone. "Who are you calling?" Nancy asked.

"The police chief. Damn, I wish the boys were here. Come on." He took Nancy's hand and pulled her from the room.

It had taken some time, but Annie had managed to get into the building that had housed the garage where Tony had worked. He had spent a lot of time there she believed that if he was alive she would feel him there with her. As she looked around, she remembered the times that Tony allowed her to help him with some of the repairs. She would change the oil and filters, allowing Tony to work on the more important repairs. She was standing at the workbench where one night after work, and Joe had gone home, they had gotten involved in a kissing frenzy that lasted for some time. She then walked over to the locker and opened it up to find a dirty jumpsuit that Tony wore when he worked there. Annie picked it up and brought it to her nose so she could smell him. She took it off the hanger and put it on, even though she almost disappeared into it. She found a corner of the garage and slid down to the floor, brought her knees to her chest and, wrapping her arms around her legs, lowered her head to her knees and cried.

Ryan had found Joe and they were just outside the garage door. Joe unlocked the door and allowed it slide upward. They rushed in and when Joe turned on the main lights, they couldn't believe what they saw. Ryan rushed over to his daughter and knelt beside her. "Sweetheart . . ." he said softly as Annie looked up.

"Oh, Daddy, what am I going to do?" She put her arms around his shoulders and he scooped her up in his arms as she rested her head on his shoulders. "I miss him so much."

Joe walked over to them. "Is there anything I can do?" He asked.

"Help me get her into the truck." Joe followed them out to the CRV and Ryan slipped her into the backseat where she laid down, crying. Ryan turned to face Joe.

"They did have something special," Joe said, worried about the girl that had brought so much light and happiness to his dingy garage and himself.

"Yeah, they did. I just hope his death doesn't take her down too."

"I really wish I could help," Joe said, understanding.

"Just pray for her," Ryan said as Joe nodded and watched his friend get into the truck and drive away.

# CHAPTER TWENTY-THREE

*"My love for you goes beyond the borders of this world and the universe. If I
lost you I would go insane."*

TROY HAD BEEN doing a lot
of work on the house, and even
though it needed a lot more, it was looking better. He had cleaned out the
chimney and got it ready for winter. He had replastered the living room painted
it, and now with a fresh coat on the outside of the home, it would look like a
million bucks. Jackie and Troy were putting on the white base coat first, then
cover it with the light gray color that Ray wanted. Jackie was standing next to
Troy, helping with the painting. She glanced at him and he looked so intense at
what he was doing. "Hey, White Boy," she said, getting his attention.

"Excuse me," Tony said as Jackie, without warning, took her paint brush and
ran it over his face from forehead to the chin. She began laughing so hard it hurt.

"Now you look like a white boy," she said as Troy picked up the paint bucket
he was using and started toward her. Jackie began to slowly back away. "Now,
come on, Troy . . . I meant nothing by it. You wouldn't dare . . . . would you?" She
saw the determination in his eyes and started to run. Troy went after her and they
ran around the yard as Jackie tried to stay one step ahead of Troy, laughing all the
time. She knew if he caught her, she would be wearing that paint.

Ray came from the house to see what all the commotion was about and
started laughing at the two of them. He hadn't seen Jackie so happy in years. He
really liked Troy and would love to have him as a son-in-law one day. The two
came running toward the house and Troy threw the paint at Jackie, just as she

ducked. The paint caught Ray full on. Jackie gasped when she saw her father and put a hand over her mouth, wondering what he would do.

Troy started to back away with fear in his eyes. "Now, Ray . . . . it's not my fault . . . your daughter started the whole thing . . . if she hadn't ducked . . ." Troy took off running for dear life with Ray close behind him while all Jackie could do was laugh at them. It was the funniest thing she had seen in ages. Ray cornered Troy at the barn, scooped him up and held him over his head as he went toward the pigpen. After the rain a couple of nights ago, the mud was deep and gooey. Ray dumped Troy into the mud and Troy came up throwing mud at Ray. Ray was not a happy camper. He jumped the fence and soon the two were wrestling in the mud until they wore themselves out. Troy looked at Ray, 'You really did look good as a white boy.'

Ray just looked at Troy. "And you don't look too bad as a black boy."

Jackie came over to the fence still laughing at them. The two men looked at each other. "You go right, I'll go left," Ray said. Troy nodded and Jackie screamed when the two men charged at her. She ran toward the house, but didn't make it inside as Troy tackled her. Ray took her arms, as Troy took her feet and they carried her back to the pig pen. "On three," Ray said as they began to swing Jackie back and forth. She was shouting at them to put her down. "One . . . two . . . . three!" Jackie flew through the air and landed face down in the mud. Ray draped his arm over Troy's shoulder. "How 'bout a beer?"

"I would love one." Tony agreed and the two men went back into the house. Jackie sat up, still in the mud, as two pigs came up to her, one on each side began to lick her cheeks.

"MOTHER!" She shouted out in frustration as she sat there with her arms folded in front of her.

*   *   *

Nancy stood at the door to her daughter's room. She had been standing there, just watching Annie sleep. Ryan came up behind her, putting his arms around her from behind. "How's she doing?" He asked.

"I'm scared, Ryan . . . scared for her. I don't think our little girl is going to pull out of this."

"These things take time."

"How could she have fallen so much in love with Tony that it would make her go insane?"

"I can understand how she is feeling," Ryan said as Nancy turned to face him. "My love for you goes beyond the borders of this world and the universe. If I ever lost you, I would go insane."

"I love you," Nancy said and they kissed. The kiss ended when they heard Annie calling out for Tony. They rushed to her side as she sat up in bed.

"We're right here, Sweetheart," Nancy said, taking her daughter's hand while Ryan's hands rested on her shoulders. Annie slowly turned and looked at the two of them.

"Mom, Dad, I want to come to work at the restaurant. I can't stay here alone another day."

"Do you think you're up to it?" Nancy asked and Annie nodded.

"Without the boys here, the house is empty and I am tired of the emptiness in my soul. I don't know who I am anymore. I see my reflection in the mirror and it's not me. My eyes are dark and lifeless. I'm scared, Mother, so scared."

Later, Annie was sitting at her computer working on her journal.

*"Mom and Dad agreed to let me work at the restaurant. They believe it would be good for me to get out of the house and I agree with them. Staying home is not good for me. Ethan is doing very well with the courses he is taking. He believes that he will be a good police officer when he finishes his training. Not only that, he has found a girl that he is interested in. Ethan Roberson . . . dating. I would have never dreamed that would happen. I wonder what kind of girl she is. Mark is having a hell of a time with the management course he is taking. The numbers are driving him crazy. We talk a lot on the phone. As far as Tyler . . . I don't hear from him very much. I am concerned that when school starts next month I am going to have to face that building. We had some of our best time there. I have talked to Mrs. Phillips at the martial arts school. I'm planning on starting my training again . . . I'm going to go for my 3<sup>rd</sup> degree black belt. The finger pointing and the blame is still there and for some, it is directed at me. They say I could have done a lot more for you, what am I going to do, Tony? My love for you grows stronger every day."* Annie shut down her laptop and once again started to cry.

# CHAPTER TWENTY-FOUR

*"Shut up and kiss me."*

AFTER THEY CLEANED up, Ray and Troy found themselves at Ray's favorite fishing spot. Ray was sitting in his wooden chair, holding a beer in his hand as he waited for a sign that he had caught something. Troy was sitting on the ground next to him, also sipping on a beer. "I have to say, Troy, your coming into our live has changed both of us. But I can't help feeling that you're not happy."

Troy looked at Ray and stood up. "I've been having these dreams, flashes of people, places, events I can't remember. I know I should, but I just can't hang onto them."

"These things take time, Son."

Troy turned to the river and signed as he took a sip from the can. "What if I am some kind of monster . . . . a killer?" He turned to look at Ray. "And these people are people I have killed. There is one face that is so strong I can almost reach out and touch her. What if I killed her?"

"Troy, I haven't know you for a long time, but I can tell that you are no killer."

"How can you tell? How do you know? He took another sip from the can.

"I am a pretty good judge of people. At least, I like to think so, and you're no killer."

"And then there's this tattoo on my ankle."

"I know . . . I saw it."

"What does it mean? What does it stand for?" Troy dropped down to the ground and lowered his head for a second, then looked at Ray again. "I find myself not wanting to remember. I am afraid of a dark past . . . and I don't want to go back to it."

"Son, you are welcome to stay here for as long as you wish. Besides, I don't think my daughter is willing to give you up yet."

"What do you mean?"

"She likes you . . . . a lot."

"Really?" That seemed to please Troy to no end . . . because he liked her too . . . a lot.

*　*　*

Annie was a little nervous about going back to the restaurant . . . alright, a lot nervous, because of the times she had with Tony there. Why did she think it would be better when his presence would be so strong? However, she was surprised about something she wasn't expecting. Ashley Moore was working for her parents. They were not busy, so they sat across from each other in one of the booths, both drinking a cup of coffee. "I've done some amazingly stupid things in my life, Annie, that I am not proud of." Ashley said as she took a sip of coffee.

"How did you get out of prison?" Annie asked her.

"That was something I had been trying to forget. I had sex with several high ranking officials for my freedom."

"Oh, Ashley, how could you?"

"It's terrible in there, Annie. I wanted out, so I sold my body to regain my freedom. I'm straight now, Annie. I don't drink, and I'm free of drugs. I have a young boy interested in me, and I am planning to go back to school."

"How did you come here?"

"I needed money. I was broke and your parents were kind enough to give me a job. They're wonderful people, Annie. You don't know how lucky you are." Annie smiled as she took a sip of her coffee. "How are you handling Tony being gone?" Ashley asked. She had heard all of the talk that was going around town.

"Not good." Annie responded as Ashley nodded, understanding where she came from.

"I cried for weeks when I heard about Tony. I can only guess what you are going through."

"It's hard, Ashley. Every day there's something that will remind me of him. And the talk around town is insane. What is wrong with people?"

"Don't blame them. My Tony was a hell of a guy." Ashley reached across the table to take hold of her hand and smiled. "I'm here now. If you need anyone, I will be here for you."

Annie smiled and sighed as she looked out the window. "Oh, Ashley, I would never have guessed that it would hurt to miss someone so much. And I do miss him . . . so very much." Annie lowered her head in sadness. "I don't know what to do sometimes."

"Everything will be all right, you'll see."

Annie shook her head not agreeing with her. "No, Ashley, it won't be. Every passing day, every passing minute, I find myself wishing for death."

Surprised, Ashley said, "Annie! You mustn't think like that."

Annie looked at her. "How am I supposed to think? Smile and be happy all the time, when the only person in my life that made me happy has been taken away from me. How am I supposed to stand here and tell the world that I don't hurt, that I don't see the sun any more or the stars at night? How can I tell you that everything is all right, when it's not?" Annie lowered her head to her arm and began to cry.

*     *     *

That night Troy was lying in bed with his back to the wall, thinking of the things that he and Ray had talked about earlier. One thing for sure, Ray sure knew how to cook fish. He only dressed in black boxers and he lay there studying the shadows dancing on the wall, wondering where the light source was coming from. Then he heard the panic sounds of the horse in the barn. He jumped to his feet and ran to the window . . . . the barn was on fire.

He flew from his room as Jackie was coming from her room, tightening her robe around her. "What's going on?" She shouted.

"IT'S THE BARN!" He shouted back. Without thinking about his own life, Troy ran into the barn to rescue the two horses and the cow. He thought he heard the roar of a Harley in the distance. He put a bridle on one of the horses, jumped on bareback.

"Where are you going?" Jackie called out to him.

"Do what you can I'll be back. "HEEYAH!" The horse took off at a full gallop. Troy decided to take a shortcut through the woods, to try to intercept the intruder that had done this to his family. "Now that was funny," he thought. He was now calling the Browns his family. The woods were dark, but it didn't seem to bother the horse as it charged between the trees. Troy came out of the woods onto the road right next to Dylan, who was shocked to see him riding hard alongside him. The horse's hooves were pounding the pavement and it was breathing hard. Troy had to wait for the right moment before making his move. He leaped from the horse and tackled Dylan from the bike. The two hit the ground hard as the bike ran into a ditch and the horse headed for home.

Troy didn't give Dylan a chance to defend himself or make any counter attack. He launched a full assault on Dylan and after a few seconds, Dylan was begging Troy to stop.

The door to the police station flew open and Troy had Dylan by the arm. As Troy marched Dylan through the wooden building, they walked by several glass enclosed offices with drop fixtures lighting everything. They passed by the wanted posters on the wall. Sheriff James Long, stood up when troy and Dylan approached the partition that separated the offices and the detectives' desks. Sheriff Long was an impressive man in his uniform. He looked at both men. "What can I do for you gentlemen?" He asked as he rested has hands on his gun belt

"Sheriff, my name is Troy Witt. I have been staying with the Browns. I have made a citizen's arrest."

"What has he done?" The sheriff asked.

"He burned down the Brown's barn."

Surprised, the sheriff looked at them. "Do you have any proof?" He hoped so, he had been trying to get something on the troublemaker for a long time.

"Just smell him . . . he's covered with gasoline. I chased him down as he was leaving the barnyard."

"TODD!" The sheriff called out. A skinny deputy jumped up and ran to the sheriff, eager to do his bidding. "Book this man! Give him his rights, get him out of those clothes and save them for evidence. Then, lock him up."

"Yes, Sir!" The young deputy said as he swung open the door, "This way, Sir," Dylan looked at each man, then followed the deputy into the back room. James folded his arms in front of him. "So you're Troy Witt. You have no idea where you came from or who you are?"

"No, Sir."

"I can take your fingerprints and run them through the database and see what comes up." Before Troy could respond, Jackie and her father came charging into the building. Jackie had some clothing in her hands and the two came to stand next to Troy. "Sorry to hear about your place, Mr. Brown."

"Thank you."

"Your guest, here, brought the man in that did it. Would you like to press charges?"

"Yes, I would."

"Then come into my office." The two men disappeared into one of the glass-enclosed offices. Troy was getting dressed in the outfit that Jackie had brought for him. Troy slipped on the jogging pants and a hoodie.

"Are you nuts or something?" Jackie asked as she punched Troy on the shoulder.

"I couldn't let him get away."

"So you wanted to be some kind of crusader, and charge off on your fiery steed to do justice?"

"I caught him, didn't I?" He couldn't help but be surprised at her reaction.

"If you ever do anything like that again, Troy . . . so help me . . ."

"Jackie . . ."

"What?"

"Shut up and kiss me."

"Damn you," she said as their lips touched.

# CHAPTER TWENTY-FIVE

*"I don't mind being your friend, but never try that again. I can't do it to him."*

ANNIE WAS STANDING by a table listening to the upset customer that had come in for lunch. "This is a piece of shit. I wouldn't feed this to my dog. How dare you serve this junk? It's over-cooked . . . burnt. I will not pay this tab! I'm going to call the police."

"I am sorry, Sir. I will see what I can do to fix the situation." Annie was getting upset. This was not what she needed right now. It was days like this that we wished to God that Tony was alive; she need him so bad.

The man stood up. "Situation? Are you saying I'm a piece of trash . . . like your cooking? How dare you?" He swung as if he was going to hit Annie, but she was able to block it and swing his arm behind him, pinning him to the wall. "Oh, you're going to pay for this big time, Young Lady!"

"Annie, let him go," Nancy said as she stood behind her daughter.

"No! He was going to hit me!"

"Annie . . . I'm only going to say this one more time . . . let him go." Ashley came from the kitchen to see what was going on. She dropped everything and ran to Annie, taking her by the hand and dragging her outside. Nancy ran to the door and was screaming for them to come back as they ran down the street.

The two were playing at the beach, chasing each other as they threw water back and forth. Ashley was able to tackle Annie into the water and they wrestled back and forth. Ashley found herself on top of Annie and the two seemed to freeze as they looked at each other. Ashley slowly lowered herself toward Annie, as if to kiss her, but Annie shoved her away and jumped to her feet. "I can't do this Ashley . . . I'm sorry."

"I meant nothing by it Annie, it was just going to be a kiss."

"I don't mind being your friend, but never try that again. I can't do it to him." Annie ran off as Ashley called after her. She ran home and up the steps to her room where she slammed the door and jumped face down on the bed, crying her heart out as she called for Tony to come home.

She soon found herself in the shower washing off the sand but all she could do was think about Tony as the water travelled down her body from head to foot. She remembered the timesi she had with him.

*"Here's an easy one." Tony said, then continued, "Captain Kirk or Captain Picard?"*

*"That's an easy one. Kirk. Going into unknown territory, I would much rather have a warrior than a diplomat." She said.*

*"That's my girl." The two did a high five over the table, and then it was Annie's turn.*

*"OK, I got it . . . . Dr. Smith or Dr. McCoy?"*

*Tony gave her a funny look as he scooped up some ice cream. "No contest. McCoy . . . I wouldn't trust Smith as far as I could throw him." They both snickered.*

*Mark looked at his younger brother when they saw the two holding hands and they marched right up to them and Mark forcefully broke the hand hold, surprising Annie to no end. "Mark, what are you doing!?" She said as Mark pushed Tony against the wall.*

*"What are you intentions toward our sister?" Mark asked.*

*"Wait . . . you're her brother?"*

*Ethan had to make himself known . . . . "Me too, bro . . ." Ethan said as he slammed his fists together, ready to do battle with anyone who made a move on his sister. Then it hit Tony was Mark had just said.*

*"Intentions . . . . what intentions? We just met."*

*Before Mark could do anything else, Annie kicked him in the shin and took hold of Tony's hand, pulling him away as Mark jumped up and down in pain.*

*"You are not to touch him. I like him!" Annie said as she left the alley with Tony in tow. Tony kind of gave the brothers a half salute as he disappeared around the corner of the building.*

Annie found her legs turning to mush as she fell back against the shower wall and slid to the floor. Her knees came up to her chest and she wrapped her arms around her legs and cried.

\*     \*     \*

Annie came from the bathroom wearing a bathrobe and was toweling her hair dry. She was surprised when she saw her mother sitting on the edge of her bed. Nancy looked at her with anger in her eyes. "What the hell was that all about?"

Annie sat down at her desk. "Please, Mother. Not now."

"Yes. Now, Annie, you need help. I think you should see a psychiatrist."

Surprised, Annie replied, "I am not crazy, Mother."

"You have got to put Tony behind you and get on with your life."

Annie walked over to the window and briefly looked out, then turned back with her arms crossed. "How can I, Mother. I love him so much."

Nancy went over to Annie and put her hands on her shoulders. "I know you do. And you always will, that will never change, but he would want you to move on . . . to be happy."

"I don't know if I can."

"It's OK, Sweetie, I will always be here for you."

A short time later, Annie was at her laptop.

*"Mother is right, Tony. I have to move on, but how can I when you're still so strong in my heart and soul? The customer whose head I was about to remove finally calmed down when my father assured him he would not have to pay for what he had already eaten, which had been half of it before he made a scene. I couldn't believe that Ashley tried to kiss me. I am not that type of girl. I am definitely a guy girl and one hundred percent loyal to you, Tony. How can I look for someone else when I already had the best there is. I am going go to back to my training tomorrow. I believe that will help me more than anything. It will feel good to have that black belt on again, but I can't help but wonder how everyone there will accept me. The feelings that I have are still there. I can feel that you are alive out there somewhere. Please come back to me . . . . come home to me. I need you. I love you."*

Annie shut down her computer and, as always, put her head on the desk and cried.

\*     \*     \*

Annie walked into the martial arts school and saw that it was a busy as ever. There were two women waiting for their children to finish class so they could get home and finish their chores for the day. They had been engaged in a conversation when Annie came into the school and their focus seemed to immediately center on her. It seemed to happen everywhere she went. Annie stood there for a second, painfully closed her eyes for a second, then went toward the two women who suddenly got quiet. "Mrs. Jones . . . I have often wondered why your husband, the Chief of Police, would leave you for another woman." She looked at the other woman. "And Mrs. Smith . . . why did you keep your ordeal out of the limelight when your husband beat you so badly you ended up in the hospital? Don't you both think those topics would be much more important than my Tony jumping from a bridge?" The two women didn't know how to respond as Annie turned and headed toward the locker room.

"Ms. Roberson . . . may I see you in my office." Annie looked over her shoulder and then followed her master into the office where they both sat down. "Ms. Roberson, I understand how you feel about Tony. I saw the way the two of you were when you were together. But, what you did just now just gave them more kindling for the fire."

"I know, Ms. Phillips. They just make me so mad. Tony was a good person. He doesn't need to be remembered as someone that jumped off a bridge."

Ms. Phillips took a slow breath, realizing how much Annie was hurting about everything. "I'm sorry, I didn't mean to be cruel."

"It's all right. It's just that the finger pointing and blame are getting to me. I don't know how much longer I am going to stay in this town. I've been thinking about going up north just to get away somewhere where nobody has heard of Tony Cross, this town, or me."

"Annie, I was very happy when you called last night. I had been hoping that you would."

'Excuse me," Annie replied as Ms. Phillips got up and walked around her desk to her. "I have an instructor opening . . . it's yours if you want it."

Annie looked up in disbelief. "Me . . . an instructor?"

"Why not? Your knowledge of the martial arts is beyond reproach. You are fine, strong and strict . . . fine qualities for an instructor."

Annie stood up and faced her with a smile. "Can I think about it for a couple of days?"

"Of course. I understand." She put a friendly hand on Annie's shoulder. "Give it time, Annie. People will forget. Tony did come from an important family here in Pine Lake . . . they did a lot for this town. You have to remember how the people felt about the Crosses."

"Oh, I understand all right, and they're blaming me for his death. They say I should have been with him more. They say I should have been more loving and caring. They say that I should have never met him . . . if I didn't he would still be alive." Annie slammed her fist down on the desk and turned and looked out the window into the class room. "That's the one that hurts the most . . . if I have never met him, he would still be alive. Maybe they're right." She turned to face Ms. Phillips. "Are they right?"

Ms. Phillips took hold of her shoulders. "No, they are not right. You were so happy together. You have to remember that time and keep that in your heart and he will always be alive."

"There's something else, Ms. Phillips . . . something that has been eating at me."

"What's that?"

"The feeling that Tony is alive, somewhere. I know he is . . . I can feel it."

"It's all right to miss Tony, Annie, but you can't let it consume you."

"I'm sorry, Ms. Phillips, but I'm not as strong as you think I am." Annie picked up her duffle bag and left the office.

A class was going on, and two young ladies were doing their stretching exercises before the next class was to begin. Annie walked by them and the brunette called Rebecca Clark spoke out. "Look who's here . . . . the princess of Pine Lake." Annie froze in her tracks.

Rebecca's partner was Lisa Hill, and the pretty redhead had to throw her two cents into the ring. "What are you going to do now, Princess? No man will want a has-been."

Annie dropped her bag and slowly walked over to the two brown belts who would soon be testing for their black belt. They stood up when she approached.

"They said Tony took the cowardly way out," Rebecca said and both girls chuckled.

"They also say that he had another woman on the side," Lisa told her.

Annie walked up to face Lisa and without warning slapped her, hard. Lisa's head moved in the direction of the blow.

"ENOUGH!!" Ms. Phillips said standing there with her hands on her hips as she looked at the two brown belts, disgusted. "How dare you treat your upper classmen like this? Do you think it's easy to lose someone you care about?" She crossed her arms in front of her. "I can see this isn't going to stop today. I'll make a deal with the two of you . . ." The two girls looked at each other. "You two are going to test for your first degree black belt. Ms. Roberson has started training for her 3$^{rd}$ . . . The three of you will fight today. If you two win, you get your black belts now, if Ms. Roberson wins, she gets her third and you two will not test again for one year. Do we agree?"

The three girls agreed and Annie continued toward the locker room to change into her red and blue uniform. She dropped down into a chair as she heard Tony's voice seemingly calling for her. "STOP IT!!" She screamed. A scream that brought Mrs. Phillips to find Annie crying. "I should not have come here. I see him everywhere I go. What am I going to do?"

"I wish I had a magic wand that I could wave and make things better for you, but I don't. Annie, you don't have to go out onto the mats."

"No . . . . I need to do this."

"Are you sure?"

"Yes, Ma'am."

Ms. Phillips ordered everyone off the mats and to the side to sit on the floor. No one was allowed to talk during the match. Annie and Rebecca stood together as Ms. Phillips went on to explain the rules of the engagement. "It's simple. The matches will be five minutes each. The first to hit the mat loses the fight, is that understood?" They agreed, then Ms. Phillips told them to face each other and bow. They did so and took their fighting stances, then Ms. Phillips gave the order for the fight to begin.

It was easy to see why Rebecca was getting ready to test for her black, she was very good, but over-confident, especially after tagging Annie a couple of times. Annie came back strong and hard. It was all Rebecca could do to protect herself and Ms. Phillips had to snicker to herself when she saw what Annie was doing, and in three moves, Annie did a throw down that slammed Rebecca to the mat. She found herself looking up at Annie who stood there for a second, the offered her a hand to help her up. Ms. Phillips called the match and the two girls bowed to each other, then Rebecca went to her spot on the edge of the mat and crossed her legs and watched as Lisa took her spot facing Annie.

Ms. Phillips gave the order for the match to begin. Lisa was not as good as Rebecca, but she was worthy of testing. She became frustrated when she couldn't lay a hand on Annie. She had hoped she would do better than her friend. Annie didn't take any time and in three moves, Lisa found herself on the mat looking up at Annie. Annie offered her hand again and helped Lisa to her feet. They bowed to each other then Lisa went to sit with her friend.

Ms. Phillips was now pacing in the center of the mat, sort of reminiscent of a drill sergeant. "This matter is finished. You will treat your upper belt classmen with the respect they deserve. If I hear any more about this subject, I will take action that won't be appreciated. Is that clear?"

All three girls at the same time responded, "Yes, Ma'am."

Ms. Phillips turned to the rest of the class. "And that goes for anyone else in this school. Is that understood?"

"Yes, Ma'am." They all responded.

"All right, everyone back to class . . . except you three," Ms. Phillips said looking at the girls. "You will do one hundred pushups, sit-ups, and jumping jacks. Understood?" The three nodded.

*   *   *

Annie was sitting at her computer. *"That was the last time that the two girls bothered me about you. In fact, we have become good friends. You would have been proud of me, the way I handled myself while fighting them. Everyone said I have to move on with my life, forget you. But the truth is, how can I? Tony, I love you more now that the first day we met."* She turned the computer off.

# CHAPTER TWENTY-SIX

*"Jim, Tony . . . Tony is dead."*

THE RESTAURANT WAS busy that day. Annie had become popular with the locals that were regulars at the restaurant. She was in a conversation with a couple that had taken a window booth, and was laughing at what they had to say. A tapping at the window got her attention and Annie looked up to see Crazy Jim motioning for her to come outside. She asked Ashley to take over for her and headed toward the door. When she got outside, she saw nobody there, in fact the street was quiet. She slowly walked by the alley and a hand grabbed her and pulled her into the alley. She was surprised and excited to see Jim. She threw her arms around him. She hadn't seen him since the storm. "What are you doing here, Jim?"

"Keeping a promise."

"I don't understand, Jim," she said as she tucked some hair behind her ear.

"I'm sorry I couldn't get to you earlier, but I was in jail for a short time."

"What for?" Annie asked, surprised.

"I stole some food in a display outside a store, and when I turned around a cop was right in front of me."

"Oh, Jim," Annie said, sounding disappointed in him.

"It's OK. I'm out and I needed to see you." Annie realized that he was holding a martial arts black belt. She didn't need to ask who it belonged to . . . she knew, and her hand covered her mouth. "He wanted you to have this, to keep it safe for him. He wanted me to tell you that he will return for you, and that he loved you very much."

The dam burst and Annie dropped to the ground, crying. Jim dropped to his knees beside her. "What's wrong, Girl?"

"He's not coming back Jim," she said, her voice cracking.

"Yes, he will. He's a smart boy . . . he'll be back for you . . . I know he will."

"Jim, Tony . . . . Tony is dead." It was like being slapped in the face as Jim sat back, shaking his head in disbelief.

"No . . . no you're wrong. He's a smart boy . . . he can't be dead . . . he loves you." Jim said as he too began to break down.

"I've lost him, Jim. He's gone." Annie said as he took her in his arms and they both cried.

*   *   *

Nancy walked up to Ashley, who was standing behind the counter. "Ashley, where's Annie?"

"I don't know, Ms. Roberson," she said, shrugging her shoulders. "I haven't seen her since she asked me to take an order for her."

"That's strange," Nancy said under her breath. She went to the door and looked out, but there was no sign of Annie. She went to the kitchen and asked if anyone had seen Annie and when nobody said they had, she began to get worried. She then walked by the ladies' restroom and heard crying from inside. She went inside and saw Annie on her knees crying hysterically as she held the black belt close to her heart.

"Annie?" Nancy said watching as her daughter slowly stood up. Nancy gasped when she saw her daughter's face and then Annie extended the belt out to her.

"This is Tony's. He told Jim he wanted me to have it. He said he would be back for me. What am I going to do now, Mother? I have been trying so hard, but he is everywhere I look. People point their fingers at me, talking about Tony and me. I can't take it anymore, Mother. I can't stay here."

Nancy took a couple of steps to her daughter. "Where will you go?"

"I want to go to Timber City University. They have a good culinary school there. I want to learn to be a chef."

"You could be gone a long time, Honey."

"I don't care . . . I just know I can't be here."

"All right, I will talk to your father and see what he has to say. Now wash your face and let's get something to drink."

*   *   *

Annie was in bed that night, but she was restless and found it hard to sleep. Seeing Jim again and getting Tony's black belt . . . it was getting to her. Annie sat up with frustration as she looked around the room. The house was quiet and usually, it meant the boys were up to no good. She was missing them so much right now . . . almost as bad as Tony, for no one ever knew what devious plans those boys were cooking up. And it usually meant that she was on the receiving end of those plans. But not now . . . they were all away, getting on with their lives, like she should be doing. But she couldn't stop thinking about Tony. He was so ingrained into her heart and soul. She looked around the room and then hopped out of bed and left her room.

Ryan and Nancy wanted to spend some time alone, something they hadn't done since the children arrived in their lives, so she assured her parents she would be all right while they went out to dinner and a movie. Since her father had gotten older, he had found he sometimes needed pain pills for his back after all those years of heavy lifting and finally gotten to him. Annie had gotten those pills from the medicine cabinet and a glass of water. The front door of the house opened and Nancy and Ryan came inside. They seemed happy and almost beside themselves, they had had such a good time. Ryan took his wife's coat and hung it in the coat closet then they turned to face each other.

"You know, Mr. Roberson, the night doesn't have to end yet," Nancy said as she put her arms around him.

"What do you have in mind, Mrs. Roberson?"

"Let me go and check on Annie and I will show you." Nancy hurried up the steps

"Yes," Ryan said with excitement.

Nancy tapped on Annie's door and when she got no response, she slowly opened the door and looked inside. "RYAN!" The frantic scream brought Ryan running into the room. He couldn't believe his eyes when he saw the medicine bottle on the floor, some pills spilled from it. Annie's arm hung over the edge of the bed, lifeless. Ryan rushed to check his daughter's pulse.

"Nancy, call 911!" Ryan said as he flung the blankets off his lifeless daughter and looked over his shoulder at Nancy who looked as if she was going into shock. "NANCY . . . . 911 . . . NOW!!" His yell snapped her out of it and she grabbed her cell phone.

Annie was talking to herself, as the ambulance raced to the hospital. *"I'm sorry, Tony. I know you must be disappointed in me, but I couldn't take it anymore. The gossip, the finger pointing, they just got to me . . . . it was something I had to do . . . please forgive me."*

# CHAPTER TWENTY-SEVEN

*"Mark, it was not your duty to take care of me all those years."*

T HERE WAS A lull at the Brown's small restaurant. It was after lunch and before dinner and Jackie and her father decided to have a little down-time before the third wave hit the place. They sat in one of the booths and sipped some coffee while they talked. Both looked up when Troy came in and walked over to them. "What brings you here, Sweetie?" Jackie asked him.

"I'm tired of staying at home all the time. After the work I need to do is completed, I usually end up doing nothing and I'm sick and tired of watching daytime TV. You can only watch so much HBO until the sex scenes start to all look the same."

Ray and Jackie looked at each other. "Well, what would you like to do?" Ray asked him.

"Well, I would like to try to cook." Again the two looked at each other.

"Can you cook?" Jackie asked him.

"I don't know, but I would like to try."

"Well, my cook did leave me, and I've been doing everything myself. Tell you what . . . if you cook and we like it, you can become my chef. If we don't like it, you can bus tables."

Troy looked at the small dining area. "I think I can deal with that."

"The kitchen is right through those doors. Good luck."

Jackie looked up at him with a smile. "I know you can do it."

The kitchen was small, but efficient. There was everything a chef needed to fix whatever he wanted. Troy was thinking about what to fix and went to the refrigerator to see what he had to work with. He smiled as he looked over the well-stocked fridge. He was going to make a Cheesy Bacon Meatloaf. He set the oven to 400 F then went to work mixing all the ingredients except the bacon . . . he would do that later. He shaped the loaf into a 9x5 loaf pan, topped it with the bacon, then put it into the oven to bake. When he was happy with the dish, he took it to the judges.

He stood by as they enjoyed the meatloaf. All Jackie could say was, "Ummmmmm." She wolfed down the food like it was going out of style or something. She looked at Troy. "That was awesome. Do you have anymore?" She sure hoped so.

"Yes, would you like some more?"

"Yes, of course." Troy took the plate from her and disappeared into the kitchen.

"That was fantastic, Father." She said to Ray who was just finishing his dish.

"He might be just what we need," Ray responded as Troy returned with Jackie's dish and she dug into it, just like before. "And you don't remember how you learned to cook?" Ray asked him.

"I don't. I guess it's like the martial arts . . . if something is pounded into you long enough, you don't forget.

"You know what . . . you are our new chef. Welcome aboard." That made both Jackie and Troy happy because it meant they would be able to spend even more time together. Jackie had to giggle at Troy because of the over-excited look he had. That smile of his had been doing something to her ever since the first day she saw him. Feelings were erupting in her that she could not explain. She was falling in love with a white boy. A year ago if someone had told her that she would have laughed in their face, but now . . . she knew she was in love.

\*   \*   \*

As what could have been a Hampton Inn hotel room focused in, Mark leaned forward with a bright smile. "You're awake?" He said with excitement in his voice. Annie sat up but the whole room went north on her and she fell back onto the bed, lightheaded and with a headache. "Take it easy, you've been out for a week," Mark said as she got her some water he helped her to take a sip. "Just small sips." When she finished he sat it down on the nearby table, then sat down himself.

"What are you doing here? Where am I?"

"You're at the Timber City hospital. Dad said you were in trouble, and that is all he had to say, so I'm here, looking after you. Always have, always will . . . . I love you, Sis."

"What about your studies?"

"Ummm, I quit."

Annie was sure she didn't hear that right and looked at him. "You WHAT?"

"Oh, Annie, it just got too much. I can't add 1 + 1 with my fingers. Remember in high school, you had to help me with the math."

"What have you been doing all this time?"

"I've been working at a Chinese fast food place, doing deliveries."

"Oh, Mark . . ."

"No, no . . . it's interesting. I have three gorgeous women wanting to have sex with me and one marriage proposal."

Annie carefully shook her head. "You're not getting married, are you?"

"Are you kidding? It was from a man." Annie tried to laugh, but couldn't. "I'd better go get the doctor, he will want to take a look at you."

"No, Mark . . . not yet . . . . please stay for a minute." Mark looked at her for a second then sat back down. She wanted to explain to him why she did what she did. "I tried to kill myself, Mark." Mark took in a slow deep breath and let it out.

"I know. Dad told me. But why, Annie? Why?" He had never understood how anyone could just kill themselves.

"It was getting too hard, Mark. I tried so hard, but he was always there . . . everywhere I looked. Then the talk around town, behind my back, blaming me for what happened. I don't know how they could think that . . . I loved him so much . . . still love him. I just couldn't handle it anymore. I wanted peace and sleep, and killing myself was the only way I thought I could escape."

"Oh, Annie, I should have been there for you. You needed me and I wasn't there. Can you forgive me?"

"Mark, it was not your duty to take care of me all those years."

Mark was surprised. "What? You mean I did all that for nothing?" Annie was able to punch him in the arm. "I'd better go get the doc." She nodded and Mark got up then he hesitated for a second. "You don't know how many times I wished you were not my sister."

"Excuse me?"

"I wanted to marry you."

Annie threw one of the pillows at him. "Will you get out of here?"

Mark laughed as he hurried from the room as Annie just shook her head in disbelief.

The next morning there was a soft knock at Annie's door. Standing there was a pretty young woman, tall and slender in a business suit. Her hair was up and she had a huge smile and was carrying a clipboard. "May I come in?" She asked. Annie didn't respond, but the woman entered the room anyway and went to sit down by Annie's bed. "I am Diana Evans." She extended her hand to Annie, but got no reaction.

"I don't need a psychiastrist."

"Well, it's my job to visit anyone when they have tried suicide."

"I am not crazy."

"Nobody said you were. I'm not here to judge you, Ms. Roberson. I want to be your friend."

"Ms. Evans, I do not need your help or your friendship. I just want to be left alone."

Diana stood up. "All right, Ms. Roberson, I get your point." She laid a business card on the end table. "If you need someone to talk to, I do have an office in Pine Lake."

Mark was coming into the room as Diana was leaving. He held the door open for her and they made eye contact. Mark's heart skipped a beat. Diana continued down the hallway, leaving Mark standing in the open door, watching her. He then went to Annie.

"Is that your doctor?" He asked.

"She's not that kind of doctor, Mark, and you can stop drooling anytime."

Mark noticed the card on the table as he ignored her last comment. "Psychiatrist?" Annie just looked at him with a blank stare.

Annie was typing on the keyboard to her laptop. *"I got stronger day by day and soon they allowed me to come home. Mark had a very long talk with Dad about the classes and how he wasn't dealing with them very well. Dad's a pretty understanding fellow. Ethan has joined the police academy, and believe it or not, I found out he is dating Ashley. Evidently they met when she went back to school. He's thinking of marrying her. I am so happy for them. Tyler is almost finished with the school in Washington, DC. He said he will be home for the holidays. It will be good to see everyone together again. Mom and Dad had agreed to let me go to the Timber City University culinary class there, the one you wanted to go to, and I have been accepted. But I have to finish high school, it's my last year and I will graduate in a few months. Thankfully, I was able to make up the schoolwork I had missed while I was in the hospital, so I can graduate with the rest of my class. It will be good to get away for awhile. I can't wait. My birthday is coming up and it will be the first one without you. I don't know how I am going to handle it. I did get my driver's license. I don't want a party, but Mom and Dad insist so I will have one. Thanksgiving and Christmas are just around the corner. I don't know how I am going to make it without you. I love you."*

# CHAPTER TWENTY-EIGHT

*"A feature that I am finding is a curse more than anything."*

IT WAS THE time of year that Ray would go to a nearby town to get supplies for the restaurant and he would normally stay overnight. In the past he had been uncomfortable about leaving Jackie alone, but this year, Troy was there and Ray was glad he was. Troy had a fire blazing away in the fireplace. It was a cold winter's night and even though Troy had done a lot of work on the house, it was still cold and drafty; but the fireplace sure helped.

Jackie had made some fresh coffee and was bringing cups into the living room. She handed one to Troy who took it as she sat down beside him. They were watching something on TV and Troy took a sip of the coffee and started watching Jackie. She noticed what he was doing. "What?" She asked, wondering why he was looking at her that way.

"Do you like me?" It was as if her hand malfunctioned, or something. Her cup dropped onto her lap, spilling the hot coffee. She screamed out as she jumped to her feet. Troy jumped up and ran to the kitchen to get a towel. He started wiping the coffee off her lap, which made her feel more uncomfortable.

"Troy, just stop . . . please." She said and, in frustration, stormed up the steps.

\*     \*     \*

Troy was lying in bed, trying to remember certain flashes that he had earlier in the day. He had not talked to anyone about the flashes since the day he had discussed it with Ray when they went fishing. They had been coming more often now, and lately, when he tried to remember them, he would suffer what was almost a migraine-like headache. He had not told Jackie because he knew she would worry about him, and he didn't want that.

There was a knock at his door and Jackie popped her head inside. Troy looked at her and smiled. She came into the room, dressed in a bathrobe. She had just finished taking a shower and her hair was still damp. "You didn't let me respond to your question earlier."

"Jackie, I really wasn't expecting an answer. Besides, you were the one that went running up the steps."

"Well, you shouldn't ask questions like that when someone has a hot drink in their hands. But . . . anyway, here's my answer." She let the bathrobe fall to the floor. Troy just looked at her, not saying anything. "Do they not please you?"

An explosion of images came at him at such speed that it was more painful than before. He screamed out and jumped out of bed. The pain was like a fire and it brought him to his knees as he held his temples. He was groaning, in pain, and scared. Jackie rushed to him and put her arms around him. "Troy, what is it? Are you all right?"

Troy's breathing finally came under control, and he looked up at her. "Help me back onto the bed." She helped him get up and he shakily, got onto the bed and laid back. Jackie started to leave the room. "Don't go . . . . stay." He said. She stood at the door for a second then went back to him and laid down beside him. "Just hold me," he said to her. Jackie allowed him to snuggle into her.

"The point is, Troy, I do like you . . . a lot. One might even say I love you." All she got in return was hearing him begin to snore as she chuckled and shook her head.

\*     \*     \*

Annie was becoming an excellent instructor and the kids liked her a lot. At the high school, the other kids were running to get to class, but she found that she could not walk up the steps to the front door. It felt like there was a force field holding her back. She was still standing there when her two new friends from the martial arts school grabbed her arms and dragged Annie into the building. Annie was sitting in class and had not heard the teacher when she was asked a question, at least not until the teacher walked up to her and slammed her pointer onto the desk, making her jump back to reality. "I said, name the Indian tribes that lived in southern Virginia," the teacher said, then waited for the answer.

"The Cherokee. They claimed territory in the extreme southwestern part of the state. If they didn't actually occupy it, at least it formed the boundaries of their hunting territory. Then there was the Manahoac group. According to Jefferson they lived on the Rappahannock River in Stafford and Spotsylvania counties."

Impressed, the teacher replied, "Well done, Ms. Roberson . . . see me after class."

"Yes, Ma'am," Annie said as the bell rang ending the class. The students piled out of the room, except for Annie, who stayed behind at the teacher's request. She went to the teacher's desk.

"You are a very smart person, Ms. Roberson. However, this past week, your mind has been wondering off."

"I'm sorry, Ma'am. It won't happen again." Annie assured her.

"I'm not worried about that . . . . is it about Tony Cross?" Annie was surprised that she would just come out and say it.

"Yes," Annie said as the teacher leaned back in her chair.

"I heard that after this year you are planning on attending the culinary school in Timber City?"

"Yes, Ma'am, I am."

"That is a very good school. I know the director of that school, I will put in a good word for you."

"Thank you, Ma'am. That is very kind of you."

Annie started to leave, but stopped when the teacher said, "Try to move on, Ms. Roberson. Don't let this take you down."

Annie hesitated. "It is very hard."

"Nothing In life is easy, Ms. Roberson. We have to fight every day just to live. We can't let it get to us."

"Tony Cross was my life force. He was my reason for living. Sometimes when I am lying in bed at night, I look up at the ceiling and pray that I don't wake up in the morning."

"Ms. Roberson . . . life is about living . . . not dying."

"Life is also about how we die." Annie said and left the room. She was walking down the hallway in the school when Rebecca Clark and Lisa Hill came up behind her, each taking an arm, just like they did when they led her into the school.

"Where have you been, Annie?" Lisa asked.

"You know . . . . here and there."

"You're turning out to be a pretty good instructor, Ms. Roberson," Rebecca said.

"Thank you."

"Rebecca and I are going to the Pizza Place. Want to come?" Lisa asked as Annie looked at the two of them.

"I don't know . . . I have a lot of homework."

"So do we, but we make time to have a little fun," Lisa said. "There's nothing wrong with sharing a pizza with your friends." Annie thought about how much fun it would be . . . she had not had a lot of fun since Tony left her.

"All right, why not?" The three girls left the school and hurried to the Pizza Place.

\* \* \*

The Pizza Place was one of the restaurants in Pine Lake off main street. It was a small place with black and white tile floor, green plaster walls with paintings of the Pine Lake area, and was well lit by the overhead fixtures. Country music was playing and they could hear the noise coming from the kitchen. The three girls were lucky the place was not busy and quickly found a booth. Annie had called her mother to let her know where she was and Nancy agreed that it was a good idea for her to spend some time with her friends. The three had been sipping their sodas, waiting for their pizza. "I think our waiter likes you, Annie," Lisa said, sipping away at her straw.

"I'm not interested."

"Oh, come on Annie, he's good looking and has a hell of a smile." Rebecca said.

"So was Tony." Annie angrily got to her feet and turned, almost bumping into the waiter with the pizza. It was only his quick thinking that kept Annie from wearing the pizza.

"You're not leaving already are you, Ms. Roberson?" Pete Conroy said as he sat the pizza down in the middle of the table.

"You know her?" Lisa asked.

Pete was a good looking man, tall and slender with bushy blond hair and light brown skin and green eyes. "Doesn't everyone in Pine Lake know her," he said as Annie slipped back into the booth. She had paid for part of the pizza, she might as well eat some of it. Pete's arms were crossed in front of him. "Haven't you started dating yet?"

Annie had a slice of pizza in her hand and looked at him. "I can't, not yet." She took a bite of the slice and it was hot and just melted in her mouth.

"I can understand how you feel, Ms. Roberson."

Annie dropped the slice down on the plate. "Can you?"

"Yes. I was a teammate of his when he was on the basketball team. His passing devastated the team."

"So, now that Tony is out of the picture, you want to move in?"

"You can't blame a man for trying. You are a very pretty woman."

"A feature that I am beginning to find is a curse, more than anything else." Her two friends just looked at each other, not believing what she had said.

"Now you really don't mean that, do you?" Pete said as he leaned down close to her. Annie just picked up her cup of soda and dumped it over his head. His co-workers saw what had happened and started laughing. Annie pushed him away and stood up.

"When I am ready for a companion, Mr. Conroy, be assured that it will NOT be you." Annie turned to her friends. "Thank you for thinking of me. I'll see you in school." Annie stormed out. There was a light dusting of snow on the ground. It was the first of the season. And usually when it came this early, it meant there it was going to be a long, rough, cold winter.

Annie was marching down Main Street like a girl on a mission. Nothing was going to stop her until she reached her designation. A black pick-up truck came alongside her. At first she didn't pay any attention to it until it blew it's horn at her. She stopped and just eyed the driver, seeing that it was Pete Conroy. "I want to apologize for the way I behaved back there," he said.

"No need." She started walking again and the truck slowly coasted alongside her like a dog following its master.

"Come on, Annie, don't be like this. I'm heading for the Hangout for a drink. Why don't you join me? You look like you could use one." Annie stopped, not looking at him. He was right about one thing . . . she needed to get drunk. She took a few steps toward the truck.

"Just a friendly drink between two people. We just talk?" She asked him.

"Just talk . . . maybe dance if you want."

"All right." Pete opened the door for her and she hopped into the truck and they drove away.

*     *     *

Pine Lake's "Hangout" was a gathering place for its young people, and this evening it was packed. There was a lot going on as the rock and roll band played and the dance floor was jumping with people enjoying the moment. Annie and Pete were sitting at the bar while Annie drank a soda and Pete was enjoying a beer. "I was helping Tony at the garage and one night we were working late and Joe had already gone home. Tony picked me up and sat me on the work table and we kissed, God that man could kiss," Annie said as she dropped her head in sadness.

"You still miss him a lot, don't you?" Pete asked and she nodded and took a drink from her glass.

"I've got to call home. Mom's goig to be worried sick."

"Use your cell phone."

"Do you really think I can hear anything in here?"

"What?"

Annie moved away as Pete put a powdery substance in her drink and stirred it until it disappeared. Annie soon returned and sat down next to him and took a drink from the glass.

"We're good," she told him.

"You want to dance?"

"Sure, why not?" As Annie stood up, she suddenly felt light headed and the room started to spin. She almost fell and Pete caught her.

"Whoa . . . . I'd better take you home," he said and Annie agreed.

\*   \*   \*

The front door opened, but it wasn't to Annie's home, it was to Pete's apartment. He helped Annie into the living room, closing the door with his foot. "Where are we?" Annie asked, groggily.

"My place," Pete said as he took her to the couch and sat her down.

"Is Tony here?" The room was spinning as Pete took off her coat.

"No, Tony is not here." Pete said as he sat down next to her.

"Is he coming later?"

"If he does, we're both in trouble." Pete grabbed her chin in a tight, forceful grip and made her turn her to face him and planted a kiss on her lips and held it. Annie fought him, trying to push him away from her. He slapped her, making her fall back onto the sofa, stunned. He pulled open the front of her sweater, popping most of the buttons. He used a pair of scissors and cut open her white cotton shirt she had on underneath. He then cut her bra, and before Annie could start fighting him again, he hit her again. The drug now had such an effect on her that her fighting skills were of little use. Annie was now lying on the couch and Pete was on top of her, kissing her neck as he cupped her breast with his hand. She was able to get one arm free and scratched his face, deep, with her fingernails. He cried out as he pulled back. He touched his cheek and his hand came away bloody.

She was able to get from under him, but was having a hard time standing or moving. The room was still spinning like crazy, but she headed toward the door. Pete intercepted her and hit her hard, knocking her to the floor. He grabbed her and pulled her into the bedroom and onto the bed. He got on top of her, using his body weight to hold her down. Annie was still trying to struggle and her hand found a small clock radio on the nightstand and grabbed it, smashing it alongside his head. Pete was stunned momentarily, allowing Annie to make her escape.

There was a police car parked on the street outside the apartment and through hazy eyes, Annie ran toward it. "Please help me!" She cried out, then collapsed to the ground.

# CHAPTER TWENTY-NINE

*"I'm going hunting, Mother."*

NANCY, RYAN AND Mark were running down one of the hallways of the small Pine Lake Hospital. They reached the emergency room receptionist. "I'm Nancy Roberson."

"Yes, I know who you are."

"My daughter?"

"She's doing pretty good, considering that she was beaten."

"Oh, my God," Nancy said under her breath. "Can I see her?"

"Just one at a time." Nancy followed the nurse through the door into the emergency room. It was small, but busy. The nurse took Nancy by a row of beds, then pulled back the curtain to allow Nancy to go to her daughter. Annie quickly covered her face with a blanket, not wanting her mother to see her condition. Nancy sat down in the chair next to the bed.

"Go away, Mother." Annie said from under the blankets.

"Annie, look at me."

"I don't want you to see me like this."

"Annie, please look at me."

Annie slowly removed the blanket so that her mother could look at her and Nancy gasped. Annie had a black eye and other facial bruises. "Oh, my baby girl." Nancy was crying as she put her arms around her daughter.

"Mrs. Roberson?" The doctor said as he came up to the bed. "May I see you?" Nancy looked at him and nodded and followed him away from Annie's bed.

"How is she, Doctor?"

"Considering everything, very good. The bruising will take some time to go away. Her attacker did not have time to penetrate her, however, we did find a foreign substance in her blood."

Nancy shook her head, not understanding. "She was drugged?" The doctor nodded. "Doctor, she's a 3rd$^{nd}$ degree black belt. She knows how to fight."

"Even the best of fighters would have a problem with this drug. We were able to clear most of it out of her system, but I would like to keep her here overnight. She should be able to go home in the morning."

"All right, Doctor."

"We will be moving her to a room shortly." Nancy nodded and went back to her daughter.

Annie was crying when Nancy sat down next to her. "I couldn't even defend myself, Mother."

"You were drugged, Annie. It's not your fault," Nancy said then looked up when Mark came in. "What are you doing here?" She was surprised to see him standing there.

"I had to see her." Mark didn't like what he saw as he went to stand at the other side of the bed.

"How did you get in here?" Nancy asked him.

"Does it matter?" Mark took Annie's hand and held it in both of his. He was shaking his head in disbelief. He then leaned over to her and whispered in her ear. "I'm going to kill the bastard. I love you." He gently laid her hand back on the bed. "I can't be here, Mother," he said as he left.

"Stop him, Mother." Annie said, scared.

Nancy ran after her son. She caught up with him in the waiting room and grabbed him by the arm, spinning him around to face her.

"Where do you think you're going?"

"I'm going hunting, Mother."

"And do what?"

"I'm going to put a gun to the bastard's head and blow it off. He deserves to die, Mother."

"I know that, but the police have him in custody. The law will take care of him."

"The law." Mark sat down with frustration and looked at Nancy as she sat down next to him. "Why did Tony have to leave her? Doesn't he know how much she needs him?"

Nancy gently touched his cheek. "I'm sure he does, Mark."

"If he was with her, none of this would have happened."

"We can't go blaming Tony, Mark."

"Why can't we?"

"I thought you didn't like him?"

"I don't . . . but he loved her, Mother. He loved her so much, even I could see it. He would have cared for her and protected her. I just wish things could go back to the way they were when she and Tony were together." Tears began to roll down his cheeks and Nancy pulled him to her and held him close.

"I know, Baby. I miss him too."

\*     \*     \*

Halloween had come and gone, but Annie still didn't feel like going out. The attack was still strong in her mind and the bruising was still noticeable. She was allowed to stay home and catch up on her schoolwork.

Troy was allowed to test for his GED, which he got under the name of Troy Witt. He couldn't remember if he had a diploma or not.

Annie was at her computer: "*Ever since the attack, I have had terrible nightmares. It's as if I relive the entire ordeal. I haven't left the house for a long time. I was actually surprised that Halloween had come and gone and Thanksgiving was knocking at the door. It will be the first Thanksgiving without you. I am not certain how I am going to handle the holidays this year. Mother understood when I said I didn't want a birthday party. I must wasn't in the mood to party after what happened. Oh, something I need to add . . . Mark is dating Diana Evans, the psychiatrist that came to see me at the hospital. I have started seeing her once a week. I believe she is going to help me get through this. Mark seems very happy with her and he's been smiling a lot lately. I don't know if I am ever going to recover from this. It would have been better if you had been with me." God I love you so much.* Annie turned off the computer, got up and walked over to her bed and laid face down.

Diana Evans' office was nicely arranged with the furniture necessary for her practice. There were heavy drapes that blocked a lot of the sunlight. Her solid oak desk was sitting in front of the window and on the right was a bookcase. There was also a couch with a chair next to it. Annie was sitting at one of the visitor chairs in front of the desk. "You seem to be doing well, Annie. I am proud of you. How are things going?" Diana asked her.

"I'm trying to keep busy. Not allowing myself to have a lot of time to think about things. People here in town seem to still be unhappy with me, but I let it slide off. I am continuing my martial arts training, and school is going OK."

"Well, it sounds like you are dealing with everything pretty well. I want to say something. You are still in pain from your loss. You are still grieving, and you have not forgiven him yet." Diana got up and went to the bookcase. When she found what she wanted she turned to Annie. "I believe you are in the last stages of grieving. You are learning to accept and deal with Tony's death and the reality of your situation. Acceptance does not necessarily mean instant happiness. Given the pain and turmoil you have experienced, you can never return to the carefree, untroubled YOU that existed before. Tony will always be in your heart and soul. It is all right to remember him. Never stop, but don't allow it to be the controlling factor in your life. Not many people are able to do this in the short time you have had to grieve." She handed Annie the book. "I want you to take this book, read it, and then bring it back to me. You are doing very well, Annie. I am pleased and I will see you next week."

Annie followed Diana to the office door and when it opened she jumped, surprised to see Mark standing there. "Ready to go home?"

She playfully punched him in the arm. "You scared the crap out of me!"

"Sorry about that. Can you wait in the lobby for just a second?"

Annie found that strange, but went out into the lobby and Mark went inside the office and closed the door. He took Diana by the arm and pushed her against the wall and their kiss went wild. They were not able to get enough of each other. The only thing that stopped them was Annie who walked up behind Mark. "Come on, Romeo." She said as she took him by the arm and started to pull him out of the office. He pulled away from her and kissed his index finger, then touched Diana's lips with his finger.

"See you later?" Mark asked and Diana laughed and nodded, then watched as the two walked down the hallway.

Later that night, after the restaurant closed, everyone but Annie had gone home. She was in the kitchen baking, and seemed happy in what she was doing. She started beating the egg whites until soft peaks formed and then gradually added the sugar and continued to whip them until the peaks were stiff. She set the dish aside and in a large bowl combined the flour, baking soda, salt and more sugar. She then added oil and buttermilk and beat it for a minute, then added the egg yolks, chocolate and remaining buttermilk and continued beating for another minute. She then poured the mixture into two greased 9 inch baking pans. When she was done, she sat alone in the dining area at one of the booths. The chocolate cake and colorful frosting sat in the middle of the table with a glass of wine next to it. She gazed at the "Happy Birthday, My Love" that was written on the frosting. She tried to smile as a tear slowly ran down her cheek. She tapped the glass on the table with her glass. "Happy Birthday, Sweetheart." She said then looked up as the restaurant door opened and Nancy walked in.

"Annie, what are you doing here?" Nancy said as she walked over to her then saw what was written on the cake. "Oh, Annie . . ."

Annie looked up at her mother, trying to smile. "I can't stop loving him."

"You've been here all this time?" Annie nodded. "What happened, Annie, you were doing so good?"

"Not really, Mother, not really."

"So, are we going to sit here and look at that or are we going to eat it?" Annie couldn't help giggling. "Go get some plates, Mom."

(Annie narrating.)

*"Diana said she was proud of me, glad I was doing well, but truthfully, I'm not. I am even fooling myself, thinking that Tony was to blame. How could I when he loved me so much. He didn't cause the attack, though Mark truly believes that if he had been alive, it would have never happened. I don't blame you Tony. I will love you, always. When I see what Mark and Diana have, I can't help but wonder if we would have been the same way, and I end up missing you even more."*

# CHAPTER THIRTY

*"Nah, I've never seen Annie look so happy."*

T HANKSGIVING HAD ARRIVED and Troy had become quite the cook. The Brown's restaurant was very popular now and had become well known in the region. With Jackie's help, Troy had been cooking all day, making a hell of a feast. He had removed the turkey from the oven and it was golden brown and smelled yummy.

There was a knock at the front door, and Jackie went to answer it, surprised to see the sheriff. "We didn't think you were going to make it, Sheriff," she said as she took his coat and hung it up.

"Did you really think I was going to pass up the opportunity to have some home cooking?" He told her. "You look lovely, Ms. Brown."

"Why thank you, Sheriff." Jackie kissed him on the cheek, making him blush.

"That was worth coming here for," he said.

"Why, Sheriff, you're just a smoothie." They went into the kitchen.

The doorbell rang and the Roberson home and Annie ran to answer it. She opened the door to see Ethan, with Ashley hanging onto his arm. He looked very handsome in his police uniform, Annie thought as she gave him a big hug, then hugged Ashley. Annie took their coats and hung them in the closet, and before she closed the door, she saw Tyler running up the front walk. She didn't even give him the chance to come in and threw her arms around him.

Annie and Ashley were setting the table. They had brought out the large dining room table for the occasion. At the same time, Jackie was doing the same thing in their kitchen. Ryan brought the turkey to the table and sat it in the center. His wife had made all the side dishes and when everybody was ready, they sat down to eat. Jackie said the prayer for her family and Annie said the prayer for her family, then everyone began to dig into their own feast.

Annie was sitting on the couch after dinner. The table had been cleared and everything put away. Her legs were crossed on the couch and she was holding her laptop on her lap. Nancy came and sat down next to her daughter. Everybody was watching the football game on TV.

"I can't eat another bite," Nancy said as she sipped a cup of coffee.

"I'm waiting for the apple pie," Annie said smiling. Nancy glanced at the computer screen to see what she was doing.

"What's this?"

"Can you keep a secret?" Annie asked her.

"Mum's the word," Nancy said, then Annie turned the laptop so the screen was facing her mother. "You did this?"

"Yes."

"What a wonderful way to remember him." Annie closed the laptop as Mark came running up to them.

"The apple pie is ready," he announced.

Annie was in her room, working on her computer. *"It is so nice to have the boys home and they are planning on staying through the New Year. Mom couldn't believe that I had download all the pictures that she had taken of us and make a nice presentation on the two of us. It was the only way I could keep you alive. I was able to get out of the house and go back to school and I'm now able to walk down the road that always took me home. It was hard the first day. I was alone and was very nervous especially when I came upon the spot where Pete had picked me up. But, I was able to conquer my fears and can walk home now, no longer afraid. It took a while for Mark to let me walk home alone, but at least I have a break now. He didn't want to leave my side for a long time. It's been snowing overnight, the largest one we've had this year. School was let out early. I had some catch-up work to do, so I stayed behind for awhile. The snow falling now is the good kind . . . good for snowballs and snowmen. Little did I know that the boys had already figured that out."*

Mark and Ethan were together on the north corner of the house and Tyler was on the south side. It was snowing very hard and there were already two inches on the ground. "She's going to kill us." Ethan said to Mark, who was standing behind him.

"Don't worry, she's a good sport." Mark and Tyler hand walkie-talkies and Mark got on his to contact Tyler, who was in a better position to spot their target. "Any sign of our target?" Mark asked.

"Negative, no sign of target," came the response over the radio.

"A simple yes or no would do."

"Affirmative, I mean yes . . . wait . . . I have a bogie coming in from the north, approaching the danger zone in one minute."

Mark looked at Ethan. "He is a Roberson . . . right?" To which, Ethan just shrugged his shoulders.

"Bogie approaching, five seconds to front door. Her shields are down and she has not picked us up yet." Tyler said into his radio as Annie made the turn that would take her to the front door. "Get ready . . . . NOW!!!"

As Annie was about to reach the door she was met by a barrage of snowballs coming from both sides of her. "I'M GOING TO KILL YOU!!!" She screamed.

Tyler got one more message into the radio. "Every man for himself . . . . RUN!!!"

The three boys headed for the woods behind the house with Annie close behind them. Ethan and Tyler were able to escape Annie's wrath, but she was able to tackle Mark at the tree line.

Nancy and Diana were coming from the kitchen when Mark was dragged into the house by Annie. Mark looked at his mother and girlfriend who, to his surprise, were not doing anything to help him. "Help me," he pleaded.

"I come from a neutral country," Nancy said as she watched the two.

"Mother, this may be the last time you see me. Diana . . . I thought you loved me?" Nancy thought about it for a second.

"One less mouth to feed. I can go for that."

"Should I help him?" Diana asked.

"Nah . . . I've never seen Annie look so happy," Nancy said as they turned to go back into the kitchen.

Mark found himself with his hands and feet tied to the bed. He was looking up at the ceiling and his boots and socks had been removed. Annie was standing at the foot of the bed, holding a large, pink, fluffy feather. She was running her fingers along the feather and she had a crazy grin on her face.

"Under the Geneva Convention, you cannot mistreat your prisoners." Mark said looking at the feather.

"All you have to do is tell me where your brothers are."

"I will never talk . . . besides, they're your brothers too."

"So be it."

"You wouldn't . . . . it's not human."

"Whoever said I was human?" Annie laughed as she started tickling his feet with the feather. First one, and then the other.

Annie is narrating. *"Mark was the weakest of my brothers. That was why I would pick on him, and sure enough, he was crying like a baby inside of 30 seconds. I don't care what the government says . . . . a nice feather is much better than Chinese water torture. Now, all I have to do is wait and the other two will come crawling back to the house. I locked the back door and turned on the backyard spotlight. With that light I could see a mouse moving around."*

Annie smiled when she saw movement at the tree lien and then the two brothers came from the darkness of the woods and slowly moved to the back door. "I thought you said you unlocked the door?" Tyler said, looking at Ethan.

Luckily for Annie, her bedroom window looked out into the backyard. She slid the window up and stuck her head out. "You boys having trouble getting back into the house?" The two looked up, but before they could react, Annie dumped two buckets of cold water on them. "You have to remember, Boys . . . I don't get even . . . I get ahead." She pulled back inside and shut the window.

The boys were pounding on the back door when Nancy came down to the furnace room. She opened the door and started laughing when she saw the condition her sons were in as they rushed into the house.

"Did you see what Annie did to us, Mom?" Ethan asked.

"Payback is hell, Boys," she said, crossing her arms. "Now you better go take a hot shower before you catch your death of cold." The boys headed for the stairs. "Wait . . . where do you think you are going?"

"To our room." Tyler answered.

"Not dressed like that. You are not going to drip water throughout the house. Now strip down . . . or do you want me to help you?" The two boys looked at each other and started to removed their clothing. They were soon standing in front of her . . . naked, trying to cover their privates with their hands. Nancy was chuckling . . . . "Now, get upstairs!"

The two boys ran up the steps as Annie and Diana, who had been sitting on the couch waiting for them to surface. Both of them had cameras and began taking pictures as fast as they could. Ryan came from his office to see two of his sons running into their room . . . naked. He could hear Mark screaming for help and just stood there for a second. "My mother told me there would be days like this," he said, then went back into his office. Diana stood at Mark's doorway, just watching him with a big smile on her face.

"You know, as a psychiatrist, I've heard stories of situations like this. You know, people's dreams and fantasies. I never really put two cents worth of truth to them, but now, seeing you here like this . . . it makes me wonder."

"Come on, Diana . . . stop playing around and untie me."

"Now why should I do that?" Diana said as she came into the room and closed the door behind her . . . and picked up the feather.

"DIANA!!!"

Later that night, Ryan and Nancy were in bed and she was cuddled to him. "You know, Honey," Ryan said, "I've been meaning to ask . . . why were the boys running through the house naked?" Nancy just buried her head in his shoulder and laughed.

# CHAPTER THIRTY-ONE

*"To my dearest love, from my heart to yours,*
*Merry Christmas. Your Tony, forever."*

THE SNOWSTORM HAD pretty much paralyzed the region with a deep snowfall. Most everything was shut down, allowing Jackie and Troy to have some fun in the white stuff. After they had taken care of the chores, it was playtime. Jackie came from the barn after taking care of the horses and caught a snowball right in her face. "TROY WITT, I'M GOING TO KILL YOU!!!" With that said, Troy cried out in pain. The flashes were hitting so hard the pain made him drop to his knee. He was supporting himself with one hand and the other was at his temple. Jackie came running to him and dropped down to her knees. "I'm here, Troy, I'm right here," she said as she took hold of his cheeks.

"Who am I?" Troy said. "Where do I come from? Isn't there anyone who can help me?" Jackie wrapped her arms around him and held him close while gently patting the back of his head.

"I love you, Baby. I love you, and that's all that matters, isn't it?" She said as she made him look at her. They kissed, and without warning a bucket of snow was dropped on them. "I don't know about you," Jackie said, "but I'm ready to hang my father up by his toenails. Go for it?"

Troy nodded and the two went 'father hunting'. A little while later, they couldn't believe that they had still not found her father. But, after all he was a Marine . . . trained in making himself invisible, and in sneak attacks. They were being hit left and right by flying snowballs and didn't have a clue where to counterattack. Ray had them running around the barnyard like a chicken with its head cut off. Finally they gave up and went into the house to get warm. They were shocked when the saw Ray sitting at the kitchen table, drinking some coffee and reading the paper. "How did you do that, Father?" Jackie asked him.

Ray looked at his daughter over the top of the newspaper. "Do what?"

"Attack us like that."

Ray took another sip of coffee and sat the cup down. Troy came to Jackie's side, eager to hear what Ray had to say. "Why would I want to attack you?"

The two looked at each other, confused. "Oh, come on, Father. You were out there throwing snowballs at us and you know it."

"I was?"

"He's playing with us," Troy said as he took Jackie's hand. "But you know what? I'm cold and I know just what will warm us up on a day like this."

"Mr. Witt . . . I like the way you think," Jackie said and the two ran from the kitchen and up the steps, disappearing into Troy's room. All anyone heard was Jackie's voice . . . . "TROY!"

*   *   *

Annie was at her laptop. *"I don't know what Diana did to Mark that day, well, maybe I kind of do. He's had this smile on his face and has been very bouncy these last few days. I can't help but wonder if I was that way after we made love on the beach that day. It's funny, I can barely remember that day . . . it's almost as if it never happened. But it did . . . we were happy and so much in love, right? What is happening to me? God, Tony, I don't want to forget you. I would go insane. The feelings I have, the dreams I have of you still being alive . . . they are eating away at my soul. Where are you? Why don't you come home to me? Christmas is just around the corner and I don't know how I am going to act without you at my side."*

The people of Pine Lake knew how to celebrate Christmas. Every building on Main Street was decked out in lights and other decorations. Mark had outdone himself this year with the house. When the lights came on it was indescribable. He was the one that had gotten the short straw, but he didn't seem to mind. He was pretty proud of himself for outdoing what his brothers had done in previous years.

Annie was in her bedroom, reaching for a box that she had to stand on her tippy toes to get. When she got the box she wanted, a smaller box, wrapped in bright Christmas paper fell at her feet. She picked it up and her hand covered her mouth when she saw who it was from. She charged from the bedroom, yelling for her mother. She found Nancy sitting on the couch in front of a blazing fire in the fireplace. Annie plopped down next to her and held out the small box to Nancy. Nancy looked at it, then her daughter, who was crying over what she was holding. "It was in the closet, Mother. It fell at my feet. Please read the note." Nancy didn't know what to say.

"Annie, are you sure? It's got your name on it."

"I can't, Mother. I can't look at it." Nancy took the note and, in disbelief, read who it was from.

"Annie . . . . it's from Tony."

"How, Mother? Annie was finding it hard to talk. "How did he put it there?""

"Tony was a special person, Annie. He loved you very much." Nancy opened the card attached to the box and ready it to her. "To my dearest love . . . from my heart to yours, Merry Christmas. Your Tony, forever"

"Open it," Annie said, crying hysterically. Nancy then unwrapped the box, opened it and gasped at what she saw. A cuff bracelet engraved with a vine of rose with CZ's at the base of the roses. It was in a green that matched Annie's eyes and had a toggle clasp to keep it in place. The bracelet was positioned around a raised area in the center of the box.

"Oh, Annie . . . . this is gorgeous." Annie had both hands covering her mouth and nose and was crying into them. "He must have saved a long time for this," Nancy said as she took it out of the box. Annie slapped it away and it went flying across the room, surprising Nancy. She stood up and headed for the stairs, but stopped about half-way up. She looked back over her shoulder. It was almost like the bracelet was calling to her and she walked back over to pick it up.

"I'm sorry, Mom. I don't know why I did that."

"It's OK, Honey, I understand."

"I wish I did."

# CHAPTER THIRTY-TWO

*"Yeah, he was cool with all those practical jokes he used to pull on you."*

ANNIE WAS WORKING on her laptop. *"I still haven't figured out how you were able to put that gift in my closet. It was definitely a surprise and I love you for it. Graduation has come and gone and I have been accepted into Timber City University. I will be going to the culinary school there and working on my Bachelor's at the same time. Mark and Diana are no longer an item. Mark was the one that broke it off. He said her work got involved with their relationship. She had to spend a lot of time away from Pine Lake and Mark wasn't ready to follow her wherever she was heading. He seems to be handling the break-up very well."*

Annie was packing the last minute things that she wanted to take along and most of her stuff was already loaded onto the truck. There was a knock at the door. She called out and Mark came into the room. She turned and saw him standing there with a long, sad face. "Come over here," she said as she sat down on the edge of the bed and patted the space beside her. He sat down and she put her arm around him. "Why so sad?" She asked him.

"I don't want you to go."

"Oh, Mark. Out of all my brothers, I love you the most."

"It's going to be strange here without you yelling at me and beating me up all the time."

Annie laughed and said, "How are you dealing without Diana?"

"All right, I guess. I kind of miss her. But it just wasn't working out with her being gone so much of the time. I guess I'm not one for long distance relationships. Do you think I will ever find what you and Tony had?"

"I don't know. What we had was special. I don't think I will be able to find anyone else like him."

"I miss him," Mark said.

"You really liked him, didn't you?"

"Yeah . . . he was cool. Especially with all those practical jokes he used to pull on you."

Annie couldn't help but giggle. "I do miss those. It made life interesting, not knowing what was going to come at you around every corner."

"GUYS . . . IT'S TIME TO GO!" Nancy yelled up to the two of them. They stood at the same time and Annie picked up her bag, but Mark took it from her. She put her hand on his shoulder and he looked at her.

"You know, Mark. Going to a new place will allow me to start over. Get a new, fresh start on life. It's what I've needed to do for a long time."

"I understand," Mark said.

"I'm glad you do." The two left the room.

Nothing was said between any of them once they got on the road. The deep winter snow that had blanketed the region was going away and signs of spring were coming. Annie sat in the back with Mark and she was watching the scenery go by. She was playing with the rose flower on a chain that Tony had gotten her for one of her birthdays. She had never taken it off. Annie narrating: *"For some reason, as we got closer to Timber City, my feelings of you being alive were getting stronger with each mile. It was as if you were there somewhere in the city. Is this where our paths will cross again? If so, I wonder how and where it will happen. I love you Tony, I will never stop. I am yours and you are my one and only. There can be no other for me."*

Timber City University was one of the largest In the country, and very popular. They pulled the truck up to the front of the dorm and they began to take her belongings up to her room. The campus buildings were all brick and nestled in with the large oak trees. It was the beautiful and peaceful surroundings that made the school so welcoming.

Annie was one of the lucky ones to have her own bathroom. The room was smaller than the one at home, but it would do. There was double everything there: two beds, two dressers, two closets and two desks. Since she was the first one there, she decided to take the furnishings on the right side.

The family said their goodbyes and left Annie so she could settle in. For the first time in her life she was on her own and was, of course, a little nervous. It was a big step for her, but she knew deep inside she could handle it. If she just didn't have these damn feelings about Tony everything would be fine. She had hoped that here, things would be different. Only time would tell. *"I have arrived at the University and my feelings for you have come alive and are even stronger than before. You must be here. You have to be here for me to have them. I will never give up hope.*

*My roommate has not arrived yet. I hear she is from Korea. It is going to be interesting sharing a room with someone from a different country. I hope I can learn a lot from her about her homeland. I love you."*

\*    \*    \*

Jackie screamed out in terror, bringing Troy and Ray running to her. They could not believe their eyes when they saw one of their horses lying dead on the front porch. Jackie turned, burying her face in Troy's chest as he held her close. Soon after, the sheriff and a couple of deputies arrived at the farm to investigate.

They were all sitting in the living room. "Sheriff, I don't know what your problem is. I know who did this . . . Blake Carter." Troy said.

The sheriff looked at Troy. "Did you see him do it?"

"Of course not."

"We can't go pointing fingers at people without proper evidence. Do I make myself clear?"

'This is crazy! I can't be here and do nothing!" Troy said as he got up and headed to the door.

The sheriff didn't even look at him. "Mr. Witt . . . . don't do something that I can't help you with!" Troy didn't say anything, just stormed out of the house and headed for Ray's pickup truck. He opened the driver's side door, only to have it shut by Jackie.

"And where do you think you're going?" She asked him.

"I'm going to pay a little visit to Mr. Blake Carter."

"Not without me, you don't!"

"Jackie . . . ."

"You don't have a driver's license. How are you going to drive? I have one . . . . let's go." Jackie hopped into the driver's seat, closed the door and rolled down the window. "Are you coming?" Troy knew he wasn't going to win that one and with frustration, he pounded on the hood of the truck and went to the passenger's side, opened the door and got in.

"What am I going to do with you?" He asked her.

"When we get back, you can make passionate love to me."

"Deal!" He said as she put the truck in reverse, backed up, and then pulled away.

Since this was the weekend, Annie decided to go to town to check it out on her own, just to see what was there since she would be in the area for quite some time.

Carter was in a meeting when one of his security men came flying into the office and crash landed on the floor. He stood up angrily when he saw Troy and Jackie come into the room. "What is the meaning of this?" He demanded.

Troy went over to the client, who was sitting there in shock at what was happening. "This meeting is over," Troy said, then sent his fist slamming down onto the laptop on the desk, destroying it. The client decided it was a very good time to leave and hurried out of the office as Troy turned his attention to Carter.

"I would like to know what this is all about," Carter said. "You can't just barge in here and order me around and throw my guests out."

Jackie walked up to him and slapped him, hard. Interrupting his meeting was one thing, but to have a woman . . . a black one at that, slap him was another. He was not about to let her get away with it and he slapped her back. The force of the blow made her lose her balance and she fell to the floor. Enraged, Troy leapt at Carter, grabbed his throat and pinned him to the wall. Jackie stood up and went to the two men. "Your beef is with us, not innocent animals." She told him as Carter began finding it hard to breathe.

"This is war, Ms. Brown . . . in war the innocent are the ones that sometimes get hurt." Troy didn't like what Carter had just said and tightened his grip.

"You listen to me, Carter. You or your goons come anywhere near the Brown's property again and I will kill you." He took Jackie's hand. "Come on, Honey. Let's go. I think we made our point." As the two moved by the table with the model on it, Troy looked at Carter, who was just stepping away from the wall. Troy grabbed the edge of the table and flipped it, watching the whole thing crash to the floor, demolishing the model. He and Jackie walked out the door.

Carter moved to the desk. "You just made a big mistake, my friend." He picked up the phone, dialed a number, and brought the receiver to his ear. "Get me Lee Du-Ho now. Yes, I know he's in Korea . . . and I don't give a damn about the time . . . just get him!" He slammed the phone down. He had just talked with Lee about coming to the States . . . now it looked like he needed sooner, rather than later. His project should have broken ground by now and this interference was going to stop.

As the two jumped into the truck to go, Troy suddenly got one of his migraines and it was a big one. He brought his hands to his temples and moaned. The images were coming at him super fast and Jackie became very worried. "Troy?"

"Just get me home . . . please." The truck pulled away as Annie came from a bookstore next to Carter's office. She stood there for a second looking both ways. *"Now I know you are here. I just had a weird feeling that you were nearby, but it went so fast, I wasn't sure if it was real or not."*

When Annie returned to her room, she was surprised to see her roommate there. She was sitting on the edge of the bed with her legs crossed, talking on her phone in Korean. She was a beautiful woman, the same age as Annie. Kim Chung-Hee was dressed in brown mid-thigh boots and had black stockings, black skirt and a dark blue summery shirt. She had long black hair, slanted eyes and fair skin. Chung-Hee waved at Annie, acknowledging that she had come into the room. Annie sat down on the edge of her bed in front of Chung-Hee. Chung-Hee finished her conversation. "That was my mother, and mothers are important," she said as she put the cell phone away into her oversized shoulder bag. "You must be Annie Roberson," she said, extending her hand.

"And you must be Kim Chung-Hee," Annie responded as they shook hands.

"You are beautiful," Chung-Hee noted.

And you are absolutely gorgeous," Annie said, making Chung-Hee blush.

"I noticed on the schedule that we are going to have at least one class together," Chung-Hee said.

"Let me guess . . . cooking class?" The two girls laughed.

"I was surprised to see a small microwave and refrigerator. I did not know that was allowed."

"Neither did I until I did some checking." Annie explained.

"It is going to be a big help saving money." Chung-Hee said.

"Agreed," Annie said, then paused. "Chung-Hee, I have to tell you something since we're going to be roommates, and hopefully, we'll become close friends."

Chung-Hee noted the sad look on her roommate's face. "What's wrong?"

"Tomorrow will be the one-year anniversary of my fiancée's death." Chung-Hee could not believe what she was hearing.

"You were going to be married?"

"Yes . . . and very soon. However, he took his own life."

Chung-Hee covered her mouth in shock as she heard the story of Annie Roberson and Tony Cross. The sun was now hanging over the horizon and it appeared that it was going to be a beautiful sunset. "What did this Tony Cross look like?" Chung-Hee asked her. She watched Annie go to the desk and reach into her backpack and pull out a photo. It was the one taken at Tony's party when he became a black belt. He had his arms around her from behind and his chin was resting on her head, and both had huge smiles on their faces. Annie turned and handed the photo to Chung-Hee. "You two looked very happy."

"We are . . . I mean we were. I mean, I am . . . I don't know, Chung-Hee. My life has been turned upside-down since his death. Sometimes I feel like I'm in a haze . . . a nightmare that never ends."

Chung-Hee shifted to sit on the bed next to Annie and handed the photo back to her. Annie just held hit, looking at it as a tear rolled down her cheek. "I still love him, Chung-Hee. I can't stop loving him."

"I lost someone close to me. Someone I loved, but not to suicide. He was murdered."

"How did you deal with it?"

"You don't. It is always in your heart and soul. You may think you have won the battle, but frankly, anything or anyplace can set it off and before you know it, you are beside yourself. You have to learn to live with it, it has become a part of your life, there is no denying it. But one thing is certain, the one you have lost would want you to be happy and move on."

"Chung-Hee, tomorrow is Sunday and there is something I must do. It concerns the anniversary of his death. Would you be there with me?" There are many traditions in Korea that allow only certain members of the family and friends to be present. Chung-Hee had only been in the United States a short time, and she wasn't sure if those customs were the same here.

"Is it permitted?"

Annie nodded. "I really want you to be there." Chung-Hee seemed to make Annie happy when she agreed to accompany her.

# CHAPTER THIRTY-THREE

*"You can't find white girl, so black girl will do?"*

ANNIE AND CHUNG-HEE were in Chung-Hee's Jeep Wrangler, traveling on the dirt service road that ran along the railroad tracks. Annie could not help having flashes of that dark day when Tony took flight and it eventually ended in his taking his own life. The images were so clear that she could almost reach out and touch them. It was a hot summer day and the sky was clear.

Chung-Hee was uncertain about her new friend, but considering they had just met, it was no wonder. She could tell that Annie was still hurting even though it had been a year since the tragedy. Even when she lost her own love, she was able to move on after a length of time. Even though there are times when one feels lost, they have to deal with it and get on with life. Chung-Hee had hoped that coming to the United States would allow her to put everything in the past, and perhaps, find someone else to love. That would be nice . . . she missed the touch of a man, his smell, his smile and the gleam in his eyes. She wanted to find that again.

Since it was a hot day, both girls were wearing sandals, summer shorts, one wore a summer blouse and the other a T-shirt. Their hair was blowing in the wind and both were wearing sunglasses. Not much had been said between them until the Jeep came to a stop at the bridge. Annie was now crying as she held a dozen red roses in her hands. Chung-Hee looked over the edge of the railing. She could not believe the height . . . nobody could have survived that fall. "Annie, there is no way he could have survived this."

"Don't you think I know that. Everybody keeps telling me he's dead, but I've been having these feelings that he's alive, and here in Timber City. I can't shake it," she said, still crying.

"It's impossible." Chung-Hee said, watching Annie throw the roses over the railing, one by one, each time telling Tony she loved him.

Once the flowers were gone, Annie gave in to her frustration and slammed both hands on the railing. "Don't you know what you have done to me?" Annie spoke as if he were standing there in front of her. Chung-Hee covered her mouth with her hand. "You took my life from me! I can't eat . . . I don't sleep . . . I see you everywhere. Dammit Tony, I love you. Where the hell are you?"

Suddenly Annie hopped up onto the railing but before she could let go Chung-Hee grabbed her, pulling her back. The two sat on the deck of the bridge as Chung-Hee held Annie in her arms, rocking her like a baby and allowed Annie to cry it out.

Later that night, after the girls had gone to bed, Chung-Hee heard Annie crying. She rolled over and turned on the light. "Annie, are you all right?"

Annie sat up, bringing her knees up to her chest and wrapping her arms around them. "No, I'm not all right. I'm so sorry about this afternoon. If you had not been there, I believe I would have jumped."

"Annie . . . taking one's life is not the answer. God gave you this life to live to its fullest. Only he can take it away."

"Then why did he take Tony from me? Doesn't he know how much I need him?"

"Annie, do you know anything about the martial arts?"

"I have a 3rd degree black belt in Tae-Kwon-Do. I have started training for the 4th degree."

Chung-Hee smiled. "I have my fourth degree. How about after class we practice together. I find that going through the routines makes me sleep better. I think I can really help you now." After Annie agreed, Chung-Hee switched off the light and the two girls finally went to sleep.

The next day Jackie and Troy went shopping and since he had been working at the restaurant he had been able to save a little money. Besides, he needed his own style of clothing . . . not Jackie's father's style. They came from the men's clothing store and Troy put the six bags into the pickup truck's cargo department. He couldn't help but wonder who was doing the shopping . . . him or Jackie. He had learned that day just how much she loved to shop. "I don't believe this . . ." Jackie and Troy turned to see five African-American males, all tall and slender, looking meaner than a used car salesman.

"What do you mean?" Jackie asked.

"Jackie Brown . . . hanging with a white dude. What would your pa think?" The leader of the group, also known as Rod Smith, asked her.

"My pa approves of our relationship." The men were surprised, as Troy, who had gotten into the truck, got out and went to Jackie and put his arm around her. Rod took a few steps to Troy and looked him over . . . not understanding what Jackie saw in him.

"So you are her new boy?" He asked Troy.

"It seems that way," Troy replied.

"You can't find white girl, so black girl will do?" Rod said, punching Troy on the shoulder.

"That's enough." Jackie was getting a little pissed off at her ex. She crossed her arms in front of her. "Back off, Rod, this dude can kick ass. They would need a spatula to get you off the pavement."

"He's good?"

"He's freaking Jim Kelley." She said, watching the men react to hearing her compare Troy to one of Hollywood's African American martial artists who had appeared in several of the Bruce Lee movies.

Rod signaled with his hand and one of his 'friends' grabbed Jackie and pulled her to the side.

"Hey," Troy said, starting to go to her, but Rod shoved him hard against the hood of the truck.

"You want her, you have to go through me."

"Don't be an ass, Rod," Jackie told him and he looked over his shoulder at her.

"Shut up, Woman!"

"Hey, she's a lady," Troy said. "You don't talk like that to a lady."

"You're going to fight me, White Boy."

"You know, I'm getting sick and tired of being call that. The name is Troy Witt, remember that."

Surprised, Rod looked at Jackie. "You sick, Gal, giving this dude one of our people's names."

"I am honored to have the name," Troy said as Rod looked back at him.

"Let's get this on, Dude."

"What happens if I win?"

"The gal goes free, with you. You lose, she's mine." Troy dropped into his fighting stance. Jackie was shaking her head in disbelief, knowing what was about to happen.

"You're a fool, Rod." She said as the fight started. It wasn't even close. Troy beat the crap out of Rod and Rod never laid a hand on him. It was over as fast as it started as Rod lay at his feet. Troy rolled him over onto his back.

"Hey, black boy, leave Jackie alone . . . got it?" Troy took her hand and they moved to the truck. He put her into the passenger's seat and took over the driving.

# CHAPTER THIRTY-FOUR

*"Excuse my son, Chung-Hee. He seems to have forgotten his manners."*

THE NEXT MORNING the girls were early for their culinary class. The other students had not reported in yet, so they were talking, wondering what kind of dishes they were going to be fixing. The culinary class was made up of about 20 students, all eager to learn how to cook. The class was a good mix of people, male and female, blacks, whites, Hispanic and others.

There were two rows of cooking stations well equipped to handle any assignment. The cooking was done right there and everyone was wearing a white chef's uniform. The room was large with tile floors and well lit by the overhead fixtures. To one side were a chalkboard and the instructor's desk. On the opposite side of the room were the windows and, at times, the aroma could be smelled all over the campus. Sometimes a group of people would form outside the building, savoring the aroma coming from inside.

The instructor was Kimberly Wooten, a tall, beautiful African-American female, who had many years of teaching cooking, and many more as a chef. She wanted to see what these new students were capable of, so the first assignment was something easy for them. She turned and wrote on the chalkboard. "General Tso's Chicken II". Kimberly repeated the name, then turned to the class. Everything you need is on the cart next to you. You have 2 hours . . . starting now." The class jumped into action and Kimberly slowly walked around the work stations, watching her students go to work.

Annie beat the egg in a mixing bowl, then added the chicken cubes, sprinkled with salt and added the sugar, white pepper and mixed thoroughly as she added cornstarch a little at a time until the chicken cubes were well coated.

Chung-Hee was already carefully dropping the chicken cubes into the hot oil, one by one, cooking until they were a golden brown and began to float. She removed the chicken and allowed it to cool as she fried the next batch. Once all the chicken had been fried, she refried the chicken, starting with the batch that was fried first. The chicken cooked until it was a deep golden brown, then she drained it on a paper towel-lined plate.

Annie was heating the vegetable oil in a wok over high heat. She stirred in the green onion, garlic, whole chilies and then orange zest and stirred until the garlic had turned golden and the chilies brightened. Then she added sugar, ginger, chick broth, viegar, soy sauce, sesame oil, and peanut oil, brought to a boil and cooked for 3 minutes.

Chung-Hee was on the last step, dissolving cornstarch in water and stirred it into the boiling sauce and stirred until it thickened. She then stirred the chicken into the boiling sauce, reduced the heat to low and cooked for a few more minutes until the chicken had absorbed some of the sauce.

The front door of the Brown's restaurant slowly opened and you could hear Jackie talking. "Sometimes Father gets so wrapped up in his work here he falls asleep and forgets to call me." She gasped at what she saw. The restaurant looked as if a tornado had come through it. Everything was turned over and all the food was left out. "FATHER!" Jackie yelled out, expecting the worst as she and Troy looked over the place. Troy went out back and heard pounding coming from the dumpster.

Troy helped Ray out of the dumpster and yelled out for Jackie who didn't take long to join them. Ray looked like a tractor trailer had run over him.

In the class, the instructor had the fun part of the exercise . . . the tasting. She finally reached Annie and the last person was Chung-Hee. She turned to face the class. "Class we do have a winner today and that is Ms. Roberson." The class cheered and applauded. "Clean up your stations and I will see you day after tomorrow." The students were able to take their creations with them when they left.

Annie left the classroom and was heading for the exit when Chung-Hee came running up to her, taking her arm. "Hey, let's have dinner at the Browns' restaurant tonight. I heard they have a fantastic new chef working there." Chung-Hee said as they left the building. The bus had stopped at the corner and Annie and Chung-Hee got off. They were caught off-guard when they saw the police activity in front of the restaurant, along with the rescue squad.

Chung-Hee looked disappointed. "Well, so much for that idea. Come on, let's go across the street." She started to leave but Annie stopped her.

"One second." Suddenly Annie covered her mouth in disbelief when she saw Troy with Jackie.

*"I could not believe what I was looking at. It was you, I was sure about it. I wanted to go to you when you fell to your knees, but the paramedics were on you in a flash. That night I couldn't sleep . . . I kept seeing that image of you."*

"It can't be you," was all that Annie kept saying over and over. She thought she was whispering low enough that her roommate couldn't hear, but she was wrong. Chung-Hee rolled over on her side and turned on the small lamp.

"Annie . . . what is it?"

"I'm sorry. I didn't mean to wake you."

"It's OK, I was awake. Is this about what happened in town?"

"That man at the restaurant . . . . he looked like my Tony."

Chung-Hee sat up and brought both knees to her chest. "I noticed that, and wondered if you did. What are you going to do?"

"I don't know," Annie said as she sat up, taking the same position as Chung-Hee. "Chung-Hee, I have to go home this weekend, Mother wants me there. Do you want to come with me?"

"That would be nice," Chung-Hee said as Annie smiled at her new-found friend.

Jackie went running to Troy when he came from the doctor's office. She threw her arms around him. "Now, now, I'm all right," Troy said to her as they sat down.

"What happened?" Jackie asked as she gently touched his cheek.

"I don't know," Troy said, although it was not exactly true. He was still having flashes of a young lady that was in the crowd forming around the restaurant.

Ray had been released from the hospital with only a few cuts and bruises. After a good meal and a shower he was feeling better and ready for a good night's sleep. Troy, however, could not sleep. He was up sketching a drawing of the woman that had plagued his mind ever since Ray had fished him out of the river. "Who the hell are you?" He said to himself. There was a knock at the door and he quickly slipped the picture into the desk drawer. He called out, inviting the person to enter. Jackie came in and went over to him.

"Dad's finally asleep," she said as she pulled him and the chair away from the desk and straddled him. "Which leaves you and me time for us."

"And just what do you have in mind?"

Jackie took off her sweater, revealing herself to him. "You are so beautiful," Troy said as he stood up, taking her with him. She laughed when he spun her around like a top.

"I love you," Jackie said to him as they kissed. They held the kiss as Troy gently laid her down on the bed and got on top of her.

\* \* \*

*"There was no cooking class today, so I was able to attend some of the other classes I need to complete by Bachelor's degree. Those classes are a little harder than I thought they would be, but I am making it. Ethan was graduating from the Police Academy and that's why Mother wanted me to come home for the weekend. Mark has definitely given up management class. He said he would rather help Mom and Dad at the restaurant. Tyler is still in Washington. My only fear is that when Mark sees Chung-Hee his hormones will kick in and if that happens . . . God help the relations between the United States and Korea. Chung-Hee's jeep is in the shop, so I guess we're going to have to take a bus home."*

\* \* \*

They Greyhound Bus soon pulled into the bus station and several passengers disembarked. Nancy and Mark were waiting and were excited to see Annie and her new friend. Annie threw her arms around her mother, giving her a huge hug. "My God, you've gotten taller," Nancy commented on the way her daughter looked.

"Mom, Mark, this is my friend Chung-Hee. She is from Korea. Chung-Hee, this is my mother and my brother, Mark." Chung-Hee bowed, as she would have in Korea.

"You are very pretty," Mark said making Chung-Hee smile and received a slap behind the head from his mother.

"Excuse my son, Chung-Hee. He seems to have forgotten his manners," Nancy said.

"It's all right, Mrs. Roberson. I think it's kind of cute." This made Mark blush like a super-nova. He held the door for the two women as they slid into the truck. Mark was about to jump into the back with them, but Nancy grabbed his belt and pulled him back.

"Mom!"

"The front." Nancy said to him in no uncertain terms, and waited until Mark had gotten into the truck before she got in. Chung-Hee whispered into Annie's ear.

"Really?" Annie responded.

Annie narrating. "*The parade grounds at the Academy were packed with people. The squad of newly graduated officers was marching to take it's place in front of the grandstand. Everyone was cheering and the excitement filled the air. And Dad . . . well I saw the pride in his eyes and Mom was snapping pictures left and right. Even Ashley was beside herself. Then, right before the Commandant was about to make his speech, Ethan walked up to Ashley, dropped to one knee and proposed right then and there. All I could think about was when you proposed to me at your high school graduation. That was the happiest day of my life, other than meeting you on the beach.*"

# CHAPTER THIRTY-FIVE

*"This Troy Witt looks so much like Tony, I can't believe it."*

ANNIE NARRATING: *"IT was just as I thought, thanks to my older brother, what was the word she used, 'interesting'. The next thing that surprised me was what my family did to me. But, considering it was my birthday, I should have expected it. Master Phillips and his wife, Ann, were there, along with Rebecca and Lisa and some of the other students from the school. It was a perfect day. The only thing that would have made it better would have been if you were by my side. Oh . . . I turned 18 today. Three more years and we would have been married. I love you more every day."*

Mark had managed to get Chung-Hee alone in his room while everyone was enjoying themselves downstairs. They sat together on the edge of the bed. "I hope you don't mind me pulling you away from the party, but I have to talk to you."

"I don't mind, Mark. This is a nice room," Chung-Hee said as she looked around the room. She was close enough to Mark that he was able to sniff her hair. She knew he was doing it, and let him. "What do you think?" She asked him.

"About what?"

"About me?" Mark gently touched her cheek and she closed her eyes to take in the full effect of his touch.

"You are so beautiful," Mark told her as he took her hand. "I don't know anything about dating someone from another country. Are you promised to anyone?"

"No, I'm not promised . . . . are you?" Chung-Hee found herself blushing as she tucked some of her long hair behind an ear. She hadn't felt this way with a man in a long time.

Mark smiled at her. "No. I think I have been waiting for you all of my life."

"I have been searching for someone for a long time . . . I believe I have found him," Chung-Hee said as the two slowly started to move toward each other, to kiss. The door to Mark's room opened and Annie was standing there.

"What are you doing? Oh great, it looks like I'm going to have my hands full trying to keep an eye on you two."

Chung-Hee was offered the guest bedroom, but the two girls thought it would be kind of fun if they slept together. "What do you think of Mark?" Annie asked, making Chung-Hee turn to her.

"He's cute. I could really see myself with him." Annie started to laugh. "What's so funny?"

"You and Mark . . . together?"

"Do you have a problem with that?"

"No . . . Mark's a great guy."

Chung-Hee had to snicker to herself. "I never thought I would fall for someone who is not Korean."

"But you two just met?" Annie said as she sat up to lean back against the wall. Chung-Hee did the same thing.

"You must remember how you felt when you first met Tony? Annie, I know you probably told yourself that there would never be anyone else. But you have to know, deep inside, that it is not so."

"There can be no other for me." Annie was now beginning to get a little defensive about the subject.

"Annie, you're going to need companionship sooner or later."

"I had my chance and I blew it."

"Annie, Tony's death was not your fault."

"Wasn't it? I could have done more to prevent him from leaving the house that night. I could have done more on the bridge that day." She was beginning to believe everything that the town had been saying about them . . . about her.

"Annie! You did what you could; no more, no less."

Annie slid back under the blankets.

"Chung-Hee, I don't want to talk about it. Tony was my life, there will be no other." Annie turned onto her side, away from Chung-Hee, who knew that the conversation was over.

"I'm sorry," Chung-Hee said as she also slid under the blankets.

\*　　\*　　\*

The sun had hardly come up when the two girls were going through their martial arts training in the back yard. Not much had been said about the conversation the night before. Chung-Hee knew now that the subject was a touchy one with Annie. She was still hurting and had not forgiven Tony for what he had done to her, even if it had been a year ago. She may never get over it.

What they didn't know was that they were being watched from Annie's window. Mark was looking through a pair of binoculars, as if he needed them, but he wasn't just watching both girls, he was focused on Chung-Hee . . . a mighty fine woman to look at.

"What are you doing?" Mark jumped, hitting his head on the window frame.

"Mom!" He said, looking at Nancy who was standing at the open door with her hands on her hips.

"Your father is going to kill you for using his binoculars."

"I'm bird watching, Mom." He got to his feet and went to her.

"Since when?"

"You know, I've always been interested in birds." Mark told her as he went by her and she smacked him behind the head.

"Put them back."

"Yes, Mom."

Nancy went to the open window and looked out. "Bird watching my foot . . . ANNIE! Breakfast will be ready shortly." Annie looked up at the window.

"All right, Mother . . . we're almost finished, we just want to go running."

Nancy nodded and slid the window closed. The two girls soon found themselves jogging on the beach and came up to the same fallen tree where Annie and Tony had first made love. They sat on the tree as the wind from the ocean seemed to have control of their hair. Annie was looking around as she held one side of her hair. "It seems every time I am home, I am drawn to this spot."

Chung-Hee looked around from where she was sitting. "What is so special about this place?"

Annie lowered her head, not sure about how to talk about it. "This is where Tony and I first made love." A tear began to roll down her cheek.

"How old were you?"

"I was almost 16 and he was 17." Chung-Hee remembered the first time she made love, but she was a little older than that.

For the first time since she met Annie, Chung-Hee now realized just how much she really loved Tony.

"Gosh, I sound so pathetic, don't I?" Annie said and pointed in front of her. "That is where I was building my sandcastle and he fell into it."

"You really do love him."

"He is my life, Chung-Hee. I know it's been over a year, but I love him now, more than ever."

"I hope I can find that kind of love with Mark." Chung-Hee was thinking about Mark and smiled.

"I hope you do. A woman should experience that kind of love once in her life . . . . come on. We've got to get back." The two hopped off the tree at the same time and took off running back to the house.

Chung-Hee wanted to cook something for the Roberson family. They had been so kind to her and she wanted to thank them, so it had to be something special. She was going to fix them Maple Syrup Korean Teriyaki Chicken. It would take a couple of hours to make, so Chung-Hee, with Annie's help, got right on it. Chung-Hee was mixing the soy sauce with water, maple syrup, sesame oil, garlic, pepper and ginger. She placed the most of it in a re-sealable plastic bag, reserving some of the mixture. She then placed the chicken in the bag, sealed it and let it marinate for 2 hours in the refrigerator. Annie placed the rice in the water in a saucepan, covered and set the heat to low so it would simmer for 45 minutes. She poured marinade from the bag into a saucepan and brought it to a boil, then mixed in the cornstarch and stirred until thickened. While Chung-Hee placed the chicken into a prepared baking dish, she allowed it to broil on each side, basting frequently with the reserved marinade. She then placed the chicken over the cooked rice and topped with the boiled marinade.

When the time was right, they served it to the family and from the way they devoured it, the girls decided they had better help themselves while there was still some left.

Annie narrating: *"The family loved the cooking, but it was time for us to return to Timber City. Fun time was over and we had to get back to school. Chung-Hee seemed to be sad to leave Mark, but he assured her that he would call her when he could. When we got back to the dorm, there was a bouquet of colorful flowers waiting for Chung-Hee . . . Romeo had struck again. I was alone while Chung-Hee was in the bathroom talking to Mark on the phone. When I finally got her away from Mark we decided to go to the Brown's restaurant for dinner."*

\* \* \*

Annie and Chung-Hee sat across from each other in one of the booths. The restaurant was busy as they looked around the place. It had been cleaned up since that day. Troy and Jackie had worked hard to get in order so they could reopen this soon. "Kind of a homey place, don't you think?" Annie said as Jackie came up to them with their water and menus. Annie looked at Jackie. "What do you recommend?"

"I like the meatloaf myself, it comes with mashed potatoes, green beans and a biscuit." Annie liked the way that sounded.

"I'll take that, please," she said as Jackie turned her attention to Chung-Hee.

"I'll have the Peppered Shrimp Alfredo, and two beers."

"Very good. I'll get your drinks and your orders will be up shortly."

"Excuse me," Annie said. "Where's the restroom?"

"Just passed the kitchen doors," Jackie told her.

"Thank you." As Jackie moved away Annie went to the restroom. However, she never made it there. She stopped short when she came upon the kitchen and looked through the windows. She could not believe it. It was Tony who was transferring a pot of old water from the table to the work stove. He let out a scream of pain, dropped the pot to the floor and brought his hands to his temples, and dropped to his knees. The images flashing through his mind were coming at him at lightspeed. Ray rushed to his side. Annie wanted to go to him so badly, but decided that would be hard to explain and went back to Chung-Hee. Jackie came running into the kitchen to see what had happened, but by that time Ray had gotten Tony to sit down.

"Your migraines again?" Jackie asked. "I thought you had them under control."

"I did. At least I thought I did. They are coming at me faster than usual." Tony said, confused.

"What triggers them?" Jackie asked as she crossed her arms in front of her.

"I don't know. That's just it . . . . I was working when it hit me."

The girls were enjoying their dinners as they tasted the ingredients, telling each other what they detected. They savored the aroma, not believing what they were eating, it was incredible. Finally Annie had to call Jackie over. "This is incredible. Is there any way we can talk to the chef . . . we are going to the university's culinary school and we would like to talk to him, if possible?"

"He's not feeling well, but I will ask him."

"What happened in there? We heard all the noise?" Annie asked.

"Don't concern yourself, he just dropped something," Jackie explained.

"His name wouldn't be Tony Cross, would it?" Annie wanted to see if she would get a reaction to his name.

"No, it's Troy Witt . . . excuse me." Jackie left them to go to the kitchen.

"What was that all about?" Chung-Hee asked, not believing that Annie would be so bold.

"This Troy Witt . . . . he looks so much like Tony. It's unbelievable."

"He really looks that much like your Tony?"

"To the point of being a carbon copy."

As the two girls were paying their bill, Troy walked up behind them. "I'm Troy Witt, did you want to see me?" Annie turned to face him, and fainted.

# CHAPTER THIRTY-SIX

*"Byung-shin."*

ANNIE NARRATING, *"I don't know what happened to me, but seeing Tony/Troy within an arm's reach kind of made by body shut down. Now, I know he is Tony. Chung-Hee may think I'm crazy, but my heart is telling me it is him. I just don't understand why he doesn't seem to know me."*

A sign of relief came over everyone when Annie came too. "Are you all right?" Troy asked as she tried to sit up without making eye contact.

"I'm sorry, I didn't mean to upset you." Annie said as she slowly slid her right hand over to the table so she could touch his hand. He didn't withdraw it.

"You didn't upset me. I'm just concerned." Troy looked at her strangely. "Do I know you?"

She stood up. "I'm fine . . . we really should be going." The two women left the restaurant, but Troy ran after them, calling out and they turned.

"Wait, please . . . I want to talk to you." Troy said, not taking his eyes off Annie.

"There's nothing to talk about, except me making a fool of myself." Annie said as Chung-Hee took hold of her right arm to steady her. She could feel those eyes taking her over.

"I can't help but feel that I know you." Troy said, having flashes from the drawing to Annie.

"I bet you said that to all the women," Annie said to him, extending her hand out to him. "It was nice to meet you." They shook hands and both seemed to have the same kind of migraine. Annie was having flashes of when they were kids together, the same as Troy. Once the pain went away, they just stood there looking at each other.

"Who are you?" He asked her.

"She's Annie Roberson, you . . ." Annie elbowed Chung-Hee to be quiet, but the damage had been done.

Troy handed her a card with his number on it. "Call me, let me know how you are feeling."

"All right . . . . I will . . . . have a good night." He stood there watching them walk away.

"What was that all about?" Jackie asked as he turned around and saw her standing there, madder than a wet hen.

"She reminds me of someone. But I don't know who she is." Troy said, taking hold of her shoulders.

"Is she the reason you've been getting these migraines?" Jackie said, feeling as if she was about to get one herself.

"I don't know, Jackie. But it could be possible." He saw the way that Jackie was looking at him. "Now don't go getting jealous." Why wouldn't she want him to remember? If this person could help, then what was wrong with it?

"I am not jealous. Is that why you want to go to the university, is it because of her?" They had been talking about him going to the university to take some of the culinary classes.

"I don't know. I don't remember seeing her until tonight. Jackie . . . don't you want me to remember who I am?"

"No." She said, shocking Troy.

"What? Why?" He ran his hands up and down her arms.

"I'm afraid if you remember you'll walk out of my life and I will never see you again." Jackie was becoming very angry at the whole situation. Like most women, she was the type that she wanted the full attention of the guy she was with . . . not some blonde chick that he hardly knew.

"Oh, Jackie, I do love you." Troy pulled her into his arms and kissed her.

Annie and Chung-Hee were walking back to their room. "Why didn't you want me to tell him who he is?" Chung-Hee asked Annie.

They stopped walking and turned to face each other. "Because, how do you think it would seem if I walked right up to him and said, 'Mr. Cross, my name is Annie Roberson and you are my fiancée. We are going to be married in two years.'"

"Ok, I know that sounds pretty bad, but come on, Annie. You know it's him, I know it's him, but the only person that doesn't is him." Chung-Hee was more than a little confused about what she had just said.

"Chung-Hee, I understand how you feel about this, but I don't want to force myself on him. It might drive him even further away. If it is amnesia, he will have to find his own way back to me. We can't force it."

"All right. I'll let you do it your way."

"Thanks," was all that Annie said as she touched Chung-Hee's arm for a second.

"What was that migraine about?" Chung-Hee wondered.

"If it was a migraine. It was strange. I never experienced anything like it. When I held his hand, I saw flashes of my past life with him going so fast, it was like watching a slide show at warp speed. Does that make any sense?"

Chung-Hee could see the pain in Annie's eyes and just shook her head. "What are you going to do?" She asked her.

"I don't know, Chung-Hee, I really do not know." Chung-Hee put a friendly hand on Annie's shoulder.

"I wish I could help."

"Your being here helps . . ." Suddenly Annie couldn't believe who she saw. "I'll meet you back at the room, I see someone I know." Chung-Hee watched as Annie walked away from her.

The person Annie was approaching was Pete Conroy, the guy that had drugged her and tried to rape her. "Hello, Darling. It's been a long time." A horrified look came over Pete as he recognized the voice. He slowly looked over his shoulder and gasped when he saw Annie standing there.

"You . . ." was all Pete could say as Annie took a few steps toward the blond that was with him.

"If I were you, I would go home before this person drugs you and tries to rape you."

The girl suddenly looked indignant and stormed away from Pete.

"Now just a second," he said as he moved at Annie and without thinking about it, she went into action and before Pete could react he was on the ground at Annie's feet and she was looking down at him.

"Come on, stand up like a man and face me." Each time Annie reached for him, Pete slid away from her on his butt. Annie finally pulled him to his feet to face her. "What's the matter, Pete? Afraid of me now that I'm not under the influence of one of your drugs?"

"Just let me go, OK? You'll never see me again." He pleaded with her, beginning to shake like a leaf.

"You know something . . . you're nothing but a low-life worm," Annie said as Pete nodded his head agreeing with her.

"You're right, I am . . ." Annie could tell in his voice that he was scared and she was loving it.

"You can't face a woman unless you've drugged them, can you?"

"I did my time." He voice cracked.

"And that is supposed to make me feel better?"

"What do you want from me?"

"I want you to suffer, the way you made me suffer. I want to take you apart, limb by limb."

"Can't we talk about this?"

"What's the matter, afraid I might mess up that pretty face of yours?" Annie pushed him away from her, then, without warning, executed an out-to-in kick and Pete went down. He slowly started to stand up, but found another kick coming at him, this time an in-to-out kick. He went down again. In the martial arts community, it is drilled into you not to use your knowledge to fight or use any violence that could cripple, or kill, someone. You should just walk away. What they don't tell you is how good it feels to beat the crap out of someone like Pete Conroy. About this time the campus police showed up and Pete was able to get up and half-way run to meet them.

"Keep her away from me . . . . please." Annie came walking up to the two officers and Pete ducked behind them.

"What's going on here, Ma'am?" One of the officer's asked.

"Some time ago, this man drugged me and tried to rape me. I can give you the case number."

"What's your name?" The office asked Pete.

"Pete Conroy," he told him.

"I'll run it." The other officer said and went to his car. Seconds later he returned. "He's got a rap-sheet a mile long. Most of it due to rape, or attempted rape."

The first officer looked at Annie. "Would you like to finish him off, Ma'am?"

A huge smile formed on Annie's face.

"Wait . . . you can't do that!!" Pete pleaded, as the officer pushed him toward Annie who let him have it with a snap kick to the groin, then swept his legs out from under him.

The two officers just watched. "She's good," the first officer said.

"Definitely . . . . pretty too. Think she's dating anyone?"

"Would you really want to date her?" The officer asked as Pete lay on the ground at Annie's feet . . . again.

"Why not?"

"What if she caught you cheating on her?"

"Good point . . ." They watched as Annie pulled Pete to his feet and hit her fighting stance again. "Twenty bucks says she puts him away in with 3 more kicks."

"You're on." However, it was only 2 kicks later that Pete laid on the ground, not moving.

The officer went to Pete and pulled him to his feet. "Feeling better now, Ma'am?" He asked.

"I've been dreaming of doing that ever since he kidnapped me."

"We had a little bet that you would take the creep down in 3 more kicks . . . you did it in 2. Here's the twenty bucks . . . . go have a pizza on us." They proceeded to put Pete into the back of the car.

"I can't take this," Annie said looking at the money.

"Please, it's on us." Annie kissed him on the cheek and hurried away.

"How come you have all the luck?" The other officer said as they got into the car and drove away.

Chung-Hee had waited to see what Annie was going to do. "What was that all about?" She asked as Annie walked up to her.

"I'll explain in the room."

"This should prove interesting."

*   *   *

Troy was in his room sitting at the desk looking at the picture. He wrote 'Annie Roberson' on the picture, then looked at the tattoo on his ankle. "Annie Roberson? Could the 'A' be for 'Annie'? "I had so many questions to ask you," he thought. "I wish you would have stayed a little while longer." Jackie came into the room, not giving Troy a chance to put the picture away and took it from him.

"What is this?" She asked him.

"Annie Roberson." Troy said, taking the picture from her and slipping it into the desk drawer.

"Are you remembering things?" Jacked asked him.

"All I know is that she seems to be the key. If I figure out who she is, and what she means to me, the pieces of the puzzle will fall into place."

"And then you will walk out of my life," Jackie said as she turned to leave, but Troy was able to take hold of her hand and pull her back to him, making her sit on his lap.

"I love you. I don't know anything about Annie."

"But what happens if you turn out to be her husband, or something like that?"

"Jackie . . . shut up and kiss me."

"Damn you."

*   *   *

"He tried to rape you. You couldn't use any of your skill because he drugged you." Chung-Hee said as she sat cross-legged on the bed, holding her pillow. Both women were in their pajamas, ready for bed.

"I couldn't do a thing," Annie explained.

"Byung-shin." (Means jerk in Korean). There were harsher words that Chung-Hee wanted to use, but this was the best one for this situation. Annie fell back onto the bed, laughing as Chung-Hee did the same thing.

Annie narrating: *"It seems I'm going to have to learn Korean . . . Mark is pretty serious about Chung-Hee. He has said he wants to go back to school to learn to speak Korean so he could understand her and have a conversation in her language. Meeting this Troy Witt for the second time and seeing him face to face . . . I am positive he is you. I'm just not sure how to proceed from this point. Oh, one last thing . . . Pete Conroy is in jail (evidently there was another warrant out for him for assaulting a woman). After what I did to him, I doubt that he will be bothering another woman. I love you so much."*

# CHAPTER THIRTY-SEVEN

*"I made a fool of myself, didn't I?"*

ANNIE DIDN'T WANT to go with Chung-Hee that weekend. She needed to catch up on some homework for her other classes. It was a beautiful June night, so Annie sat outside on one of the many wooden benches found on the campus grounds. A slight breeze was playing havoc with her papers and she was having problem trying to control them so she could study her notes. She was so involved that she didn't hear someone talking to her, until he had spoken several times. She looked up to see who was there and jumped up, forgetting about the papers on her lap and they scattered over the ground, some getting caught by the breeze. The two gathered the papers and sat back down on the bench. "What are you doing here?" Annie asked Troy.

"I'm looking for the registration office."

"They close early on Friday's. You just missed them. You going to register for the next term?"

"I want to take some cooking classes."

"Why do you need cooking classes? You're already a great chef?"

"One can always learn new things . . . need to keep the mind sharp. Besides, having that piece of paper never hurts. Have you eaten?" Annie picked up the open container that had once had a ham and cheese sandwich in it. "That is not eating."

"It seemed OK to me."

"Let me buy you dinner."

"Not at your place."

"Would I do that to you?"

"I hope not." Annie finally agree to go with him and they walked away. Annie found her hand going to his and it felt so good. He was definitely her Tony, no two ways about it.

*"Why didn't he have his flashes? I don't know. Perhaps his mind was at peace being with me . . . finally realizing it's where he belongs,"* she thought to herself.

The two were sitting across from each other in a booth at a busy Italian restaurant. Troy had ordered a chicken pasta dish and Annie ordered a pasta salad and a soda. "This may be none of my business, but I would like to ask you something, if it's all right?" Annie said to him.

"You can ask me anything," Troy said to her with that sexy smile of his that always did something to her.

"Where do you come from? I mean, where is your home and family?"

"I know this will sound crazy, but I really don't know."

"Amnesia?"

"That's what the doctor said. I keep having these flashes of people and places I should know, but I just can't grasp them. The odd thing is, some of those flashes have been of you."

Annie just sat there stunned. *"Was he remembering?"* She thought to herself.

"I don't know why I'm not having those flashes now . . . like the other night. It's all very confusing. Do you know why I would have those flashes of you? Do you know who I am?"

"I think it would be better if you remembered on your own. Trying to force things might not be good for you. Hold that thought for a moment." She was cut off by her cell phone ringing. She grabbed her backpack and started to pull things out . . . . her compact, keys, makeup kit . . . notebook, pens. Troy could help chuckling.

"Did you pack the kitchen sink, too?"

Annie giggled. "It wouldn't fit." She had realized that she had pulled out the photo of the two of them. Troy picked it up and looked at it and the flashes came faster than ever. Annie couldn't believe what was happening and told her mother that she would have to call her back later. The flashes in Troy's mind were out of control, and he was afraid he might pass out. He excused himself and went to the bathroom where he washed his face. Soon the flashes passed and the rest of dinner went without any further problems. Later that evening, Annie and Troy stood outside Annie's dorm.

"I had a wonderful time, thank you." Annie said and gently kissed Troy on the check. "I love you," she whispered, then darted up the steps into the building. Troy stood there touching his cheek and couldn't understand why she had said those three words to him. He walked away.

*"By the time I returned to the room, Mother was calling me again. She was very upset and I can understand why when she told me the news. I couldn't believe it myself.*

*Ethan had been shot. He walked into a bank robbery in progress. He is still in the OR but the doctor has said that he should pull through. Ashley was climbing the walls. I hung up the phone, rested my elbow on the table and cried."*

I know that at times I have fought with my brothers, but they are my brothers, my family, and I love each of them dearly. I know it's seemed like I love Mark more, but we are family!

Chung-Hee came into the room and Annie didn't give her much time to get comfortable. She ran and threw her arms around Chung-Hee who was, needless to say, surprised. "Annie, what's wrong?"

"He's been shot!" The first thing Chung-Hee thought about was Mark.

She made Annie look at her. "Who's been shot?"

"Ethan." In a way Chung-Hee was relieved that it wasn't Mark, she had already lost one loved one to a bullet, she didn't need to lose Mark this soon. She was just developing strong feelings for him. She took Annie to the bed and made her lie down, then called Mark.

*"I really needed you today. Ethan getting shot and still being in the OR hit me hard. Granted we were never as close as Mark and me, but he was my brother. Please, if you are out there, please come home to me. I need you."*

Several hours later Annie rushed into the Brown's restaurant and even though Jackie shouted at her, she barged passed her and went into the kitchen where Troy was cooking. He turned to find Annie hugging him, crying. At first he wasn't sure what to do, but slowly put his arms around her and held her. Chung-Hee couldn't stop her, but she knew what Annie had in mind, so she came rushing into the kitchen followed by Jackie, who couldn't believe what was going on. "Come home to me . . . please come home." Was all that Annie could say.

Later all of them were sitting at a booth and Annie was drying her eyes with a napkin, trying to compose herself. Chung-Hee was sitting next to her and Jackie and Troy across from them. "I am so sorry, I didn't mean to have done all of this. I just kind of lost it when I got the word that my brother had been shot and was still in the OR. For some reason, I came here to you . . . two years ago I lost my fiancée. You remind me of him. I promise, it won't happen again."

"I am honored that you think I look like your fiancée, Ms. Roberson. If you ever need a shoulder, Jackie here can vouch to the fact that I have a good one." Jackie punched him on the arm.

"Thank you for being kind. I assure you it won't happen again." They got up to leave and Jackie and Troy followed them out with Jackie holding Troy's arm as if she would never let go. Annie turned and waved at Troy, who smiled and waggled his fingers back at her.

*  *  *

Everyone was in class way before the teacher. This was a first . . . she was never late. Everyone was adjusting their uniforms and cleaning their workstations. Chung-Hee, who was at the station behind Annie, got her attention and Annie turned to look at her. "How are you holding up kiddo?" Chung-Hee asked.

"I made a fool of myself, didn't I?"

"Who could blame you? He does look like your Tony."

"What am I going to do Chung-Hee. I don't know how much longer I can endure this."

"I don't want to hear talk like that. Looks like I'm going to have to spend more time meditating with you. Oh, by the way . . . . I got good news for you. "Ethan is in a regular room and is expected to make a full recovery. Mark called in the middle of the night. You were sound asleep and I didn't want to wake you." Annie sighed a breath of relief then turned when the teacher came in clapping her hands to get everyone's attention. Annie could not believe who was with her.

"We have a new student joining us today. I believe you all know him as Troy Witt, head chef of the Brown's restaurant. I know it's the middle of the term, but he told me he can always learn something new. However, to me, he already an excellent chef. Let's give him a warm welcome." Everyone applauded. "Do you know Ms. Roberson?" The teacher asked Troy.

"Yes, Ma'am," he said with a smile.

"Good. Take the work station next to her."

"Yes, Ma'am," Tony said and headed to the station. Annie watched as he walked behind her on his way to the station. He put his books on the nearby shelf. He flashed her that smile that melted her insides and she tried to collect herself so she could do the class.

The teacher began writing on the chalkboard. "Today's class is Piazza Pasta." She turned to the class. "As always, the stove has been preheated and everything you need is available. You may begin."

*  *  *

Jackie was out on the porch, pacing back and forth. She was scared and nervous, all rolled up into one. She felt as if she was losing the man she had come to love so much. Ray came out and sat down in the rocking chair that Troy had seemed to claim for himself and now he was going to enjoy it. He just sat there, watching his daughter.

"I don't want to have to fix the porch tonight," Ray told her, making her stop the pacing.

"I don't like this, Father. Troy is taking the same class with the Roberson girl."

"One thing you have to learn to have in a relationship is trust. You have to trust him, Jackie."

Jackied folded her arms in front of her and leaned back against the railing of the porch. "I do trust him. Just not with her." Ray started snickering. "What's so funny, Father?"

"My little girl . . . jealous of a white boy."

"He's not a white boy . . . he's Troy Witt and I'm not jealous . . . why do you think I am? All right . . . I'm going over there right now!" Ray burst out in a full laugh. "Stop laughing . . . this is not funny!"

\* \* \*

The teacher called out, stopping the work and she began tasting. "We do have a winner today. It is Mr. Wilson." Everyone politely applauded. "Clean up your stations before you leave." Annie, Troy and Chung-Hee left the building together and were surprised to see Jackie run up to Troy. Annie had to look away when they kissed. If this was her Tony, she couldn't stand seeing him kiss another woman. Chung-Hee was watching her closely.

"You OK?" She whispered to Annie.

"NO!" Annie said, not even looking as Troy and Jackie walked away arm in arm.

Troy and Jackie were riding back to the house on their horses. "Why did you come to the school just now?" Troy asked her.

"To see you," Jackie said as they stopped the horses for a second.

"You knew I was going to come straight home."

"What is wrong with me coming to escort you home?" Jackie said as she leaned forward and petted the horse's neck.

"This is not about us. It's about Annie, isn't it?" Jackie just flashed him a look. "Jackie, she's hurting. I'm just trying to be nice to her."

"What makes her so special?"

"Jackie . . ."

"Have I become so obsolete that you wouldn't go to bed with me?"

"Jackie . . ."

"I don't want you to see her anymore."

"We're in the same class. That would be hard." Troy took a deep breath and let it out. "I have no desire for her."

"Yeah . . . right. I've seen the way you look at her." Jackie was not happy and Troy could not blame her.

"You know something. I'm not going to just stand here and talk about Annie Roberson. The last one home has to wash down the horses."

"You just made a deal with the wrong girl . . . . HEEYAH!" Jackie's horse took off like lightning. What Jackie didn't know was that Troy had found a shortcut back to the house and took off through the woods. He had his horse at a full gallop, he could almost feel that the horse knew the way home.

# CHAPTER THIRTY-EIGHT

*"You're not getting passed me, Mister."*

JACKIE COME TROTTING onto the farm believing that she beaten Troy, however, her victory was short lived when she saw Troy sitting in his favorite rocking chair. "Are you going to tell me how you did that?" She asked him.

"Nope." He said to her as he held a can of beer. She walked up to him, took the beer and drank from the can.

"Are you going to help me with the horses?" She asked . . . still holding the beer, planning on finishing it herself.

"Nope."

"I hate you."

"You love me."

"You're a monster!"

"I know."

Jackie moved away to take care of the horses.

\*   \*   \*

There was a knock at the door and Chung-Hee hurried to answer it. She opened the door surprised to see who was standing there. "MARK!" The entire campus must have heard her. She plastered him with kisses and closed the door behind him when he came into the room.

"What are you doing here?" She asked him.

"Well . . . if you don't want me here . . ."

"You're not getting passed me, Buster."

"Bo Go Shi Paw Yo . . ." (I miss you.)

Chung-Hee's face lit up. "You're learning very well."

"Yeah Ppaw Yo." (You are very pretty.) She had not heard that in a long time, not even her ex had said it to her as often as Mark. She knew she was going to love this guy.

"Ja Gi Ya Sa Rang He." (Baby, I love you.) Chung-Hee said to Mark, which made him smile. Then she said, "Na hante kiseu." (Kiss me.) Mark didn't even think twice . . . he kissed her. The only thing Chung-Hee could think about was how Mark did something to her that no Korean guy ever had. Suddenly, the door opened and Annie walked in.

"Ooops. I didn't know you had company." They were suddenly acting as if nothing had happened. "Hi, Mark," Annie said, as she put her things on her desk.

\*     \*     \*

Jackie finished washing down the horses and still had a lot of water left in the bucket. She quietly walked up to the porch where Troy was now sleeping in the chair. He let out a scream of bloody murder as he got drenched from head to toe. The scream brought Ray out to see what happened and began laughing as Troy chased Jackie around the yard. He could not believe how much Jackie had grown up since Troy came into their lives. He couldn't help but wonder what would happen to her when Troy finally remembered who he was and where he came from. And this Annie Roberson . . . who was she to Troy. The day he brought Troy there and got him out of the wet clothing he saw the tattoo on his ankle. Was the "A" for "Annie"?

Ray went to his truck and hopped in, starting it. Jackie ran to him. "Father, you must save me from this maniac!"

"Can't . . . . got something to do. See you later." Ray backed the truck up and took off just in time to see his daughter being tackled to the ground by Troy.

Annie answered a knock at her door. "Why, Mr. Brown."

"Can we talk?"

"Of course," Annie said and they went to sit on a bench outside the dorm. "Tony and I met when we were kids. We were both from popular families in Pine Lake. Both families ran restaurants and just about everyone in town knew us. A tornado came through town and changed our lives forever. Tony's parents were killed and, believing he was going to be sent to an orphanage, he ran away. He got into some, actually minor, trouble and when the police caught up with him, he committed suicide rather than going back. We were going to be married when I finished college."

"And you think Troy Witt is your Tony?" Ray asked her and she nodded.

"I know it is. It has to be him. Why do you ask?"

"I saw a tattoo on his ankle."

Annie took off her shoe and pulled down her sock to reveal the same tattoo. Ray couldn't believe it.

"My God, he is your Tony."

"His name is Tony Cross. Mr. Brown, please don't mention this to either of them."

"Why. You and Tony were meant to be together . . . you should be happy."

"For one thing, it would tear Jackie apart," Annie said. "For another, I've been reading about amnesia and they say that to force someone to remember could be dangerous. I couldn't hurt Tony. I would rather lose him that cause something worse to happen to him."

"You are an amazing woman, Annie Roberson." She looked at him oddly.

"I don't understand."

"Here you are, in pain, and in arm's reach of the man you love, but you are worried about someone else."

She smiled at him. "I guess that's just the way I am."

Ray nodded. "All right. Look, there's a carnival coming into town in a few days for the 4th of July. How about going with me and let me show you a good time."

"I would like that. Thank you."

"Good."

Annie watched Ray walk away. She sat there almost relieved that her feelings were right. But now, what to do? She didn't have a clue.

# CHAPTER THIRTY-NINE

*"You were all over her like a jackass in heat."*

ANNIE NARRATING: *"RAY treated me like a queen at the carnival. He won a lot of stuffed toys for me. He was very good at the games. I don't think Jackie was very happy about the way he hung all over me. But, truthfully, I wasn't happy the way she was draped over Troy all the time. I can't help but wonder if, and when, he remembers everything, who he will stay with. Jackie Brown or me? If he goes to her, I will have to force myself to accept it and I'm not sure I can do that. Mark and Chung-Hee didn't come with us, instead they went to town to go to a movie and have dinner. I wonder about those two. They are really getting serious about each other. Ethan is home and recovering. Everyone there is going nuts over planning the wedding for him and Ashley. They want to marry around Christmas time. Ethan says it will be the best present he could ever receive. Tyler is now working as a private chef for a billionaire in New York City. Mark and Chung-Hee are going hot and heavy. Maybe there's another wedding in the works for the Roberson family . . . I just wish it was ours. I love you."*

The fireworks lit up the night sky. Annie was sitting with Ray on the Ferris wheel and they were stopped at the top while passengers were unloaded and reloaded. Ray had noticed Annie looking over her shoulder at Jackie and Troy and the way they were acting. "It really does hurt, doesn't it?" He asked her, making her look at him.

"More than anyone could know."

"I can only imagine what you are going through. When my wife died from cancer I was angry with her, the world, myself and my daughter. But, it was because of my daughter that I overcame that anger. I saw my wife in her; her smile, her eyes and her mannerisms. Believe me, there is not a day that I don't think of her."

Annie took a deep breath and exhaled. "There are nights when I wake up crying. I denied the fact that he was dead because I could still feel him. Everyone believed I was going insane. At times I thought they were right. I even went to a psychiatrist. She helped me to a point, but it seemed that everywhere I went, everyone blamed me for what happened. When I found Troy, my heart sunk to my gut when he didn't know who I was. I still don't know what to do." Ray put an arm around her, hoping to make her feel better.

Jackie was with Troy, but could see what her father was doing and the thermometer started rising. "He's just being nice to her." Troy told her.

"There's a point of being nice and a point of being disgusting, and that is disgusting."

"Jackie . . . she lost her fiancée."

"I don't care. That is my father . . . hell, he could be her father!"

"Jackie, look at me."

"No!"

"Come on." Jackie slowly turned her head to him and he flashed her that smile that he knew she couldn't resist.

"Damn you." They kissed and the wheel started moving again. Annie took in a breath as she watched the fireworks from where they sat.

"They are so beautiful." She said.

"You know, if I was younger, I would scoop you up in my arms and take you to a place where they never heard of Pine Lake, Timber City, or Tony Cross. I would make you not want any of them but me," Ray told her.

"You are sweet," Annie said as she touched his cheek. "But I'm afraid that man with your daughter has already locked up my heart.

"That is a pure shame."

After several hours at the carnival, they went to the local steakhouse to have a late dinner. Once Ray parked the truck he got out and ran around to Annie's side, opening the door for her. He then took her hand and helped her out. Jackie was standing with her arms folded and tapping her foot as she watched what she believed was her father making a fool out of himself. As they went inside, he opened and then held the door for Annie. Later, after dropping Annie off at the dorm, they rode back to the farm in silence. "All right, Daughter. What is it?" Ray finally asked. Jackie looked at her father.

"You should be ashamed of yourself."

"For what?"

"The way you were acting with Annie."

"Oh, I see. And how was I acting?"

"You were all over her like a jackass in heat."

"Jackie . . ."

"I wouldn't be surprised if Mom was turning over in her grave seeing you hanging around a white girl . . . and one young enough to be your daughter, at that!"

"You're with a white boy."

"That has nothing to do with it." There was a tapping sound at the small glass window. Jackie slid it open. "What!?"

"Are we there yet?" Troy asked from the bed of the pickup.

"NO!" She slammed the window closed.

When they arrived at the farm Troy hopped down and opened the door for her, offering her his hand but she slapped it away.

"I'm not some helpless little white girl!" She pushed him aside and stormed into the house as the two men stood in front of the truck.

"What's got her all fired up?" Troy asked.

"She hasn't been this fired up since I . . . . we won't go into that right now." They looked at each other.

"You don't think she would . . . ." Troy said, then both at the same time . . .

"She would!!"

They ran to the front door only to find it locked. That was what they had feared. Ray started pounding on the front door, yelling for Jackie to open the door but got no response. He turned to Troy. "Looks like we're sleeping in the barn tonight." Troy said.

Ray thought about it for a few seconds. "Come with me." They ran around to the east corner of the house and stopped at a basement window. "I can never keep this window closed, but you're small enough to slip through and open the front door. Do you think you can do it?"

Troy nodded his head. "I know I can." Troy started to climb through the window but Ray grabbed his arm to stop him. Troy looked at him.

"If you are caught or killed, I will disavow any knowledge of your existence." Troy just looked at him and didn't say anything. As he was about to disappear into the house, Ray stopped him again. "Remember, if you are tortured, it's name, rank and serial number only."

"Ray, she's your daughter."

"I rest my case." Ray said and left Troy to do his mission. Troy had a little trouble climbing through the window but he finally got through and fell into a stack of boxes. He ran up the steps to the main level of the house.

"Dad made you climb through the bad window, didn't he?" Jackie said as she sat on the couch with her legs crossed and her arms folded.

Troy took a couple of steps toward her. "Why are you acting like this?"

She stood up. "My beef is the way you two act when you're around her." There was a pounding at the front door and they heard Ray's muffled voice calling out for them to let him in.

"What should I do?" Troy wanted to go to the door, but waiting until Jackie told him to.

"Let him in." Jackie stormed up the steps as Troy opened the door for Ray.

"I see you're still alive." Ray looked Troy over just to make sure. The two went over to sit down on the couch. "What happened to you boy, did she torture you?"

"Hardly," Troy responded. "Did Annie say anything to you about us?"

"Yes, but she made me take a blood oath not to discuss it with you." Troy sat back against the couch.

"Who is she, Ray? Who is she to me?"

Ray put a friendly hand on Troy's shoulder. "It will come to you."

"And if I remember? Do I go with Annie or stay with Jackie?"

"You will have to listen to your heart. It will guide you."

"I don't know, sometimes I wish you had left me in that river."

"Troy, I don't want to hear talk like that. I've known soldiers that were in worse shape than you and they lived through their torture."

"Perhaps, but they had friends and family to help them. What do I have?"

"You have us . . . and we both love you very much." Troy's face lit up with a bright smile.

# CHAPTER FORTY

*"You can't, he belongs to someone else."*

ANNIE NARRATING: *"THE time I spent with Ray at the carnival was amazing. He is a special man and knows how to treat a woman. I think I might have left some of the toys he won for me in the back of the truck. I wonder what Jackie will do with them. I can't believe that Ray figured everything out. But, he is a very smart man and proved to me that Troy Witt is my Tony. Now I am glad that he talked to me into getting that tattoo. It may be the only thing that will link us up and bring Tony back where he belongs."*

Jackie was behind the barn. She had built a fire in an old oil drum and was drinking beer. She had one in her hand and there were several bottles at her feet. She had found the stuffed toys in the truck and one by one, she was throwing them into the fire. She was remembering everything that had happened since Troy had come into their lives. And now there was Annie. She wondered what her future was going to be like when Troy left her. A tear started for fall down her cheek. "I love you, you bastard."

"You love that toy?"

Jackie knew he was standing there, but how long, she had no idea.

"Go away."

Troy slowly walked up to her. "What are you doing?" He was looking at the fire, the bottles and the toys.

"I'm getting myself drunk." She said to him and took another drink from the bottle. Troy took it from her and finished it in one gulp and threw the bottle over his shoulder. They looked into each other's eyes. Troy took her by the shoulders and slammed her back against the barn and they kissed.

\*     \*     \*

Everyone came into the classroom one-by-one. Now, knowing for sure that the man next to her was her Tony, Annie could not bear to look at him, knowing that if she did, she would want him to hold her and if that happened she would never let him go again. And Troy, well, he was trying everything he could to get her to look at him. Then Troy looked at Chung-Hee who just shrugged her shoulders, having no idea what was wrong with her.

The teacher began to write on the chalkboard. "Ok, everyone, today we are doing Bulgogi." Chung-Hee had gotten Annie's attention. Bulgogi was a Korean dish served with rice.

"I've got this one," Chung-Hee mouthed to her. Annie giggled and turned back to her station and just for a second her eyes locked with Troy's. She tried to shake it off and turn away from him. The teacher ordered everyone to begin. Chung-Hee jumped right in. she grabbed a large bowl and missed together the soy sauce, pear juice, sugar, garlic, sesame oil, sesame seeds, black pepper, and monosodium glutamate. She also placed beef and onions into the mixture and stirred to coat. She covered the dish and refrigerated it for one hour. It was a good thing she had two hours to complete dish. However, the refrigerators were special, just made for the glass and they cooled things down very fast. When the mixture was almost ready, she preheated the grill and brushed oil over the grill pan and added beef and onions. She cooked them until browned evenly, then mixed everything together and added rice to the dish. She was very happy with her work today and knew that her mom would be proud of what she had done.

Finally, the teacher called time and began her enjoyable task of tasting the dishes. "We have a winner today, Ms. Kim Chung-Hee. Chung-Hee let out a scream of joy and started to do the moonwalk as everyone laughed at her. The two women exited the building and saw Jackie who ran to meet Troy. She threw her arms around him and smothered him with kisses. Chung-Hee could see the pain on Annie's face as she looked away from the two. She put her arms around her friend. "Let's order Chinese tonight," she said, trying to get a smile out of her but it didn't work.

The two entered their room and Annie went right to the bed and sat on the edge of it, hiding her face in her hands. Chung-Hee sat down next to her and put her arm around Annie. "I can't do it, Chung-Hee. I can't see him with her like that . . . it hurts too much."

"Come on, Annie . . . you're a strong woman. I know you."

"I am not strong . . . not unless he is at my side."

"Are you sure he is Tony Cross?"

"Ray told me he has a tattoo on his ankle." She removed her shoes and socks to reveal the tattoo on her ankle. She then went on to explain. "The T is for Tony, his tattoo has an 'A' for me."

"What are you going to do?"

"I don't know. Revealing who is is may hurt him more than saying nothing. It's a double-edged sword, Chung-Hee. I'm damned if I do, and damned if I don't."

"Look, it's not good to decide anything on an empty stomach. How about that food? I'm starving." She hadn't much more than got that out when her cell phone rang. She took it out of her pocket.

"Don't tell me . . . . ?" Annie said as Chung-Hee answered, then her face lit up and she went into the bathroom.

Annie narrating: *"So much for Chinese. It is off to the cafeteria to leave the two love birds alone. It's not that I have anything against them . . . . I am happy for Mark and Chung-Hee . . . I really am. All right . . . I guess I am a little jealous. I should be living like they are with Tony right now. I miss him so . . . his baby blue eyes, his smile, and his lips. Just thinking about him still gets me flustered. It is late September and the signs of winter are all around. The forecasters are saying that this winter is going to be a bad one. But, since when are they right? I've been trying to pay less attention to Troy, figuring that is the best for everyone involved, but it does hurt."*

Annie was between classes and walking across the campus grounds when she saw Troy sitting on a nearby bench looking depressed. She went over and sat down beside him. He didn't realize she was there until she put a penny in front of his face. "Penny for your thoughts," she said to him. Suddenly he got one of his migraines and this one was so intense it brought him to his knees. He was in extreme pain and he remembered walking on a beach. He didn't know where, or who he was with, then everything went black.

Annie was shaking him by the shoulders trying to get him to respond. She planted a kiss on his lips, hoping she might be able to break the episode, but the only thing it got her was being pushed to the ground by him. "Just leave me alone," he said and ran off.

That night Troy found himself on the rocking chair, just rocking and thinking of the kiss that he had received from Annie. He was still trying to figure out who she was, and what their connection was. He looked up to see Jackie come out of the house, dressed in her oversized nightshirt. It was a good thing that Indian Summer had kicked in and it was a lovely evening. She folded her arms in front of her as she leaned on the porch rail. "I was wondering where you were," she said as he looked up at her.

"What would you do if I left here?" He asked, surprising her.

"Do you remember something?"

"No, I was just wondering."

"I don't know. I love you, Troy. I've never felt this way about anyone before. He extended his hand out to her and she took it as he guided her onto his lap and she sat down.

"I don't know where I belong. It's been almost two years since your father fished me out of the river and I still don't know who I am."

"Does it matter? You're with us and we both love you, and we will take care of you." She said, snuggling against him.

"I need to find out, Jackie. Don't you understand?"

"No. I do not. Why can't you be happy being Troy Witt and loving me?"

"I don't know, Jackie. I may have a wife and family out there somewhere who are in pain that I am not with them."

"And is this wife Annie Roberson?"

"I don't know . . . . but don't you think that it's odd that I am at peace with her. And what about my tattoo?"

"You think the 'A' stands for Annie?"

"It could be." Jack stood up and looked out at the barnyard.

"Then go to her. See what I care." She turned and went to the front door, but he took hold of her and pulled her back to him.

"Don't, Jackie. Don't do this."

"What about me, Troy? Don't you think this is hurting me too? When I know that you are thinking about her."

"Jackie, please."

"You're going to have to make up your mind, Troy. You can't have both of us." Troy made her kiss him and at first she tried to fight him, but the power of his kiss took her over and she melted into him.

Annie narrating: *"I guess I can understand how Jackie is feeling about this whole thing, because I feel the same way. And I have been waiting for him since I was ten years old and he fell into my sandcastle. It was like we were supposed to meet on that day. But if we were supposed to be together, why was he taken away from me?"*

The next morning Ray had come from the house to see the two snuggled on the rocking chair. Troy was talking in his sleep but Jackie couldn't understand what he was saying. She looked up at her father and put a finger to her lips, asking him to be quiet. Then, without warning, Troy screamed out and jumped up, making Jackie fall to the floor on her butt, then Troy ran out into the yard screaming as loud as he could as he looked up at the sky. "Who am I?!! Who the hell am I?!! Someone help me!!" He dropped to the ground, hiding his face in his hands. Jackie ran to him and dropped down beside him, pulling his hands away from his face. "Who am I, Jackie. Where do I belong and who is this Annie Roberson? I can't get her out of my mind. What is happening to me?"

Jackie had her arm around his shoulders. "I wish I knew, Baby. I really do. I hate seeing you in pain all the time."

"Why has God done this to me? What have I done to deserve this torment? Did I kill someone in my past and now I'm paying for it? I just want to be a normal person. A person worthy of marrying you."

That hit Jackie like a lightning bolt. "What did you just say?"

"I would marry you if I could; but not like this. I have to know if I have someone in another life. I'm not the kind of guy to do this to her. I can't keep going on like this." Jackie hugged him, allowing him to cry on her shoulder.

Chung-Hee came into the room to find Annie sitting on the edge of the bed sobbing into her hands. She went and sat down next to Annie. "Annie, what's wrong?"

"I feel like I need to be with Troy."

"Annie . . . he belongs to someone else."

"I know that. Just hold me."

# CHAPTER FORTY-ONE

*"I just talked with him, Sheriff, and sometimes talking is better than action."*

DYLAN STOOD IN front of Blake Carter's desk. Carter couldn't help but notice that the man had finally gotten the message and had gotten a shirt and was wearing it. "That's all to report, Sir. We've been watching the Browns and, as you said, it looks like the Witt guy is romantically involved with the daughter." Carter got up and walked around the desk and leaned on it.

"So, Jackie Brown has a lover. Then who is the other woman?"

"I don't know anything about her. You would need a court order to get a look at the school records."

"I should have thought of that. So the key is Jackie Brown. We get her and this Witt guy will do anything we say. Bring me Jackie Brown."

"And if she refuses?"

"Do I have to think of everything?"

"Yes, Sir. I understand."

Jackie came into the house, not expecting to see Dylan and his group of goons holding her father at gunpoint. "What's going on?" She demanded, scared at what was developing.

"Carter wants to see you." Dylan told her.

"Tell him to go to Hell. Now let go of my father and get out of here."

"Can't do that." Dylan said as both Jackie and her father were knocked out at the same time.

Jackie soon regained consciousness and realized she was in Carter's office. She was in a chair with her hands cuffed behind the chair. "What the hell . . . ?"

Carter took hold of her chin to make her look at him. "I hadn't realized this before, but you are a beautiful woman."

"This is kidnapping!. When Troy hears about this . . . ."

Carter cut her off. "Oh, I hope he does. Because you are the bait that will bring him to me. Have you two slept together yet?"

"That is NONE of your business." Carter walked around her, looking her over. He then put both of his hands on her shoulders, making her jump.

"I wouldn't mind trying out that tight little package of yours."

"You disgust me." Jackie said to him as he moved around in front of her.

"It's a shame. You probably wouldn't know what to do with it."

"I'd cut it off and feed it to the dogs. It's the only thing it's good for . . . . on second thought . . . maybe not give it to the dogs . . . might give them heartburn." Carter slapped her, hard. Then bent down to face her.

"When I get your home, I am going to enjoy making you mine. You have a lot of spirit and I like that in a woman."

Troy was surprised to see the front door of the house open. It was not like to Browns to do that . . . the door stayed closed, even on the hottest days. He jumped through the door, and went into his fighting stance only to see Ray lying on the floor, just coming around. Troy went to him and helped him onto the couch. "JACKIE!" Troy yelled out, hoping to hear a response. When he didn't he panicked and started to go up the steps but Ray called him back. "Where's Jackie, Mr. Brown?"

"He has her."

"Who?"

"Carter. His men were here, they took her to him." Troy headed for the door. "No, Troy! That is what they want. We need to call the sheriff."

Troy looked at Ray. "It may be too late already. No, I'm not putting Jackie's life in the hands of the police. If you want to call them, that's fine. I'm going."

One of Carter's men came flying through the door to his office and crash landed on the floor. Troy followed and Dylan came at him, but all Troy had to do was give me an evil look and he backed away. Carter marched up to Troy and extended his hand which Troy ignored. "Let Jackie go," Troy ordered.

"Of course," Carter said as he released Jackie who jumped up and ran into Troy's arms.

"Leave the Browns alone," Troy ordered again and Carter seemed to think about it.

"I'll make a deal with you, Witt. You come to work for me and I will leave them alone."

"Don't do it, Troy, he's a monster," Jackie said making Troy glance at her for a second, then look back at Carter.

"I'll make sure you have a good position in my organization, along with a good paycheck."

"Don't do it . . ." Jackie was scared that Troy might actually accept. He let go of Jackie and took a few steps toward Carter who did not back away, but stood up to him.

"Destiny has chosen a path for me. What that path is, I am not sure yet. It may, or may not, be with the Browns. But there is one thing I am sure about, and that is that my path is in no way connected to you." He turned and went back to Jackie.

"You're making a mistake, Witt."

Troy looked over his shoulder at Carter. "Touch the Browns again and you will find your head hanging over that fireplace." Again Dylan tried to block Troy's path, but all Troy had to do was growl and Dylan backed away, letting Troy and Jackie leave.

"What the hell is the matter with you, Dylan?" Carter shouted at him.

"I know what he can do, Sir."

"You chicken shit." Carter said as he went to sit down at his desk.

"Yes, Sir. I know."

Jackie ran to her father, hugging him, happy to know that he was all right. The sheriff walked up to Troy. "You always seem to surprise, Mr. Witt. How did you do it?" He asked looking back at Jackie and the way she was checking her father over to make sure he was OK.

"I just talked with him, Sheriff. Sometimes talking is better than action."

"And you didn't lay a hand on him."

"I did not . . . let's just leave it at that."

Jackie call Troy over to them and he excused himself to the sheriff and went to the Browns.

Later than night the two faced each other in Troy's room. "I do love you," Jackie said as she touched his cheek."

"You must know by now how I feel about you," Troy said to her, looking right into her eyes.

"I do." She said, getting lost in his look.

"Will you lighten up on Annie? You know my loyalties are with you."

"I know I have been shameful toward the two of you . . . I am sorry." Troy scooped her up In his arms never looking away from her eyes as he carried her to the bed, gently laid her down and got on top of her. She smiled, nodded, and he began to unbutton her blouse.

# CHAPTER FORTY-TWO

*"I know you, but right now I can't be the person you want me to be."*

ANNIE WAS ALONE in her room, sitting at her laptop, typing into her journal. *"I see Chung-Hee less and less these days. It seems that she and Mark are spending more and more time together. I have to say, those two are really in love and sometimes I wonder if I have a roommate or not. Every other day Chung-Hee and I still practice our martial arts training. That seems to be the only constant thing in my life that is holding me together right now. The holidays are coming up fast this year. It has been a cold winter, with snow constantly on the ground, it seems. This will be the third round of holidays without you. Sometimes I lie awake at night, looking up at the ceiling just wondering what you and I would be doing right now if you were at my side. God, I miss you so much. I continue to ignore Troy and I do know that it is driving him nuts."*

Annie was in class way before anyone else and was cleaning her workstation, thinking about everything that had been going on in her life and wondering if she was happy with the path it was taking. She was so lost in thought that she had not even notice that Troy was standing there watching her until she ran into him. They moved to the right, then to the left, as if they were dancing. Troy took her by the shoulders and made her look at him.

"Why wouldn't you look at me?" This craziness had gone on long enough for him.

Finally Annie spoke. "Because you look so much like him."

"Who, Tony?"

"Yes. You are a carbon copy."

"Am I him, Annie? Am I Tony Cross?"

Was he remembering? She wondered if he knew who he was to her and what they had? She had so much to ask him.

"Troy, please, just leave me alone . . . it hurts to be with you." She turned away from him.

"Tell me, Annie. Tell me about Tony Cross."

"I can't it hurts too much. Don't you understand? I need him." People started to come into the room for the class and she pushed him away from her. Tears were beginning to fall and she was trying to dry her eyes when Chung-Hee walked over to them.

"Annie, are you all right?" She asked her.

"No, I am not. I can't be here today . . . I'm sorry." She started for the door, just as the teacher came into the room.

"Ms. Roberson, are you all right?" The teacher asked.

"I'm sorry, I thought I had forgotten something in my locker."

"Does it have to do with this class?"

"No, Ma'am."

"Then return to your station."

"Yes, Ma'am." Annie went back to her station and Chung-Hee got her attention. She didn't say anything, just shook her head no and turned her attention to the front of the class.

"OK, Class," the teacher said, getting everyone's attention, "we are going to do something different today." She went to the door and opened it to allow someone to push in a big cart of shopping bags. She thanked the person who then left. "In the shopping bags are the same ingredients. Each person will take a shopping bag and you may fix whatever you wish using those ingredients. You have two hours to prepare your dish, or dishes. You will come up by station. Station 1 will be first, and so on. Once you have returned to your station, you may begin.

Annie still wasn't thinking straight and went up at the same time as Troy and reached for the same bag. When she discovered that she was holding his hand, she pulled it back and put it into the pocket of her jeans. Being a gentleman, Troy allowed her to get her bag first. She stood there for a minute, not believing how much he was acting like Tony. The teacher was watching and walked over to them. "You two have a class assignment to complete . . . I suggest you get started." Annie snatched one of the bags and went back to her station.

After two hours the class had been working hard and the teacher finally called time. They stopped immediately and the teacher began to check their work. She took her time with each student and then she came to Annie, Troy and Chung-Hee. She turned to the class. "Attention, Class. We have a tie today between Ms. Roberson and Mr. Witt. We cannot allow this to happen, so there will be a cook-off this Sunday. Now, you are dismissed as soon as you clean up your stations." She turned to Annie and Troy. "I want to see the two of you after class."

"Is there something going on between the two of you," the teacher asked them after everyone else had left. Annie could not believe that she would ask that.

"As in romantically?" Annie inquired. "Me and him? You've got to be kidding. I would never be involved with someone like him." Annie pivoted and marched out of the room as the teacher looked at Troy.

"Does she love you?"

"I don't know." Troy said, then left. He caught up with Annie outside the building, making her stop and turn as he took her arm. "What was that all about?"

"I don't know what you're talking about. Just leave me alone." She started to go down the steps, but he blocked her way.

"We're going to talk about this, and we're going to talk about it now."

"We have nothing to say to each other."

Without warning Troy picked her up and flung her over his shoulder like a stack of potatoes and carried her back to her dorm. Annie was hitting his back, calling him all kinds of names, making people stop and look at them. When they reached the door to Annie's room it was locked. "Either put me down or turn me around so I can use my key." Annie told him. He was not about to let her go, so he turned around and knelt down so she could reach the lock. They went inside and Troy sat her down and slammed the door with his foot. He pushed her back onto the bed and hopped on top of her and started to tickle her. Annie was trying to get him to stop but was dying of laughter in the process. Unintentionally, his hand went up inside her shirt and gently touched her breast. Like an atomic bomb went off in his head and he fell back, crying out, "NO!!" The pain was so intense it was making him sick. Annie threw her arm around him, to hold him and laid her head on his shoulder.

"Shhhh. It's all right, I'm right here, Tony." She had not realized what she had called him and when it was over she stayed in his arms on the bed.

"I'm sorry. I didn't mean to do that."

"The headache?"

"No, my hand going under your shirt . . ." Annie remembered how good his hands felt on her body.

"It's OK . . . I don't mind." For a second neither of them spoke, then Troy wanted to talk.

"I just want to know who I am, where I belong." He began to cry. "Do you know what it's like to look in the mirror and see a face you don't recognize."

"I'm so sorry." Annie said, know he was hurting.

"Who am I, Annie?" He now looked directly at her. She wanted so much to tell him what there were to each other but was afraid of hurting him more. They sat on the bed facing each other.

"Ray found me floating in the river. I was near death and he took me back to his place. When I came to my mind was blank. I didn't know who I was or where I came from or how I got there. They took me in and became my family. I love Jackie with all my heart, she means the world to me. But, there's something nagging at me that keeps pulling me away from her. I keep feeling that there's someone else. Who, I don't know. And then there's you. Why do I seem to know you? And the tattoos . . . . Annie, did we love each other?" Annie's hand covered her mouth

"Troy, I . . ."

He shook his head. "No . . . don't tell me. I have a feeling that in a different time and place . . . . perhaps one day we may be together again. Only God knows. Please remember that in this time and place, I belong to Jackie." He got up and went to the door.

"I love you . . ." Annie said, making him stop just at the door and look over his shoulder at her.

"I know you do, but right now I can't be the person you want me to be." He left the room and she lay back onto the bed.

# CHAPTER FORTY-THREE

*"You know, you've got a great laugh."*

ANNIE WAS IN her room by herself. She had no idea where Chung-Hee was and had pretty much given up on her. She sat up in the bed with her back to the wall, thinking. "I cannot believe the conversation that Troy and I had. I can understand how he feels about Jackie and her family, but how am I supposed to be just a friend, and not a lover. How am I supposed to do that?"

It was Sunday and Annie and Troy found it strange that they were the only ones in the class. The teacher had come in and sat down with them. "This whole cook-off thing has gotten out of control." The teacher said as Annie glanced at Troy for a second.

"What do you mean?" Annie asked.

"I don't know if you're going to like this or not, but the cook-off is going to be held next weekend in the school auditorium. There will be four judges that will decide on the cooking and a one-thousand dollar reward will go to the winner. Also, the Food Network channel will be filming it."

"This is crazy," Annie said. "I'm not sure if I want to do this."

"You may not have a choice. I have contacted your family, Ms. Roberson. But Mr. Witt, I can't find anything on your family."

"It's the Browns. I will tell them." The three stood up.

"I will be sending you a letter and I expect a full report on the dish that will be made. I will see you next week."

A few minutes later Annie and Troy were standing outside. "Well . . . a Sunday afternoon and nothing to do," Annie said, looking at him.

"I don't know about you, but I would love a hamburger." Troy said with a smile that made her heart skip.

"I suppose you know a good place that has good hamburgers?"

"I sure do . . . come on." Troy took her by the hand and they ran off, not knowing that Jackie was standing behind some nearby bushes. She lowered her head in sadness.

The two were sitting at a booth enjoying their burgers and fries. Annie looked around. "McDonald's is not what I would call a good place for hamburgers."

"Come on, they're great. And reasonable."

"Now I understand." Annie said, sipping at her soda.

"I don't get much of an allowance from the Browns." That made Annie laugh.

"You know, you've got a great laugh."

That made Annie blush, he was sounding like the old Tony. They took their time eating, not in a hurry to get back to whatever awaited them. They found they were really enjoying each other's company. Laughing at the jokes. Soon they stood just outside Annie's dorm.

"Thank you. I really needed this afternoon." Annie kissed him on the cheek and disappeared into the building.

Troy seemed happy. He was really at peace with the universe. His mind was quiet and he had a happy bounce to his walk, whistling some kind of song. He had no idea where it came from, but he liked it. However, his mood changed when he saw Jackie standing at the porch, her arms crossed in front of her, looking madder than hell itself. Troy slowly walked up to her, but was met by a slap. Ok . . . he deserved that one.

"Where the hell have you been?" Jackie demanded to know.

"I was hungry, so I had a hamburger with a friend." Troy actually felt he had done nothing wrong.

"A friend? What kind of friend?"

"All right, if you must know, I had a burger with Annie Roberson."

Jackie threw up her arms in frustration. "Why are you even associating with her?"

"Jackie, she needed a friend." He said, trying to sound innocent.

"So you volunteered."

"It was just a friendly conversation over hamburgers. That's all." Jackie started to swing at him again, but Troy stropped the swing and tucked her arm behind her, pulling her close to him. "You only get one slap, Jackie."

She looked up at him. "I don't know you any more."

"Maybe you're finally seeing the real me."

"Well, I don't like it."

"Jackie, please, can we go back to the way we were?" He wanted so badly to do that.

"That's up to you, Troy." He planted a big kiss right on her lips, but she pushed him away. "Damn you." She busted out laughing when he scooped her up in his arms and carried her inside.

Ray was sitting on the couch watching TV when the two came in. He started to laugh at them. "Ray, I need to talk with you, but not right now." Troy said as he raced up the steps with Jackie still in his arms. He went into his room and laid her gently down on the bed. "I want you to tell me, when I'm finished, if I am Troy Witt, or not." She didn't say anything, but nodded her head and he started to kiss her.

The following day, Troy was in the Browns' restaurant kitchen, doing some work. Even though they were not busy, there was always something to do. Ray was there, helping when an overly excited Jackie came running into the kitchen with an envelope in her hand. She gave it to Troy. "What's it say?" She asked him as he opened it.

"Roasted New York Strip Steak with Port Wine Mustard Sauce." Troy read aloud as Jackie looked at him oddly.

"Can you do that?" She asked with some excitement in her eye.

"I don't know." Troy looked at Ray, who was wiping his hands with a towel. "I need to take some time off to work on this. Is that all right?" Troy asked.

"Sure . . ." Ray said as Jackie gave Troy a kiss and he left.

Troy was sitting in the library at one of the many computers. He was doing his homework on the dish. It was the dish he would have to make for the contest. After all, the teacher wanted a ten-page report about the dish, where it came from, how it was made and so he was surfing the internet to find out as much as he could. A bad storm had come up by the time he had reached the library and there were thunder, lightning, and a heavy downpour of rain. The power kept flickering and was threatening to go out. Troy was just hoping he would get his research done before than happened.

As he was working hard at the computer a pair of hands covered his eyes. "It's not Jackie." Troy said, trying to guess who the hands belonged to. "It's not Patty McCall." He recognized the giggling. "It's Annie Roberson." He said as he stood up and turned to face her just as there was a huge clap of thunder that seemed to shake the whole building, along with a blinding flash of lighting. The power went out. Annie panicked and jumped into Troy's arms. He had flashes as he brought his hand to his head, but for some reason, the pain was not as bad this time.

*"She's a beauty, Tony," Jim said.*

*"That she is, Jim and I'm the luckiest guy in the world to have her." Tony said after taking a sip from the whiskey bottle and handed it back to Jim so he could take his turn.*

*"Have you two had sex yet?"* Have you had sex seemed to echo through his mind. Then a voice called out of the darkness.

'THE LIBRARY IS CLOSED. EVERYONE MUST LEAVE NOW!"

"Oh, great. Now what?" Troy said as he started gathering his stuff.

"I have a laptop in my room and it's fully charged." Annie told him.

"And you don't care what the other girls may think?"

"Hell, no." Troy grabbed his soda cup and took it with him. Once outside he dumped the soda and filled the cup with the water that was running off the roof of the building. Annie was using her backpack to cover her head. She was hoping to keep her hair dry, but with this downpour that didn't seem to be in the cards.

"Annie    ?" The voice from behind her made her turn only to get a cup full of water in her face.

"I'M GOING TO KILL YOU!!" And by the way she said, she meant it. The two chased each other around the courtyard not seeming to care about the rain. Annie dropped to the ground and did a reverse leg sweep and knocked Troy on his butt into a puddle, then jumped to her feet. Troy was laughing as she took a few steps to him, extending her hand to help him up. He took hold of her hand and pulled her down to him. She let out a yelp as she went down. They wrestled back and forth until Annie found herself looking up at him as he hovered over her. He pulled her soaked hair away from her face.

"Why do I find you so fascinating?" He asked her as he moved in for a kiss but she held him away from her. "You have the prettiest eyes I have ever seen."

"Don't say that!" Annie said as she pushed him off her and jumped to her feet and started for the building but Troy ran after her, grabbed her arm and swung her back into his arms. "Please . . . don't."

"It's what we both want, isn't it?"

"If I kiss you, we will have to go to the next step. I am not the type of girl that gets herself involved with a man who is seeing someone else."

"Annie, please . . . let me say this . . . I'm remembering things . . . people, places, events, but they are all still a blur to me."

"Why tell me?"

"Because you're the key."

"You make me feel like some kind of relic. Can we go inside?" They gathered their things and went into the dorm.

# CHAPTER FORTY-FOUR

*"We are doing research."*

ANNIE WAS ALREADY taking her shower by the power came back on. There was only a light shower outside now. Troy was sitting at Annie's desk when he noticed a ring that was sitting in a knickknack box. He picked it up and examined it. He suddenly had flashes of his graduation. He closed his eyes prepared for the pain would have brought him to his knees. He was shaking it off when Annie came from the shower. She was wrapped in a towel and using another for her hair. She saw that Troy had her ring and rushed over and snatched it away from him.

"There's only one man that can touch that ring," she said and put it back where it belonged.

"Did he give that to you?"

"Yes, a long time ago. It's all I have to remember him. If I lose this, I lose him."

"You love him that much?"

"He is my life."

"I'd better go take my shower," he said.

"Good idea." Annie watched Troy go to the bathroom and soon heard the shower start.

Later that evening as Troy's clothing was drying in the bathroom under the heat lamp. Annie was sitting on the edge of the bed with the laptop on her lap as Troy was sitting on the bed beside her, and they had papers spread about them. "That looks good, can you save that and transfer it to a flash drive," Troy asked her and watched as she plugged in a flash drive. They were only dressed in their towels and were surprised when Chung-Hee came into the room. She was just as surprised as they were.

"I didn't know you had company," she said to Annie. "Is this a new way to study?" She asked, talking about how they were dressed (or not, depending on the way you looked at it).

Troy looked at himself and Annie, then Chung-Hee. "We are doing research." He finally told her. "For the competition." He continued, trying to clarify things for her.

"I bet." Chung-Hee said, shaking her head.

"I'll go get dressed, my clothes should be pretty dry by now." As he got up, the towel fell to the floor revealing himself to both women, who wolf-whistled at the same time. He just marched to the bathroom with dignity, ignoring them. Chung-Hee went over to sit by Annie.

"Nice butt," she said to Annie.

"The front is not too bad either," and both girls chuckled.

# CHAPTER FORTY-FIVE

*"You are going to my sister?"*

THE TEACHER WAS happy with both reports that Annie and Troy submitted. They both showed that a lot of time and research had been done. The auditorium was filling up fast and there was media all over the place. Everyone who was anyone in Timber City was there. Annie narrating: *"The teacher was right about one thing, this cook-off had gotten out of control. I can't believe the amount of people that were here to watch us cook. It was good to see Mom and Dad. Tyler couldn't be here, but told me he would be watching on TV. Mark, of course, was hanging around with Chung-Hee. I just had a funny feeling he was going to pop the question. I hope he knows what he is getting into . . . marrying someone from another country. Hell, I hope Chung-Hee knows what she is getting marrying Mark. Ethan and Ashley are here. I can't believe how happy those two are."*

Mark and Chung-Hee were outside and had found a quiet spot where they could be alone. He took hold of her shoulders. "Chung-Hee, you are the most gorgeous person I have ever known. I haven't stopped thinking about you since we met. I can't imagine life without you. I don't even want to think about that." He dropped to one knee. "Dangsin-eun nalang gyeolhon hae jullaie?" (Will you marry me in Korean.) Chung-Hee brought both hands to her mouth then gasped as she saw the engagement ring that Mark was holding. It was the most beautiful thing she had ever seen.

"Oh, my God . . . . are you kidding?" She said, starting to cry tears of joy.

"I still don't have an answer, darling?" He said.

"NEH, NEH, NEH!" (Yes) Mark slipped the ring on her finger and stood up. She threw her arms around him and they kissed and what a kiss it was. "Saranghaeyo," Chung-Hee continued. (I love you.)

Troy was looking into the mirror, adjusting his chef's hat, wishing he was somewhere else when a pretty young thing stuck her head into the room. "It's time, Mr. Witt." He took a deep breath, let it out and left the room and ran into Annie.

"We still have time to make a mad dash for the door," Annie said, looking him.

"I have a feeling that all of Timber City would be after us."

"Not if we disappeared to a tropical island."

Troy thought about that. "I can definitely see you in a bikini." She giggled and punched him on the arm.

As Mrs. Kimberly Wooten came to the podium the place was packed . . . not a seat was vacant. "I am Kimberly Wooten and welcome to the Timber City University cook off between Ms. Annie Roberson and Mr. Troy Witt. In my many years of teaching culinary classes, this was perhaps only the second time that we had experienced a tie. The judges for today's event will be Chief Wilson of the Timber City Police Department and his wife along with Chief Roberts of the fire department and his wife." The place erupted in cheers and applause. "Today's recipe is New York Strip Steak with Port Wine Mustard Sauce. And, if there is another tie, I have a secret recipe that only I know. The workstations behind these partitions are just like the workstations in our classrooms. There is a partition between them and, as always, the equipment and the ingredients have been prepared for our chefs. The Food Network Channel has set up cameras so they can film the event and it will be shown later on their channel. And now, let's meet our chefs . . . . Annie Roberson and Troy Witt." The auditorium went nuts when the two came onstage. Nancy's mouth hit the floor, as did the other members of the family when they saw Troy. How could this man look so much like Tony Cross . . . they could be twins? Ashley looked at Ethan and by his reaction, he was seeing it too. The teacher continued, "They will have one hour to prepare the dish. Chefs, will you take your stations?"

The two moved behind the partitions and the place went crazy again as people called out encouragement to their favorite chef. "I love you," Annie said loud enough for Troy to hear, but nobody else. There was no response from Troy, but then again, she wasn't expecting one.

The teacher then said, "All right everyone help me out as we countdown from five and when we hit zero, they will begin cooking." The whole audience counted down and when they hit 'zero', Troy and Annie went to work. The first thing they did was to season the New York Strip Steak with salt and pepper, then began to heat a layer of olive oil that they placed in a heavy metal roasting pan.

They seemed to be proceeding at the same time and when the oil began to give off wisps of smoke, they carefully put the meat into the pan, presentation side down and turned the heat down to a medium-high. They then scattered the trimming scraps around the sides of the steaks. They seared the meat until it was evenly brown. They turned the meat and put the roasting pan in the oven and cooked until done (medium-rare) for about 45 minutes.

Both Annie and Troy could not believe how long that one hour could be. Both of them were working hard and neither cared which one would win. Mark got up and went over to kneel in front of his mother. "Did you see how much this Witt guy looks like Tony?"

"Yes, we did, Sweetie."

"What are we going to do?" He looked at both his parents.

"There's nothing we can do, Mark," Ryan said, leaning down to him. "We can't walk up to a stranger and say, 'hey, you look like Tony Cross'. There are billions of people on this planet, Mark. There are bound to be similarities . . ."

"But a carbon copy?" Mark knew it was Tony and couldn't believe that his parents couldn't see it.

"Mark, honey," Nancy said to him, "try not to think about it and go to your girl. I think she's missing you."

"Oh, yeah. Speaking of my girl . . . we're engaged." He moved off as Nancy and Ryan looked at each other and it hit them what he had just said.

"WHAT?" They both shouted out as Chung-Hee held up her ring finger. Nancy covered her mouth in excitement as everyone started the countdown once again to stop the cook-off.

The wait was agonizing as the judges tasted the dishes. The whole place was quiet . . . you could almost hear a pin drop. Annie was standing next to Troy, very nervous. She found her left hand taking hold of his hand. They glanced at each other for a second and smiled, not letting go during this phase. They couldn't see the glare that Jackie was giving them as they held hands.

The teacher finally concluded talking with the judges and went to the podium. "May I have your attention, please?" Annie's grip on Troy's hand got tighter. "What I feared, has happened. We have another tie." There was a loud, collective gasp from the audience. "The tie-breaker recipe is . . . . New York Cheesecake." Annie and Troy just looked at each other, wondering how they were going to get out of this situation. But, they knew that there was no way out . . . if they tried, they would be burned at the stake. The teacher continued, "OK, the stations have been prepared for the second part of the cook off, so Chefs, go to your stations."

Everyone but Jackie laughed when Annie kissed Troy on the cheek and they went to their stations. There was another countdown and Annie and Troy went to work greasing a 9-in spring form pan. They then proceeded to the next step and mixed graham cracker crumbs with melted butter in a medium-sized bowl.

They then pressed the mixture into the spring form pan. Soon, the second part of the cooking was over and everyone waited through the second phase of the judging. The teacher returned to the podium. "Both chefs should be proud of the work they did today. Both have performed beyond our expectations. So, this time we do have a winner, by ONE point. The winner of the Timber City Culinary School is . . . . Annie Roberson!"

The whole place went ballistic. Troy wrapped his arms around Annie, picked her up and spun her around like a top and sat her back down. By that time, Annie was being mugged by everyone in the place. A few seconds later she looked over her shoulder to see Troy, with his arms around Jackie, who was giving him a kiss. She couldn't help but sadly look away.

Nancy was finally able to pull Troy from the madness to talk to him in the lobby of the auditorium. "Mr. Witt, I am Nancy Roberson, Annie's mother. I must apologize for taking you away from the celebration, but I need to talk with you."

"It's OK, Mrs. Roberson, what can I do for you?"

"It's about my daughter . . . . I can't believe I'm standing in front of you after all these years."

"Is this about Tony Cross, Ma'am?"

"Yes, then you know?"

Troy nodded at her. "I know part of it, but not the whole story." Nancy reached into her oversized bag and pulled out a small photo album and handed it to him. Troy took it. Nancy had been working on putting it together for a long time and was going to give it to Annie.

"There are pictures of Annie and Tony together, from the day they met, until the day she lost him. Look at it when you're ready. It might help explain to you, how much she loved Tony."

"I don't know what to say." He was holding the book, almost afraid to open it.

"Mr. Witt, if you are our Annie's Tony, please . . . she needs you to live . . . I'm worried about her."

"Mrs. Roberson, I am sorry for your daughter. I have gotten to know her as a wonderful person and I can understand how she and other people think I look like this Tony Cross, but honestly, I can't remember."

Annie came running up to them and put her arm around his. "Hi, Mom. Troy, they want to interview us and take some pictures." After Annie gave her mother a hug, she dragged Troy away. Ryan found his wife and slipped an arm around her. When Chung-Hee and Mark came up to them Nancy put her arms around Chung-Hee to hug her.

"Welcome to the family, Honey. I had a feeling about you two."

Afterwards Chung-Hee gave Ryan a hug. "Thank you. You have all been wonderful about this."

Mark looked at his father. "Now, I have to go to Korea." Ryan looked at his son, bewildered. "I have to ask Chung-Hee's parents for her hand in marriage."

"You know, Son. Many moons ago you came into my office all worried about Annie. Seems I remember that you said something about never falling in love . . ."

"But that was when I was a kid." Mark said as he put an arm around Chung-Hee.

"I'm very proud of you, Son. You two look very happy together. Now, I've just got one more son to marry off, and an impossible daughter."

"You might as well forget about Annie. She'll never love anyone other than Tony."

"I know . . . that's what I'm afraid of."

Later that evening, Annie was working on her laptop. *"I am so glad this whole cook off thing is over. It was a real headache and I would have run off with you to some tropical island. I hope you are not too unhappy with the outcome, but from what I heard it was a very difficult decision that the judges faced. I am very proud of you. I have a feeling that Mark is going to propose to Chung-Hee. He has really fallen head over heels for that girl. I love you, Tony . . . always."*

Annie closed her laptop as Chung-Hee came into the room. She told Annie to come sit next to her. She had something to say to her. As they sat on the foot of the bed, Chung-Hee ran her fingers thought her long hair, trying to figure out how to break the good news to her best friend. "Mark and I are engaged."

It took a moment for the news to sink in, but when it did, Annie's face lit up like a solar flare. "It's about time! You are going to be my sister!" Annie said excited. Chung-hee nodded and showed Annie the ring and they hugged each other.

# CHAPTER FORTY-SIX

*"Don't, if you love Jackie, don't look at this."*

R AY'S OLD FORD pickup came to a stop in front of the house and Jackie was the first to get out and run into the house. The two men got out and looked at each other. "She's really mad, Ray," Tony said, stating the obvious.

"The last time she was like this it took her days to calm down."

"Should I get a hotel room?"

"No. This is your home, too. Did you notice how the Roberson family was looking at you?"

"Yes, I did. I had a chit chat with Mrs. Roberson."

"What did she say?"

"She said that I looked like Tony Cross and that Annie and Tony were to be married in a few years. She also gave me this photo album of Annie and Tony's life together. I'm a little afraid to look at it." Troy handed the photo album to Ray, who's eyebrow went up.

"Would you mind if I looked at it?"

"Not at all." Troy went into the house and up to Jackie's room. The door was locked so he started pounding on the door. "Open the door, Jackie!"

"GO AWAY!" The angry voice from within shouted. Troy, knowing that she would never open the door, took the matter into his own hands (or to feet, so to speak) and did a snap-kick bursting the door open and rushed into the room only to be met by a flying lamp heading right for his head. He ducked to avoid the lamp that exploded when it landed on the hallway floor. A vase came at him next and then Jackie went to him and started beating him on his shoulders. She finally tired herself out.

"Are you done?" Troy asked her.

"No, I just ran out of things to throw at you."

Troy led her to the bed and they sat down on the edge of it. "Now, what's wrong?" He asked, although he already knew what the answer would be.

"Annie Roberson . . . that's what's wrong."

"Now, Jackie. There is the possibility that we were once deeply involved." Jackie just snapped her hand at him.

"As in love?"

"Yes. Apparently we were to be married."

Jackie jumped up. "As in man and wife?"

"Yes."

"Then what am I supposed to do, Troy . . . look the other way?' Jackie was not happy with this situation at all.

"Jackie, please listen to me . . ."

"I'm tired of it all, Troy. You say you love me, but you're thinking about another woman. How do I know that when we make love, you're not thinking about her."

"Jackie . . ."

Get out, Troy. Just get out and leave me alone."

Troy stood and moved to the door. "If that's what you want." He left the room as Jackie threw herself onto the bed and cried.

Troy walked into the kitchen to find Ray sitting at the table drinking some coffee. He quickly closed the book so Troy would not see what was in it. Troy made himself a cup of coffee and sat across from Ray, eyeing the book as he took a sip of the coffee. "Anything interesting?" He asked Ray and started to reach for the book.

"Don't," Ray cautioned. "If you love Jackie, don't look at this."

Troy didn't say anything, he just had an odd looked about him. He couldn't understand what Ray was saying. Troy tried to lighten the situation. "What? Are they nude pictures or something?"

"Please, don't look at this," Ray said, standing up.

Troy looked at him. "Then take it away from me." Ray picked up the book and started to leave the room, but Troy stopped him.

"Ray, were Annie and I . . . . ?

Ray looked over his shoulder at him. "Close." Was all Ray said and left the kitchen. Troy ran both hands through his hair and rested his elbows on the table with his chin on his hands. A tear fell from an eye.

Annie narrating: *"This year's Christmas was no different than the past ones. I was down and depressed, missing you horribly. It seems that as the years pass I cannot stop thinking of you . . . loving you. Come back to me soon. I don't know how much longer*

*I can keep this façade up. Everyone thinks I'm happy, but in the long run, I am not. I still have dreams of you jumping off that bridge. There are times I wish Chung-Hee had let me jump off that damn bridge, oh well. To happier thoughts, we just had one of the happiest days in the Roberson family. It was the wedding of my younger brother and his girl. When I first met Ashley, I never dreamed she would be part of this family, but she and Ethan are so much in love. I can see it in their eyes. A lot of Pine Lake turned out for the wedding and a lot of Ethan's fellow officers from the police force were there. He looked so dashing in his dress uniform, I almost cried thinking that this handsome man was my brother."*

It was a cold winter day, the church at the south end of town was all decked out in wedding decorations. It was beautiful. The church was as old as the town, with wooden siding, slate roof and the inside had wood floors, walls and ceiling. The benches were wood and not a vacant spot could be had for the wedding.

Annie stepped into the small room where her mother and Ashley were. Ashley was sitting at the makeup table and she looked stunning. There was a veil hiding her long hair. She was wearing a white satin dress and with the makeup, Annie could see why her younger brother could fall in love with this woman. The Roberson boys sure could pick them. Annie could see how nervous Ashley was as she approached her. Who wouldn't be on a day like this. A day that would change her life forever.

"It's time," Annie said to her, making Ashley look up at her.

"And Ethan?" Her voice showing her nerves.

"He is so handsome in his uniform. I can hardly believe he's my brother."

Ashley stood up to face her. "Annie, I am so happy," she said, her voice breaking.

"Stop crying," Annie admonished her, "you'll mess up your makeup. You and Ethan better make lots of babies." Now Ashley chuckled.

"I wish this could have been a double wedding. You and Tony . . . ." Annie flashed her a smile.

"I know . . . come on, before Ethan thinks you're backing out on him."

"NEVER!!!" Ashley said as they left the room. Since the wedding was in the late afternoon, the sun was hovering over the horizon, casting a beautiful sunset sky. The wedding was over and the reception was at a local hotel where everyone was eating, drinking and dancing.

Then it was time for Mr. and Mrs. Ethan Roberson to leave. A police helicopter was sitting on the roof of the hotel, waiting for its passengers. On the side of the chopper was a sign, "JUST MARRIED". Everyone went to the roof and Ethan had hold of Ashley's hand as they turned and waved to the crowd. Ashley grinned and threw her bouquet at Annie. The bouquet didn't have time to take root in her hands as Annie handed it off to Chung-Hee. Ashley just shook her head and she and Ethan then boarded the helicopter. After they took off, everyone started to leave the roof as Annie walked to the railing and looked out at the night. Her father came up behind her.

"Annie?"

"Dad, will I ever be that happy?"

Ryan made her turn to face him. "I don't know, but what I do know is that I am very proud of you, and I love you so very much."

"It hurts, Father, every day it hurts." She started to cry.

"I know, Sweetheart, I know." He pulled her to him and wrapped her in his arms.

"I love you, Father. I don't know what I would have done if you were not in my life." He kissed the top of her head and they swayed, as if dancing to music.

# CHAPTER FORTY-SEVEN

*"Your brother is absolutely insane."*

A NNIE NARRATING: *"THE holidays passed by very fast and spring was upon us like a wink of an eye. This was my favorite time of the year. The sun was warming the earth and things were coming alive. There was love in the air; however, not for me. Today the class had a field trip to the farmers' market. The teacher had given instructions that we were to find our ingredients at the market. Whatever we wanted and we were to make a report on why we picked those ingredients and why we wanted to cook that particular dish. It was kind of exciting to do something different."*

Chung-Hee was one of the first ones to board the bus that would take them to the farmers' market. She was sitting at a window looking out, just thinking of the man she loved, wishing he was with her. "Is this seat taken?" Her face lit up with a smile as Mark sat down beside her.

"What are you doing here?" She asked him.

"Well . . . if you don't want me here . . ." he started to get up, but she quickly grabbed his arm and pulled him back down next to her and planted a huge kiss on his lips. Each time that happened, reminded Mark just how much he loved that woman. "I got the day off from work and I wanted to spend the day with you." He reached into his cargo pants pocket and pulled out a long, black, shiny box.

"Mark?" Chung-Hee could not believe her man.

"You are worth it." He said to her. "Now open it."

She gasped when she saw what Mark had gotten her . . . a gold chain and cross. "Mark, it's beautiful."

"I am not a wealthy man, but I will try to give you the things that make you happy."

"I don't need this stuff," Chung-Hee said. "All I want is your heart."

"I love you, you know."

"I know you do. I can see it in your eyes, the way you look at me," Chung-Hee replied and they kissed again. Once everyone was on the two busses, they took off. The farmers' market was large. It was situated on the top level of a three-tier parking garage. There were many stalls and shops. The shops stayed open all year, but the farmer's market area was only open at certain times of the year.

Annie was ready to shop until she dropped. She had her list and a small shopping cart that she pulled behind her. She was wearing sneakers, shorts, a white over-sized T-shirt that had a picture of a sailing boat on it and she had her hair up in a half ponytail. She was also wearing dark sunglasses. She was at one of the stalls, going through the produce when she heard Troy's voice behind her. "I would not buy that if I were you," she heard. She looked up as he came up behind her.

"And why not?" She wondered.

"It's not fresh for one thing. Not everything here is in season."

"You seem to know a lot about produce. Did you work in a grocery store?" She asked him.

"No, just studied a lot online . . . you can learn a lot there." Annie started to put her backpack on. "Here, let me help you." Troy said as he took hold of the backpack, but one of the clasps came undone and before he could adjust it, the backpack fell and most of the contents came out. Being flustered at talking with Troy, Annie had not realized she had not zipped it up. She knelt down to gather her things, and Troy spotted a drawing on a piece of paper and was able to grab it before she did. "What is this?" He said, pointing to the drawing. He desperately wanted to know, since it was a sketch of the tattoo on his ankle. When Annie stood up she snatched the paper form him and stuffed it back into her bag. This time she made sure it was zipped.

"That is personal, and none of your business." She started to walk away from him, but Troy was faster and grabber her arm, stopping her. He knelt down and pulled down her sock to reveal the tattoo. He suddenly had a flash of them getting the tattoos at the tattoo shop in Pine Lake, but this time, there was no pain . . . it seemed that those days were over.

Annie and Troy were sitting at a table outside a concession stand and Troy was having a hotdog and Coke while Annie just had sipped on a Coke. "I've been having these flashes," he explained. "The pain has finally subsided, but the flashes are still there. They don't seem to be coming at me at light speed any more. Now I can see the people and places that I should know but don't. I especially see you . . . . I have the same tattoo on my ankle except mine as an 'A' and yours has a 'T'. Annie, were we lovers at one time?"

Annie slowly took a drink as she tried to figure out what to say. "I was in love with Tony Cross, and we were planning to be married when I finished school. He committed suicide when he jumped off a bridge. I see a lot of him in you. That is this why I have been hanging around you, hoping that if he survived, that maybe you were my Tony and would remember me."

"I am remembering," he said as he ate his hotdog. "I am remembering places and people. They are so clear to me, but I just can't remember their names . . . or how I am related to them. I think I am from a place called Pine Lake and I think my mother's name is Angela. You're from Pine Lake, aren't you? Are my mother and father still there?"

A tear started to fall from Annie's eye. "Troy, they are . . ." before she was able to say anything else Chung-Hee and Mark came running up to them.

"You brother is absolutely insane." Chung-hee said as she sat down next to Annie. "We were looking at beds at the antique store and we don't even have a house yet."

"Isn't that where a family is started in the first place?" Mark said as Chung-Hee just looked at him.

"I have showed you some interesting ways of doing it . . . but there is still a lot that we can do without a bed." That surprised Annie.

"Are you saying that you two have already had sex?" She asked them.

"Oh, Annie . . . he is absolutely wonderful. And he seems to know just where to touch me . . . in places that I never knew existed."

Annie looked around and found that Troy was gone. She scanned the area but he was nowhere in sight, but there was a post-it note next to her on the table. She picked it up and read it to herself. "I do love you." She had a smile on her face and slipped the note away in her pocket as she noticed what Mark and Chung-Hee were doing.

"Will you two stop it!! That's disgusting. They were French kissing and stopped to look at Annie, trying to figure out why they should stop.

"You and Tony used to do this." Mark said to her.

Annie slammed her fist on the table. "You are not to mention his name!" Both Chung-Hee and Mark called out Annie's name . . . they couldn't believe what she had just said.

Annie took a drink of her soda and the two were back at it again. She looked up at the sky. "Hey look up there . . . there's a dog." Getting no response, she stood up. "Well, if this is the way you're going to act, I'm going to go shopping. After all, this is an official school field trip." She continued to explore the market on her own. There was a lot to see, then she was suddenly pulled into a stairwell, her back was pushed against the wall and she was kissed. At first she fought the kiss, but the power of it took control over her and she found her hands sliding up the person's back to grip his shoulders. As the kiss continued, the flashes came and he was fighting them back, but could not. He broke the kiss, holding his temples and dropped to the ground. Annie knelt down beside him.

"What's happening, Troy?"

"Who the hell are you? Just go!" Annie wanted to stay with him, but abided by his wishes and left.

# CHAPTER FORTY-EIGHT

*"And if he doesn't remember?"*

ANNIE NARRATING: *"AFTER meeting Troy at the marketplace I believe he was remembering, but for some reason, he has blocked me out. When I left him that day at the market I hadn't realized how bad he was. Was it because of the kiss? I don't know, but I did find out that he had ended up at Timber City Hospital."*

Troy was sharing a room with a teenager. He had activated the Nurse Call button, trying to get someone to come in and see him. Finally, a nurse came in. "Yes, Mr. Witt?"

"Is there a psychiatrist here at this hospital?"

"Yes, Dr. Diana Evans is on staff here." The nurse informed him.

"I would like to speak with her. Do you think she could come see me?"

"I believe so. Let me give her a call."

"Thank you." Within the hour, Diana came into the room and went over to Troy, extending her hand to him.

"I am Dr. Diana Evans," she said as they shook hands. "May I sit?" Troy nodded his head. "Now, Mr. Witt, what is troubling you?" She couldn't figure out what this man looked so familiar to her.

"I have amnesia," Troy said.

Surprised, Diana asked, "And what makes you think you have amnesia?"

"A doctor that examined me when I was pulled out of the river told me."

It hit her like a brick. "Are you Tony Cross from Pine Lake?"

"That is what people keep telling me, Doc, but I just don't know who I am."

Diana crossed her legs. "Let's do it this way, Mr. Witt. What do you remember?"

"Ray Brown fishing me out of the river, then he and his daughter, Jackie, taking care of me. I started helping out at their farm and then began working at their restaurant. I started taking cooking classes at the university; but there's this girl in the class, Annie Roberson, and when I first me her it was very painful. Even now there are times when I think about her, I get these headaches."

"You did say Annie Roberson?"

"Yes. Do you know her?"

"She came to me for help after she lost her fiancée."

"She did tell me that I look like someone that was very close to her. It's like my mind is trying to remember, but the flashes come at me so fast that I can't take hold of them. And the pain . . . it makes me go to the floor."

"Well, Mr. Witt, it seems to me that you are definitely trying to remember. However, the mind is very protective of the body. It will not allow you to remember that dark day in your life. Now, can you tell me when these flashes occur?"

"I cannot control them and I don't remember the order that the flashes come in, but I will try. The first time they happened was when Jackie Brown revealed herself to me and said, "Do they not please you?" That was one of the worst one I believe. Another one was when I met Annie and another was when Annie showed me a picture of us together. That was a bad one. Another time was at the Browns' restaurant. I was working in the kitchen and that one hit very bad, I still don't know what set it off. There was one just recently when Annie and I were playing around and I . . . ." He motioned her to come closer so he could tell her what he did.

Diana looked at him. "Really?" He nodded without saying anything. She sat back down.

"The most recent one that put me in here was when I kissed Annie."

"The key to all this is Annie Roberson."

"I know that Doctor, but what makes her so special?"

"It could be that Annie represents a time in your life when you were most happy." She stood up. "I have to go, I have another patient appointment, but I will come back and see you later."

"Thank you, Doctor." Diana smiled at him and left the room. Just outside the room, she dialed a number on her cell phone.

"Hello, Annie. How are you doing these days? That's great. Listen, I have a patient that you should meet he is here at Timber City Hospital. I can come get you if you like. OK . . . I will see you shortly." Diana hung up the phone and walked away.

Diana drove through the University's parking lot and soon came upon the main gates of the University. Annie was waiting for her, holding her books in front of her. She hopped into the passenger seat of the Corvette and they took off.

Annie glanced at Diana. "Who is this special patient you want me to see?"

"Troy Witt."

"Stop the car!"

Diana didn't understand.

"I said, stop the car!" Once the Corvette pulled to the side of the road, Annie got out and started walking away from the car and Diana ran after her.

"Annie . . . . what's wrong?"

"Every time I'm with him, I get these strange feelings. The same feelings I had when I was with Tony."

"Annie, he is Tony Cross . . . he has amnesia. He is starting to remember certain things and events, but when it comes to you and your life together, it is very painful for him."

"Then what do you want me to do?"

"Talk to him. Being with him for a while, perhaps you can mention certain events in your past that might help him remember."

"And if he doesn't remember?"

"I can hypnotize him. Once he remembers the past life the two of you had, Tony Cross will come back. If he does not remember that life, he will remain Troy Witt. Also, perhaps, I can ease the pain that he goes through." Soon after that, Annie stood at Troy's side. Diana stood away from them, but observed them closely.

Troy slowly reached up to Annie to touch her cheek with his fingers. "I love you," he said and then without warning another migraine sent pain through his body and the flashes came even faster than before, causing him to cry out in pain. Diana alerted the doctor and nurse as Annie left the room and stepped out into the hallway. Without realizing it, she ran into Jackie.

# CHAPTER FORTY-NINE

*"Will you stop it? Have you ever considered that this
negativity is pushing me away from you?"*

ANNIE AND JACKIE were the
only ones in the waiting room.
Annie was watching Jackie pace back and forth, very upset and frustrated. "What
is it you want?" Annie asked her, making her turn to look at her.

"I want you to leave Troy alone. He belongs to me," Jackie said poking herself
in the chest.

"The last time I checked, this was a free country." Annie said and Jackie came
at her as if she was going to slap her. Annie grabbed her hand the tucked it behind
her back and shoved her face to the wall, pinning her there. "Next time you come
at me, you'd better have a damn good reason, because I'll put you on the deck so
fast you'll think you've been run over by a truck. I have been waiting for him since
I was 12 years old. You have no right to come and take him away from me." Annie
stepped away from Jackie, releasing her as Jackie turned to face her.

"Who is he to you? Why is he constantly thinking about you?"

Annie could tell how upset she was. "Let's just say my acquaintance with him
goes back years before you came into the picture." Just then a nurse stuck her
head into the room.

"Ms. Roberson, the doctor is looking for you." The nurse told her.

"I think Ms. Brown is quite capable of answering any questions the good
doctor wants," Annie said and left the room.

Diana was waiting for Annie in the hallway just outside the room, but was
surprised to see another woman walking up to her. "I'm Jackie Brown. Mr. Witt

and I are what you would call 'involved.'" Diana was trying to figure this one out. This was getting better than General Hospital.

"He is trying to remember Ms. Brown, but, as you know, it is very painful for him to remember. One possible way of helping him is through hypnotism. I could do that here, or in my office."

"What is this hypnotizing you were talking about, Doctor?"

"It's a way to help him remember." Diana told her, "It could help him with the pain . . . it was the pain that brought him here."

"Is it a way to help him forget?" Jackie wonders as she crossed her arms in front of her.

"Yes, it can be used that way. But I don't think that would be a viable option since he is trying so hard to remember."

"I have my reasons for not wanting him to remember."

Both of the women were surprised when Troy came out of the room and up to them. "Stop it, Jackie."

"Is this about Annie Roberson?" Diana asked.

"Yes. I want him to completely forget about her," Jackie said.

Troy couldn't believe how cold it sounded to him, like it was nothing to her. Remembering was everything to him. He had a life out there, somewhere. A life that, for some reason, he left . . . and that life had been with Annie Roberson. He took a few steps to Jackie taking her by the shoulder and made her look at him.

"Will you stop it? Have you ever considered that this negativity is pushing me away from you?" Diana had to break this up before an all-out war erupted between the two of them. She stepped between them, pushing them apart.

She looked at them. "Both of you . . . come with me now!" They stepped into an empty waiting room, the same room where Jackie and Annie had been. They sat down and Diana just looked at them. "I don't know what relationship you two have, but this attitude must stop." Her voice had gotten very harsh. Both Jackie and Troy crossed their arms in front of them and clammed up at the same time. Diana looked at Jackie. "Why do you care about him, Ms. Brown?"

"I love him."

Diana looked at Troy and asked, "Now, Troy, what is Ms. Brown to you?"

"I love her." Troy said

Then Diana asked Troy, "And what is Ms. Roberson to you?"

"I don't know. That's what I want to find out."

Diana turned to Jackie. "And what is Ms. Roberson to you?"

"I hate her."

Troy couldn't believe what he had just heard. "Jackie . . ." Diana waved her hand and Troy stopped.

"Why do you hate Ms. Roberson, Ms. Brown?"

"She wants to take Troy away from me."

"You do know that she is his fiancée? That they were to be married two years after his disappearance?"

"Excuse me?"

"Be quiet, Troy." Diana said to him. He got up and went to the window to look out. There wasn't much to see, just the parking lot. Diana wanted to talk to Jackie some more.

"I'm still waiting for an answer, Ms. Brown."

"All I care about is Troy Witt and I want him with me."

"And what happens if he remembers? What then?"

"I will deal with that situation, if and, when I come to it," Jackie said to her. Troy turned from the window to look at the two women. He did not like the way this conversation was going. He was finding out just how Jackie truly felt and he didn't like it.

"You don't want me to remember, do you, Jackie?" He said angrily.

Jackie went to face him. "Troy, Sweetheart, I love you."

"I would have thought that you, of all people, would want me to remember. To stop the pain I've been having. I was someone, Jackie. Perhaps . . . someone important."

"You are someone, Troy. You're important to me." Jackie stepped up to him, putting her arms around him, wanting him to hold her, but he pushed her away. Jackie couldn't believe what he had done. That was the first time he wouldn't hold her.

"What's the matter?" Jackie asked, worried.

"Just leave me alone for awhile, OK?" Troy went back to his room and Diana stood as Jackie turned to her.

"Are you happy, Doctor?" Jackie said as she started to leave the room, but Diana stopped her.

"This would have happened eventually, Ms. Brown . . ."

"I'm losing him, Doctor . . . I'm so scared." Jack said to Diana as she left.

*   *   *

Troy was in Diana's office at the hospital. The office was small, but efficient. She got up from behind her desk and walked up to face Troy. "How are you feeling today, Mr. Witt?"

"OK, I guess. But I am a little afraid of doing this."

"And why is that?"

"I'm afraid that I will remember some evil person that has killed and should be locked up in a prison."

"You're not that type of person." Diana said as she leaned back against her desk.

"How can we be sure?"

"I have done a lot of research on you. I know who you are and where you came from. Who your parents and family are and what Annie Roberson is to you." That surprised Troy as she continued, "Please sit down and be comfortable." He did and she sat down next to him.

"I'm fine," Troy said. "Will this hypnotizing help me to remember and stop the pain?"

"Yes, to both questions, Mr. Witt. Are you still scared?"

"I've never done anything like this and perhaps I am a little afraid to find out who this Tony Cross really is. If I remember that I belong with Annie, what happens with me and Jackie. She and her father have been so kind to me. How can I betray them?"

"I don't think leaving them would be a betrayal, Mr. Witt. If you find you do belong with Annie, don't you think you should be with her . . . . happy and perhaps start a family of your own one day?"

"I can get that with Jackie, Dr. Evans."

"All right. Can you tell be about Annie?"

Troy snickered. "Annie Roberson is something special."

"What kind of relationship have you had with her?"

"Relationship? We have no relationship. We're just friends that met in high school."

"OK, Troy . . . this is what we're going to do. I'm going to dim the lights and you are to watch the colorful light over my desk. I will put on some mood music and I want you to relax and clear your mind. Let the music take you to a different time and place." She got up and turned the light off and turned on a strobe light over her desk. She placed a headset over Troy's ears with some soothing music playing, then closed the curtains. Even though Troy could hear the music playing, he could still heard Diana talking to him. "How did you meet Annie Roberson?" She asked, as she sat down in front of him.

"I was eleven years old and running from a gang leader named Glenn Baker. I was friends with his girl, Ashley Moore. I loved hearing her stories about her father, a fighter pilot. Glenn caught us together. I was able to get away. They chased me through Pine Lake and I was running on the beach and fell right into a sandcastle that Annie was building." Troy said, now, fully under the hypnotic state.

"Do you remember what you did during your graduation ceremonies a few years later?"

"I got my diploma and we had a party."

"Do you remember seeing Annie Roberson there?"

"I think she was at the party, but other than that, I don't remember anything with her . . . it's all blurry when it comes to her."

"Can you remember your parents?"

Troy began to get very nervous. "No . . . I don't remember."

"Please, Troy. Try to remember your parents."

Troy tried, but it became very painful for him. "No . . . . I can't . . . . I don't want to go there."

"You are Tony Cross."

"No . . . I am Troy Witt."

"One more time . . . your name is Tony Cross."

"Stop it! I don't want to remember him . . . . please stop!" Troy jumped up and ran to her door but Diana was faster and intercepted him. Troy dropped to his knees in pain and began crying.

"Don't you understand? They're dead. I saw her bloody hand in the wreckage of the house . . . . I don't want to be there . . . . please let me come back."

"OK, Troy, I will snap my fingers and when you hear the sound you will be here in my office. You will remember everything we did today in this office. When you wake up, you will feel refreshed, like you had a wonderful nap. And, in the future, when you have these flashes, you will no longer have the pain that used to be with them. Now . . . I will count to three and when I snap my fingers, one . . . . two . . . . three . . . ." Diana snapped her fingers and Troy came too. She helped him to his feet. Once on his feet, she restored the lights in the room and turned off the strobe and opened the curtains. "How do you feel?" She asked him as he watched her go back to her desk and sit down.

He smiled. "I had a good sleep . . . I feel at peace. Did you learn anything?" Troy asked as he sat back down in the chair.

"A little bit. You remembered Glenn Baker and Ashley Moore. You even remembered Annie to a point. When you remembered your parents' deaths, your mind went into defensive mode. That event was very painful for you and the pain you have been feeling is the way your body protects itself. It puts up a pain shield to keep you from remembering too much. I was actually hoping to get a lot more."

"So what now?" He was hoping that she had an answer for him.

"We can take a field trip to Pine Lake. Just the two of us. We can walk Main Street."

"I don't want to go there."

"Why not?"

"I don't remember . . . just that it's dark and evil there. I just want to be as far away from there as I can."

"All right, Troy. I'm going to let you go home today."

"Good. The food here is terrible, but the nurses are pretty." Troy brought his hand to his forehead with the beginning of a headache. Diana got up and moved around the desk to face him.

"What is it, Troy. Do you remember something?"

"I, I remember being in this hospital before. I remember someone bringing me food that they had cooked."

"Was it Annie, or Jackie, or somebody else?"

"All I can see is that it was a female. I'm sorry . . . that's all I remember."

"I want you to keep a small notebook at all times and when you begin to remember things, no matter how small it is, write it down." There was a knock at the door and Diana called out and a nurse came in with a wheelchair to get Troy.

"His ride is waiting for him out front," the nurse informed the two and then Diana and Troy said their goodbyes as the nurse took him away.

The familiar pickup truck belonging to Ray Brown was waiting patiently in front of the hospital, like a horse waiting for its rider. The nurse pulled the wheelchair up next to the truck and he stepped to the passenger door and climbed in and the truck pulled away.

At first nothing was said between Jackie and Troy, then Jackie looked at him. "Are you OK?" She asked, wondering if he was Troy or Tony Cross. He slowly turned to look at her.

"No, not really. I just don't know what's going on in my life. I so confused about everything. A part of me wants to remember and another part is afraid to remember. That part doesn't want to remember the dark days I had. That's where the pain is coming from. But it's a part of my life. I can't deny that something bad happened to cause my amnesia."

Jackie didn't quite understand what he was talking about. "What are you going to do? What are we going to do?" She couldn't help wondering about it. He looked away from her for a minute, but turned to her again.

"I need to get away from everything to clear my mind and figure things out. It won't be long . . . just a few days." He was tired and she could tell.

"Where do you want to go?"

"I don't know, Jackie. I truly do not know. I do know that I love you . . . but yet . . ." He closed his eyes for a second and there was pain in them when he opened them again. "I love Annie Roberson." That was a slap in the face to Jackie. She didn't know what to say, or do. She knew she was losing him and there wasn't anything she could do or say that would keep the two of them together.

Once again, silence filled the cabin of the truck and nothing was said between them as they headed down the two-lane road back to the farm. That was until the silence was broken by the thunderous sound of a big black Ram Charger with smoked windows slamming into the rear of the truck. Jackie tried to hit the brakes, but there was no response. Now the Charger was in control of the situation and pushing the pickup off the side of the road. It bounced down the hillside, out of control and came to a stop as it slammed into a tree and smoke began to come from the engine compartment. Neither Troy, nor Jackie, was moving.

# CHAPTER FIFTY

*"She really did love you, you know?"*

T HE SMOKE COMING from the engine compartment was getting worse. Troy was the first to regain consciousness. He unbuckled himself and Jackie then got out of the truck and went around to the driver's side and pulled Jackie from the truck. He had barely pulled her clear when the truck exploded.

The truck was fully engulfed in flames. Troy could see that there was a bad cut on Jackie's head that was bleeding badly. He gently rolled her onto her back and placed her head on his lap. He could see the life force draining from her eyes. The gleam that he had fallen in love with was slipping away. "You taught me so much. You told me that the color of one's skin didn't matter, that there was good in all people." She started coughing and he could see that she was coughing up blood. As he leaned over and kissed her lips he could feel her slip away from him . . . he knew she was no longer with him . . . at least in this world. He just sat there with her in his lap and cried.

\*　　\*　　\*

By the time Troy made it back to the farm he could barely stand. He was carrying Jackie in his arms. He dropped to his knees, but never let go of her body. Ray came out to see what was going on and could not believe it when he saw his daughter's lifeless body. He walked over to Troy who looked up at him. "We were rear-ended, then forced off the road. The truck hit a tree and exploded. I barely got us out, but for Jackie . . . it was too late. I wasn't quick enough." Ray was beginning to cry with him and the two stayed well into the evening, not saying anything more, just crying.

\* \* \*

Three days later, at the Timber City Church, Troy and Ray were standing at Jackie's gravesite, next to her mother. Troy stood there staring at the headstone that had Jackie's full name, date of birth and the date she died. Troy wanted to make sure he would remember that name and that day for the rest of his life. Ray put a friendly hand on Troy's shoulder. "She really did love you, you know?" Troy heard what Ray said, but didn't take his eyes off the headstone. "I don't blame you for what happened," Roy continued. "You are welcome to stay with me at the house for as long as you want."

"Thank you, Ray, but I don't know what I'm going to do now. What do I do now?"

"I wish I had an answer for you, Son, but I don't." He patted Troy on the shoulder and walked away as Troy stood looking at Jackie's grave.

\* \* \*

There was a pounding at Annie's door and she ran to answer it, shocked to see the condition that Troy was in. "Troy . . . what happened?" He dropped to the edge of the bed and lowered his head in sadness as Annie sat down next to him.

"She's dead," was all that he would say to her.

"Who is dead, Troy?" Annie was trying to get information from him so she could understand what had caused him so much pain.

"Jackie . . . she's dead . . . he killed her . . . I know he did."

"I don't understand. What is going on? Please help me to understand so I can help you." She watched Troy get up and go to the door. He stopped just at the door and looked over his shoulder at her.

"That really was a cool castle you were making."

"What castle?"

"The one I fell into."

Annie covered her mouth in shock and when she stood up she reached out to him. "Tony?" Her voice cracked.

"That name means nothing to me. I'm sorry." Annie stood there watching him leave, not believing what was happening. She ran out of the building and looked left and right but there was no sign of him. She saw Chung-Hee and Mark walking toward her, holding hands.

"Did you see Troy?" She asked them.

"What's wrong?" Chung-Hee asked her.

"I don't know. Troy was here . . . he said that Jackie was dead."

Chung-Hee took hold of Annie's hand. "Come on, we're going to check this out." The three hurried off.

A thunder storm rolled into the region. The rain was coming down in buckets and Troy was packing back and forth on the porch, shouting out for Jackie, telling her to leave him alone. Ray came out onto the porch to see what was going on. "I thought you were talking to somebody." Ray said to him.

"I was . . . to Jackie."

"Troy, Jackie has passed away."

"No . . . she's standing right there."

"Troy . . . we are the only ones on this porch. Let's go inside. This is not a good night to be outside." Ray retrieved two beers from the refrigerator and handed one to Troy and sat down on the sofa. "I remember the first time I brought you home. Her face just lit up like a lightning bug. I had never seen her so excited about a man before. Remember when the two of you started painting the house?"

Troy nodded his head. "Yes, I do. You really did look good as a white man." They both laughed.

"And you looked good as a black man." Again the two laughed as they sipped their beers. "Jackie was a wild thing. She was angry at the world when her mother died. She did not handle that very well. I tried to raise her the best I could, but she was always getting into trouble at school and in town. Then she met you and fell so much in love that she changed. You changed her Troy . . . . for the better. Oh, don't get me wrong, she was still a wild thing, but she calmed down quite a bit."

"She might be still alive if you hadn't found me in the river and brought me here." The two continued to sip their beers.

"I wasn't going to leave you there. I had to bring you home and save you, it's the way I am."

"I will always be grateful to you for that. I will never forget you. I have to go Ray. I can't stay here."

"I know, Son, I know."

"Jackie is still strong in my mind. I see her wherever I look. I still will help you in the kitchen, but I feel I must go get an apartment in town. You do understand?" Ray nodded his head. "However, I feel strange to leave you alone."

"I will be all right, Boy. My sis and nephew is coming here. My nephew wants to go to the culinary school and my sister wants to take care of me and ride the horses. So I will have my hands full. I plan to stay with a lady friend for a while, and then she is going to help me clean up the house before my family arrives."

"You have a lady friend . . . I would never have guessed." Ray nodded his head.

"She is a wonderful woman, she helped me when my wife passed away, I never told Jackie about here cause I know how upset she would have been if she found out I had a new lady friend. A man has to have a woman at his side for him to be happy. Please don't let my daughter's death deny you the happiness that you need."

"I don't think I will be able to be happy with anyone for a while."

"I think you will," Ray said as he picked up the photo album and handed it to Troy. "When you are ready, look through this book and you will understand what I was talking about. I'm going to bed now, good night." Ray walked up the steps and Troy noticed that he was moving a little slow now. He wasn't sure if it was old age, or the death of his daughter, or both. At first Troy was afraid to open the book. It seemed to be calling to him so he pulled it across the table to him and opened it. Nancy had done a hell of a job putting it together. She had included dates, times and what was going on when the photo was taken. Troy closed the book and sat back in the chair.

"I understand now," he said to himself.

*     *     *

A door opened to a small two bedroom apartment that had a kitchen, living room and a few pieces of furniture. He was going to be sleeping on the couch and there was no food in the refrigerator. It looked as if he would have to go shopping tomorrow. Troy sat down on the couch and then laid down resting his head on the armrest of the couch. A tear started to fall from an eye. "I miss you, Jackie," he said and closed his eyes.

# CHAPTER FIFTY-ONE

*"I find sometimes this helps."*

ANNIE HAD GONE to the Browns' house to find out what happened to Troy. She had not seen him for over a month and was getting worried. Ray brought Annie some coffee and sat down in one of the wing chairs. "I'm truly sorry, Mr. Brown. Troy told me that Jackie had passed away, but he didn't say how. I wasn't sure if I would be intruding if I came out here sooner . . ." she said taking a sip of the coffee.

"You would not have been intruding. Troy could not stay here any longer. The happy memories that he and Jackie shared were too painful for him. He really did love her."

"Do you know where he went?"

"He's in Timber City, but where he is staying . . . . I don't know." Annie reached into her backpack and took out a personal information card that had her cell phone number on it and handed the card to Ray.

"If you should see him, or hear from him, please let me know." They stood up and walked to the door. Ray looked around from where he stood.

"One more thing . . ." Ray said as he went to the kitchen to retrieve the photo book and brought it back to Annie. "Your mother gave him this at the cook off."

Annie took the book and looked at him. "Is there anything I can do for you?"

"This place seems so empty without her . . . . I still can't sleep at night." He opened the door for Annie.

"If you need me, call me, OK?" She told him, giving him a hug.

Annie narrating: *"It was sad visiting Ray today. I can understand your sadness . . . your sorrow. I hope you don't let it consume you as it did me. I am here for you. All you have to do is come to me and I will help you through these dark times. The next cooking class seemed empty without you there. It's funny, I've been feeling empty since I thought you took your life. The trip to the farmer's market was a success and the teacher is planning on doing it again next summer. The neat thing about this class is that we get to taste everybody else's cooking. Chung-Hee and Mark's romance keeps getting stronger. I really do believe that those two were meant for each other. I am proud of Mark for learning Korean. It is not an easy language to learn and he's thinking about going back to the university to study management again. So, when Mom and Dad really do retire and hand the business over to him, he will be able to keep it running smoothly. It has been three years and my feelings for you are the same as they were when we first met. I love you."*

\*　　\*　　\*

"I find that sometimes this helps." A whiskey bottle appeared in front of him, and Annie sat down next to him, crossing her legs. She popped open the whisky bottle and took a sip from it, then handed it to Troy, who did the same. "I remember sitting with Crazy Jim in his cave and drinking whiskey. He said we were both good drinkers," Annie told him. "It's amazing how things have changed since that day." Troy started to say something, but Annie put a finger to his lips to quiet him. "I am truly sorry for what happened to Jackie. Believe me, if anyone knows what you are going through, it's me."

"Annie, I'm sorry." He took another sip from the bottle and handed it to her.

"There's nothing to be sorry about. This is what God has chosen for me. I have pretty much accepted it. There are times when it still hurts . . . like today." She handed the bottle back to him.

"I'm sorry that I can't be the person you want me to be." He handed the bottle to her.

"I'm not asking you to be my companion . . . I'm asking you to be my friend."

Troy extended his hand toward her. "My name is Troy Witt . . . I'm glad to meet you."

Annie flashed him a corner-of-the-mouth grin and shook hands with him. "I'm Annie Roberson, it's very nice to meet you Troy Witt."

"Likewise."

"See, we're friends now," Annie said with a snicker. Troy returned that snicker when he notices the gleam in her eyes. He knew he had seen it before. Annie pouted when the bottle was empty, she even turned it upside down to make sure nothing came out. "I saw a movie once where the hero lost his memory and when his girlfriend kissed him, he remembered everything . . . who he was, who she was . . . everything. Why don't we kiss again and see what happens?" Annie watched to see what kind of reaction she was going to get from him.

"I'm sorry . . . I can't."

"Jackie?"

"Jackie." They both stood up.

"I understand, I really do. And it's not all bad today . . . I made a new friend. See you in class?"

"I don't know if I'm going back or not," Troy told her.

"It would be a shame if you don't," Annie said. "See you around Troy Witt," she turned and started to walk away, but Troy called out to her and then caught up with her and the two walked away together.

\*     \*     \*

The door to Carter's office flew open and one of his men went flying through the air and crash landed into the desk, but didn't get up. Carter jumped to his feet reaching into the desk drawer and pulled out a pistol, but he didn't get a chance to use it as Troy did a flying sidekick over the desk and pinned Carter to the wall. He grabbed Carter's gun hand and slammed it against the wall several times until he made him drop it.

"How dare you come barging in here, Witt?!!"

"I should rip you apart," Troy said angrily.

Carter tried not to show it, but he was scared. "If this is about the Brown girl, I'm sorry."

"And that is supposed to make me feel better?" Troy threw Carter aside like he was a wet dish towel, making him fall into the bookcase, knocking several books to the floor. He went to the floor and sat there.

"Jackie was never the target. It was you I was after."

"Well, you made a fucking mistake. If I ever hear of you bothering Mr. Brown again, I will kill you." Troy said grabbing Carter by the front of his shirt.

Suddenly a hand appeared on Troy's shoulder. He looked at it. "If I were you, Pal, I would remove that hand, or lose it." The hand forced Troy around. Troy ducked as a fist came straight for him and, instead, caught Carter directly in the face, knocking him out cold. Lee Du-Ho was the man behind that punch. The man that Carter had brought from Korea to deal with the situation. The two men went into combat mode and proceeded to make kindling of Carter's office. Both men were quite capable in the martial arts and neither was going to back down from this fight.

Du-Ho was there to protect Carter, and Troy had the frustration of the last few years inside him. He released it into Du-Ho. He sent a sidekick into Du-Ho's chest, sending him flying backwards into Carter's pride and joy . . . the model which had been rebuilt. Some of Carter's men heard the ruckus and headed to the office. Troy knew they would be armed and no matter how good you are in the martial arts you cannot stop a bullet. There was only one way out of the office . . . the window. They were three stories up, and Troy could only hope that there would be something soft that would keep him from hitting the pavement below . . . or this day, and life, would come to an abrupt end. The men came into the room and opened fire, but they couldn't hit a moving target and Troy crashed through the window.

# CHAPTER FIFTY-TWO

*"Hey, Buddy, let me off at the next red light . . ."*

D U-HO RAN TO the window and looked out, then shook his head in disbelief. Troy had landed on a flatbed truck carrying a load of mattresses on their way to the city dump. Troy looked up and saw Du-Ho and flashed him the bird. Then he pounded on the roof of the cab. "Hey, Buddy, let me off at the next red light . . ."

Annie narrating: *"I was sad when Troy didn't show up in class today. He did say he didn't believe he would come back, so, I guess the rest of the semester is going to be very boring without him there. After class I decided to go to the Brown's restaurant and have dinner. I didn't really want a whole lot, so I just got a house salad and a beer. I also gave the new waitress a note for the cook."*

\*　　\*　　\*

The two were sitting on Troy's couch at his place. He had gotten them a couple of beers and Annie was looking around the near-empty apartment. "This is a nice place you have here, Troy."

"It's a place to keep warm, dry and sleep. That's about it."

"You know what?" Annie said. "Let's go shopping tomorrow. I want to get you some things to make your life here a little more comfortable."

"Annie . . . you don't have to. I really don't need anything else."

"It's not that I don't have to, it's the fact that I want to." She stood up, picking up her backpack. "I need to go, Troy. I'll see you tomorrow?" Troy nodded his head, not saying anything. Annie smiled and headed for the door as Troy stood up.

"Annie?" She turned to him. "Don't go . . . I need you tonight." She dropped her bag and he went to her. "I do need you tonight," he said as Annie looked into his blue eyes. He slowly moved to her lips and they kissed as they never had before. As they held the kiss, everything came back at Troy. Everything he had been through since the tornado in Pine Lake, the feelings he and Annie had for each other everything. "You know, you were right about the kiss . . ."

Annie looked at him, confused.

"I remember, Annie . . . everything . . . you, me, what we mean to each other. I am your Tony Cross."

At first Annie was beside herself, but didn't want to say anything that would 'upset the apple cart'.

"I never stopped loving you, Tony. Never. Even when everyone told me you were dead and I had to let go . . . I knew you were alive. I knew you were out there somewhere."

"I am so sorry. I have been gone for so long."

Annie gently touched his cheek, "You are home now, where you belong and that is all that matters."

"When I hit the rapids under the bridge, I think I must have hit everything that was floating in that river. I was knocked out and when I came to, Ray Brown was trying to save my life. The only thing was I couldn't remember anything. I didn't have my wallet, no ID on me."

Annie picked up her backpack and unzipped it and pulled out his wallet. It had seen better days, but she handed it to him. "The boys didn't like the job the police did looking for you, so they went searching. This was all they found."

'I don't understand why all this pain and suffering happened to us. To two people that were so much in love . . . how could it keep us apart for so long?"

"We are together now, and we will never be separated again." Annie smiled at him. "Make me yours tonight." Tony scooped her up in his arms and spun around. They both laughed as he took her to the couch and sat her back down. He sat down next to her and ran his hand through her hair. She closed her eyes, savoring his touch. "I love you."

Annie narrating: *"That night was incredible. Even though we made love on that beach so long ago, he still remembered how to touch me. I came over and over for him that night. It seemed like we didn't stop making love all night. Chung-Hee had called me in the middle of the night. She needed to see me about something so the next morning, before I left, I returned the black belt that belonged to him and the ring."*

*   *   *

A file dropped on Carter's desk and Lee Du-Ho picked it up and looked through it. There were several papers and a photo of Chung-Hee and Mark. "That is the man that is going to marry your girl," Carter said to him as he sat back down in his chair. Du-ho just looked at him.

"He is of no concern to me, but Chung-Hee is. I am here to take her back to Korea with me." Then he found a photo of Troy. "He is the one that is making it hard for me to obtain the Browns' property . . . he is the one that was here the other day."

"This one, I will kill. But I will be sad when he dies."

Carter looked at him strangely, "I don't understand."

"He is a good fighter . . . he deserves the respect and honor of a warrior."

"I don't give a damn if you dance the Watusi on him. Get him out of my hair. With him gone, I can deal with Ray Brown." Du-Ho wasn't paying attention to Carter, he was looking at the photo of Chung-Hee and smiled. "Soon, you will be home where you belong, and we will be married."

# CHAPTER FIFTY-THREE

*"At least we had our night."*

ANNIE WAS SURPRISED to see Chung-Hee sitting on the steps in front of the dorm. "This is the first time I have seen Chung-Hee scared to death," Annie thought as she sat down beside her. Chung-Hee's knees were drawn to her chest and her arms were wrapped around her legs as she rocked back and forth. "Chung-Hee . . . are you all right?"

Chung-Hee looked at her, trying to figure out what to say. "He's here," she finally said. "He's here to take me home."

"Who is here?"

"My ex."

"Oh, My God," Annie said, then continued, "where's Mark?"

"I sent him home."

Annie couldn't believe that. "But why?"

Lee Du-Ho is a dangerous man, Annie. He would kill Mark, or anyone, that tried to keep him from getting to me."

The two women looked up as Tony sat down next to Annie. Chung-Hee looked at him. "Troy."

He smiled back, "The name is Tony Cross."

Chung-Hee looked at Annie, who was smiling and nodding at her.

"Really?" Chung-Hee then threw her arms around Annie, and looked at Tony. "Welcome home."

The celebration was short-lived as they heard a voice. "Kim Chung-Hee." Lee Du-Ho said then continued, "jib-e waseo sigan." (Come home in Korean.)

Chung-Hee responded, "Bil-eo meog-eul dwe jyeola." (Go to hell in Korean.) Du-Ho didn't give her a choice and grabbed her by the hand and started to pull her away from the others. Tony wasn't about to sit by and watch what was happening and jumped to his feet, but Du-Ho ignored him.

Two of the three men with Du-Ho cornered Tony, with weapons drawn, one of them pointed at Annie. Before that man could do anything, Annie made her move and executed one of her throw-downs, then charged after Chung-Hee and Du-Ho. Tony wanted to help so badly, but with two guns pointed at his chest, there wasn't much he could do but watch. Suddenly, there was what sounded like a war-cry come from the building behind them. Mark and several students from Pine Lake martial arts school were upon them. All Mark had needed to say was that Annie Roberson was in trouble and they were right there. The students were able to take care of the two goons as Tony headed after Annie.

By this time, Annie had caught up to her friend and called out to Du-Ho, making him stop. He swung around slapped her and she went down. Tony leaped over her to take out the man that had hit his woman. Du-Ho pulled a gun from his belt and fired, hitting Tony in the side. Tony cried out in pain and dropped to his knees. Chung-Hee screamed and went into combat mode. She kicked the gun from his hand and there was nothing Du-Ho could do to defend himself against the enraged woman. She was an expert at martial arts and was out of control. This was not the way it was supposed to be. Korean women were supposed to bend to the demands of their men. Chung-Hee was not supposed to be beating the crap out of him.

Annie had Tony's head in her lap and was crying, out of control. He was bleeding badly and starting to cough up blood. "At least we had our night." He tried to say to her as Mark came running up behind Annie. He could see how much blood Tony had lost.

"No . . . no . . . . you can't go . . . please . . . I just found you," she sobbed.

Tony's bloody hand slowly reached up and touched her cheek. "You have the prettiest green eyes . . . ." Tony started coughing and then his hand fell to the ground. Annie dropped her head onto his, as Mark rested his hand on her shoulder.

"Hang in there, Tony," Mark said. "I've called 911 . . . they'll be here any second."

Before Chung-Hee could execute the final blow on Du-Ho, a black van skidded to a stop and the side door opened. Du-Ho was able to get away from Chung-Hee and dived into the van, which then sped away. Carter was in the back of the van. "You asshole . . ." he said angrily. "You told me you could handle the girl."

"I used to be able to . . . I've never seen her that insane before."

"You fucked up, you idiot. I didn't want you to kill Witt. I wanted you to rough him up . . . I don't need the cops snooping around me right now."

Du-Ho had heard enough of the man's bitching. He leaped at Carter, pinning him to the wall of the van. "I don't care about your situation . . . I came here for the girl."

"You screwed that up too . . . . now what?" Carter asked him.

"I have to leave the US . . . . I just killed a man and the cops are probably looking for me right now. As for you . . . . you will have to find someone else to do your dirty work . . . if you can."

# CHAPTER FIFTY-FOUR

*"Don't come near me, Mark; cause if you do, I may do*
*something we both would regret."*

ANNIE WAS PACING back and forth in one of the hospital hallways. She had been there all night and still hadn't heard any news about Tony. She kept telling herself that no news was good news, but if that was the case, why did she have such a bad feeling about things.

Chung-Hee and Mark were with her but, off to the side. "I told you to go home, Mark," Chung-Hee said.

"If I am to be your husband, I must prove to you, your family and the world that I can protect you and keep you safe."

"Oh, Mark, I love you," Chung-Hee said as she threw her arms around him, not paying attention to two orderlies that were walking by them.

Annie couldn't help but hear what they were saying as they stopped to look out a window at the sun that was just coming up. "Did you see that dude that came in last night?"

"The one with the gunshot wound? What about him?"

"I heard he died on the operating table a little while ago. Come on . . . let's get some coffee."

"Sure . . . what a hell of a way to start a day." The two walked away. Annie found she no longer had legs and fell back against the wall, both hands covering her mouth. She dropped to the floor. Seeing what was happening, Chung-Hee and Mark ran to her.

"Annie?" Chung-Hee said to her. Annie didn't respond, just pushed her away, got up and ran off.

They came into Annie's dorm room that afternoon and found Annie packing. She was just throwing things into the suitcase, not caring how they went in. As she turned to leave, she found that they were blocking the door. "Get out of my way!" Annie ordered the two.

"Where are you going?" Chung-Hee asked her.

"Does it matter? I can't stay here any longer."

"What's wrong? What's happened?"

"Tony's dead . . . isn't that enough?" Chung-Hee looked at Mark in shock as Annie continued. "I heard them talking, he died on the operating table this morning. Now get out of my way, or so help me I'll put you on the deck, and you know I can do it."

Chung-Hee and Mark moved apart to give her a pathway to the door.

"Go with her, Mark," Chung-Hee said.

"Don't come near me, Mark; 'cause if you do, I may do something we both would regret." Annie turned and left the room.

Mark looked worried when he glanced at Chung-Hee. "Do you think there's any truth to what she said about Tony?"

"I don't know, but I think we should go back to the hospital and find out." By the time Chung-Hee and Mark got to the hospital, Ray had already been notified and was at Tony's bedside when they came into the room. Ray stood up. He knew Chung-Hee, but not Mark.

"I'm Mark Roberson," Mark said to him.

"So you're Annie's brother?"

Chung-Hee had gone to Tony's side. "How is he, Mr. Brown?"

"He's doing pretty good." Ray told them. "He lost a lot of blood, but the doctor feels that he should make a full recovery."

"Mr. Brown," Chung-Hee said. "Annie thinks that he's dead?"

"I don't understand."

Annie said that she heard two employees talking about a gunshot victim that had died in surgery. She thinks it's Tony."

"Oh, Dear God. How could she think that?" Ray couldn't believe what he was hearing."

"I've got to call Mom," Mark said as he stepped to the side to use his cell phone.

"Where is Annie?" Ray asked Chung-Hee.

"She packed her things and left."

A groggy voice asked, "What do you mean she left?"

"I'll get the doctor," Ray said as Chung-Hee sat down in the chair next to the bed.

"Tony . . . it's me, Kim Chung-Hee."

Things were still fuzzy for Tony, but he knew who she was. "I know you . . . . and him." He looked at Mark.

"You had us worried, Dude."

"Where's Annie?"

"We don't know, Tony," Chung-Hee said as Tony tried to sit up, but fell back as the whole world tilted on him.

"I've got to find her," Tony insisted.

"You have to rest and get strong. We will look for Annie," Chung-Hee told him. Tony was slipping back to sleep when the doctor and nurse came back into the room, followed by Ray.

\* \* \*

Two days later, Nancy came into focus. She had a huge smile on her face when she saw Tony open his eyes. Tony, for a few seconds thought it was Annie. "Annie?" He was disappointed when he realized it was Nancy instead. "Any word from Annie?"

"We're looking for her, so is the police. Don't worry, we'll find her."

"I want to sit up."

"Do you think you should?"

"Please." Nancy adjusted his bed to where he wanted it and it seemed to make him feel a little better.

"Mark said that you remember who you are." She said to him.

"Yes . . . . everything. When we met, what we were to each other . . . she must hate me for what I put her through."

"I don't think she hates you, Tony. She still loves you very much."

"Then where is she?"

"Tony, she heard a couple of the orderlies talking about a patient that had died of a gunshot wound while in surgery. She thought it was you. I guess that was the last straw. She probably just wanted to get away by herself for a while. She'll be back. Look, Tony, I have some news for you. Your parents had life insurance and you were the sole beneficiary. They also had insurance on the restaurant. Those funds have been put into a trust fund for you. There's close to two-hundred and fifty thousand dollars waiting for you. You can start your own business . . . whatever you want."

"Excuse me . . . can you fly that by me again? Did I hear you say two-hundred fifty thousand?"

"Yes, I did," she smiled at him.

"I can start my own business . . . with Annie?"

"Whatever you want, Tony."

Then it hit him . . . . "Oh, God . . . I didn't need to run. I put her through hell all because . . . ."

"Stop it, Tony! You had no way of knowing; besides you were grieving. A person doesn't always think straight when they go through something like you did."

"Do you think she'll forgive me?"

"Just give her a chance . . . I don't think you'll have anything to worry about."

# CHAPTER FIFTY-FIVE

*"No need to worry about me, Detective. My life doesn't mean much to me."*

ANNIE CROSSED THE street after leaving the convenience store and disappeared into her motel room. *"I had no way of knowing that Tony was alive and seemed to be well on the way to recovery. I just needed to sort things out and be by myself for a while. I had been approached about an opportunity abroad and I decided that now was a good a time as any."*

Tony was standing at Jackie's grave. He had been there for some time, just talking to her. "I remember everything, Jackie. Everything that Annie and I had . . . were. We were going to be married after she graduated from college. I've put her through a lot . . . . I just hope she will be able to forgive me. I don't think I would blame her if she never wanted to see me again, but I do love her. But, Jackie . . . I will never forget you, and what we had together. Our paths only crossed for a short time. I don't think we were ever meant to be together . . . and I don't blame you for being angry . . . I did love you, Jackie . . . and I meant it . . . I will never forget you."

"Mr. Cross," a voice said behind him. Tony stood and turned to see a tall muscular man in a business suit with a big smile on his face. "I am Detective Billy Jones. We spoke on the phone."

The two men moved away together. "You look familiar," Tony said. "Have we met before?"

"Many years ago, in school. Annie Roberson beat me up." Tony stopped walking. That skinny red headed kid sure looked different now. Annie would sure be surprised at how he had turned out. "We appreciate your help, Tony. We have been trying to get Blake Carter for a long time, but he always seemed to slip through our fingers. He's a very clever man." They came to a blue Ford Taurus that belonged to the detective. The detective opened the passenger door to allow Tony to enter, then moved around to the driver's side and got in.

"Carter took something very precious to me, Detective. He must pay for it."

"It could be very dangerous," Billy said as he started the car.

"If I get him to confess what he has done, will it get him locked up?"

"Yes, but it is you I'm worried about."

The car pulled away as Tony glanced at the detective. "No need to worry about me, Detective, my life doesn't mean much to me anymore."

Billy pulled the car off the road and looked at Tony. "I can't let you go in there with that kind of attitude."

"Do you want Carter or not?"

"Yes, we want him, but not at the cost of your life."

"I appreciate your concern, but right now, my life is not worth the energy."

Billy didn't like what he was hearing and got out of the car and marched around to Tony's side, opened the door and pulled him out and slammed him back against the car. They were standing so close they were almost touching noses.

"ALL life is important, Mr. Cross. God gave us this life for a reason. Only he has the right to take it away from us."

"Is that why Jackie Brown died . . . because God decided it was her time to go?"

"We all die, Mr. Cross. That is a part of life. Ms. Brown had served her purpose in this life. She saved you from a death that was not planned for you. Now she has moved on to what I believe is another life. A life without you . . . yes . . . she was special to you, and you will always keep her close to you, but there is another life, and other people that need you. Since the day Annie beat me up for putting glue on her chair and making her stick to it, I have been watching to the two of you. And I can see that you two belong together. That is what God wanted." Tony couldn't believe he had done that to Annie.

"You put glue on her chair?" Tony asked watching Billy as he leaned back against the car.

"Pretty cool," Billy said. "They had to cut her out of her jeans." Tony found himself almost laughing. Something he hadn't done in a long time.

"I wish I could have seen that."

"You're the one that put a frog in her desk . . . she was pretty mad about that one." Now Billy had started laughing.

"She cornered me in the restroom. I thought my life was over then."

"She is special, Tony. There are not many girls that will stand up for themselves like that."

Tony nodded, "She is special."

"Now . . . why don't we go get Carter?" Billy opened the door to the car and Tony started to get back inside, but looked at him.

"Thank you," Tony said as Billy smiled.

"What are friends for?"

*   *   *

The door to Carter's office flew open and Carter saw one of his men come flying into the room and crash land on the floor, down for the count. Carter had a funny feeling who was behind this escapade. It seemed like every time this man showed up, he lost a man. "Mr. Witt, I do wish you would make an appointment if you wish to see me."

Tony walked right up to the desk, put his hands on it and leaned across, looking Carter in the eyes. "My name is Tony Cross."

"All right, Mr. Cross, you have every right to call yourself whatever you want. Now what is this all about?"

"Answer one thing for me."

Carter thought about it for a moment. "All right . . . what?"

"Why? Why Jackie Brown?"

Carter could see the hurt in his eyes. "As I said before, she was never the target, you were."

"Why?"

"Because with you there, the Browns were strong."

Billy was in the hallway with his men, listening to his radio receiver. "The wire's working great, we have him now," he said, tapping the man on the shoulder. He then spoke into his radio, "OK, Men, get ready, we go in on my command."

"Was your damned project worth her death?" Tony was decidedly trying to hold back his anger.

"I would kill the President of the United States if he got in the way of what I wanted," Carter slowly reached for the drawer in his desk where he had a gun, but Tony saw what he was doing.

"Go ahead, Carter. Give me a reason."

Carter thought about it, then removed his hand from the drawer. He had seen this man in action and knew what he could do.

"The barn . . . the horse . . . and the restaurant?" Tony asked.

At first Carter didn't say anything until Tony barged around the desk and pulled him to his feet. "Fuck you, Cross!" Tony pulled the man up by his jacket collar and pushed him into the bookcase.

"You bastard . . . you ordered everything, didn't you?"

"All right . . . . I gave the orders to burn down the barn and kill the horse, and to rough-up Brown."

"You son of a bitch," Tony said then threw a right cross that sent Carter to the floor. Billy and his men rushed into the office and Billy's men pulled Carter to his feet and cuffed him.

"You're under arrest, Blake Carter, for assault, arson, animal cruelty, and murder. Take him away men . . . and, oh yeah . . . read him his rights."

"You've got nothing on me       " Carter said, struggling with the officers.

"We've got plenty, Carter," Tony said as he lifted his shirt to reveal the recording device strapped to his chest.

"You'll pay for this, Cross . . . mark my words," Carter said as he was being dragged from the room.

Billy turned his attention to Tony. "Thank you, Tony."

"Did you get enough to lock him up?" Tony asked as one of the officers removed the wire device from his chest.

"Plenty," Billy said as he put a friendly hand on Tony's shoulder. "I have found this hell of a website that has damn good practical jokes that I've been dying to try. Let me know when you want to get back at Annie and I'll be glad to help."

"I don't know if that will happen, now."

"Don't be a fool, Tony. You let her go and you'll regret it for the rest of your life. Any place I can take you?"

"No . . . I think I'll just take a walk."

"All right. Keep in touch. I'll need you to testify when the trial comes up."

# CHAPTER FIFTY-SIX

*"Chung-Hee, take me to Pine Lake."*

TONY STOOD AT the railing of the railroad bridge at the exact spot where he had jumped. Chung-Hee was with him. "She came here on the anniversary of your death," she told him. "If I had not been with her, Tony, she would have jumped."

Tony leaned on the railing. "I can't imagine what she went through," he said, and turned to Chung-Hee.

"She went through hell, Tony. That girl loves you."

"Loved, Chung-Hee . . . the word is loved."

Chung-Hee crossed her arms in front of her, letting the breeze blow her hair. "I think when you find her again, you will see that she still loves you."

"I don't know. A friend once told me that God has things planned. Perhaps Annie and I have had our time. Maybe it was over the day I jumped off this bridge."

"I don't think so, Tony. What are you going to do now?"

"There is a restaurant in Washington, DC that is interested in making me their head chef. I'm thinking about taking it."

"Don't be a fool, Tony. If this happened to Mark and me, by God I would fight. I love Mark with all my heart and if there was a chance of us being together again, you'd better believe I would take it. I would hold onto Mark and never let him go again."

Tony thought about all the good times that he and Annie had shared and he looked at Chung-Hee. "Chung-Hee, take me to Pine Lake." She let out a yell of joy and high fived him, and the two left.

# EPILOGUE

*"We had our time, Mother."*

NANCY RAN TO the front door and was surprised to see Annie standing there. She put her hands on Annie's shoulders and looked her over. "Where have you been? We've been looking for you."

Annie smiled at her mother; it was good to see her again. "I really would like some coffee," she said.

"Yes, of course," Nancy said as she took Annie's hand and led her to the kitchen.

A few minutes later, they both sat at the table drinking their coffee. "I'm sorry to have worried you, Mother. But I had to go somewhere and think . . . clear my head." She took a sip from the cup.

"Annie . . . Tony is not dead." That news didn't seem to faze Annie. "Didn't you hear me . . . he's alive."

Annie sat back in her chair, holding the cup with both hands. "I don't care, Mom."

Nancy looked at her oddly. "What do you mean you don't care?"

"It's just been too much. When Glenn stabbed him . . . the jump from the bridge . . . then the shooting . . ."

"Annie, you love him."

"Yes, I love him . . . always have, always will. But that was in the past. Something has been taken from me. I can't go back. I'm not staying here, Mother. I just came to get a few things that I will need, then I am leaving."

"What do you mean you're leaving?" Nancy asked, surprised to no end.

"I have been in contact with a hotel chain in France. They are interested in having me as their head chef. I will be gone for a long time . . . away from this place."

Nancy took a sip from her coffee, not liking what she was hearing. It was hard, but if it was what Annie wanted, she wouldn't stand in her way.

"You're a fool, Annie. You can't leave someone like Tony."

"We had our time together." Annie looked at her mother then sat the cup down on the table. "If you should see Tony, don't tell him my plans." She stood up. "I'm going to walk on the beach one last time, then I'll return to pack my things." She started to leave the table then turned and went to hug her mother. "I love you Mom. I am sorry for what I have put you through."

"Annie, can't you wait for a little longer . . . at least until Chung-Hee and Mark have married. Can you imagine how hurt they will be if you're not there?"

"Their day should be a happy one, I will just put a damper on it."

"What about Ashley and Ethan . . . . their baby is due soon?"

"Just have them to Skype me when the baby comes . . ." She turned and left the house.

*　　*　　*

As the sun approached the horizon, Tony entered the Roberson's restaurant. Ashley was at the cash register and gasped when she saw Tony standing there. He still had that wonderful smile that she remembered. She ran around the corner to hug him. "I can't believe it's you . . ." she told him. He looked at her and couldn't help but see the signs of her pregnancy.

"You're married?"

"Yes, to Ethan."

"You married Annie's kid brother?" She nodded. "But he's at least ten years younger than you."

"Age has nothing to do with it as long as two people love each other. And I love him very much."

"So . . . . boy or girl?"

"Boy. Ethan is already buying baseball gloves and bats . . ."

Tony laughed, he was so happy for her. "I'm glad you got your life in order."

"I'm very happy, Tony . . . couldn't be happier."

"TONY!!!"

He had hoped that it would be Annie calling his name, but it was her mother. Nancy came running to him from the kitchen and threw her arms around him. A few minutes later they were sitting at a window booth across from each other. "She's still hurting, Tony. She says she's all right, but I don't believe her."

"I've looked everywhere I could think of, Ms. Roberson. Do you know where she is?"

"She's planning on leaving the country, Tony. I don't think she's planning on returning any time soon."

"I've got to find her, I can't let her go . . . . I love her too much." He stood up.

"The last time I saw her she said she was going to take a last walk on the beach, but that was a couple of hours ago. Do you think you can convince her to stay?"

"I guess we will know soon."

Annie had not realized how long she had been standing looking out at the lake. The only thing that brought her around was the sound of the seagulls. She tried to smile at the beautiful sunset and slowly took a deep breath and let it out. It was time to go. She turned toward the house . . . . and froze.

"I knew you would be here," Tony said. "Why I looked in all those other places beats me." He slowly approached her, not wanting to make her run from him.

"Did Mother tell you where I was?"

"Just that you wanted to walk on the beach. This is where we first met when I destroyed your sandcastle." He was finally standing in front of her. He looked around the area. "I've been away too long. I'm sorry."

"Tony . . . . I'm not staying here. I have a flight that takes off at midnight."

"I know . . . allow me that time to change your mind."

"My mind is already made up."

"And your love for me? Are you leaving that behind too?"

"No . . . just the past we had together. It's too painful to stay here anymore."

"But I'm here now."

"Yes . . . . you are . . . but I can't . . ."

She stopped talking as Tony reached into his pocket and pulled out the ring he had given her so many years before at his graduation. She couldn't believe he had it.

"I tried to give this to Mark, but he said it belonged to you . . . to us. I know I have a lot of making up to do. If you stay, I promise you won't regret it." He dropped to one knee. "Annie West Roberson, will you marry me?" He looked up at her, holding the ring in front of her left hand . . . . waiting.

"Yes," she said and he slipped the ring onto her finger where it belonged. Annie threw her arms around him knocking him backwards into the sand.

"Annie . . . !!"

## THE END

Please see my other book


LOVE SO TRUE


Contact info:
Stvasilas58@gmail.com